P9-BJF-126

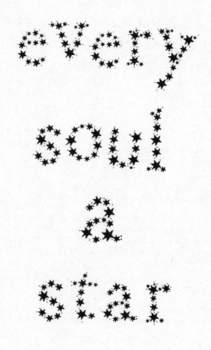

every soul a star

wendy mass

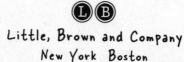

Little, Brown and Company
New York Boston

Also by Wendy Mass:

A Mango-Shaped Space

Leap Day

Jeremy Fink and the Meaning of Life

Heaven Looks a Lot Like the Mall

The Candymakers

This book is a work of fiction. Names, characters, places, and incidents are the product of the author's imagination or are used fictitiously. Any resemblance to actual events, locales, or persons, living or dead, is coincidental.

Copyright © 2008 by Wendy Mass
Reading Group Guide copyright © 2009 Hachette Book Group, Inc.
Cover photography by Pat LaCroix/The Image Bank/Getty Images

All rights reserved. In accordance with the U.S. Copyright Act of 1976, the scanning, uploading, and electronic sharing of any part of this book without the permission of the publisher is unlawful piracy and theft of the author's intellectual property. If you would like to use material from the book (other than for review purposes), prior written permission must be obtained by contacting the publisher at permissions@hbgusa.com. Thank you for your support of the author's rights.

Little, Brown and Company • Hachette Book Group • 1290 Avenue of the Americas, New York, NY 10104 • Visit our website at www.lb-kids.com

Little, Brown and Company is a division of Hachette Book Group, Inc.
The Little, Brown name and logo are trademarks of Hachette Book Group, Inc.

The publisher is not responsible for websites (or their content) that are not owned by the publisher.

First Revised Edition: November 2010
First published in hardcover in October 2008 by Little, Brown and Company

Library of Congress Cataloging-in-Publication Data

Mass, Wendy, 1967-
  Every soul a star / by Wendy Mass.—1st ed.
    p. cm.
  Summary: Ally, Bree, and Jack meet at the one place the Great Eclipse can be seen in totality, each carrying the burden of their own problems, which become dim when compared to the task they embark upon and the friendship they find.
  ISBN 978-0-316-00256-1 (hc) / ISBN 978-0-316-00257-8 (pb)
  [1. Solar eclipses—Fiction. 2. Friendship—Fiction. 3. Coming of age—Fiction.] I. Title.
  PZ7.M42355Ev 2008
  [Fic]—dc22   2008009259

20

Book design by Alison Impey

LSC-C

Printed in the United States of America

For Steve, Kathy, and Judi Brawer, with love

"In our world," said Eustace,
"a star is a huge ball of flaming gas."
"Even in your world, my son,
that is not what a star is,
but only what it is made of."

—from *The Voyage of the Dawn Treader* by C. S. Lewis

"Space isn't remote at all. It's only an hour's drive
away if your car could go straight upwards."

—Fred Hoyle, British astronomer

And when he [the author of the universe] had compounded the whole, he divided it up into as many souls as there are stars, and allotted each soul to a star. And mounting them on their stars, as if on chariots, he showed them the nature of the universe and told them the laws of their destiny.

—from "Timaeus" by Plato (427–347 BCE)

Eclipse:

from the ancient Greek word ekleipsis,
meaning abandonment or omission

ALLY   BREE   JACK

ALLY

1

In Iceland, fairies live inside of rocks. Seriously. They have houses in there and schools and amusement parks and everything.

Besides me, not many people outside of Iceland know this. But you just have to read the right books and it's all there. When you're homeschooled, you have a lot of books. I also know how to find every constellation in the sky, and that the brightest star in any constellation is called the Alpha. I know all the constellations because my father taught them to me, and I know about the Alpha because it is also my name. But my family and friends call me Ally.

Okay, that's not entirely true. I don't really have any friends. Not within hundreds of miles, anyway. And it's not because I am unlikable or smell bad or anything like that. In fact, I take a bath every single day in the hot spring outside our house, and everyone knows that the minerals in hot springs make you smell like fresh air all day long.

The fact that we live somewhere with a hot spring outside our house pretty much explains why I don't have friends nearby. Basically, my house is as close to the middle of nowhere as a person can get and still be *somewhere*. Our town is not even on the map. It's not even a town. It's more of an *area*. There's the Moon Shadow Campground that my family owns, where I know every tree and every rock and which foxes are friendly and which aren't, and a tiny general store a mile away, where most everything expired in the last millennium. That's it. The nearest real town is an hour away. Sure, maybe it gets lonely every now and then, but I love it here. I was only four when we moved, so I don't really remember life in civilization, which is what my ten-year-old brother, Kenny, calls anywhere other than here.

It should be pointed out that Kenny's only knowledge of civilization besides our books is based on what he can glean from the ancient black-and-white television at the general store, and since the only show that comes in is the soap opera *Days of Our Lives,* he thinks civilization is very dramatic. And until a few years ago, he thought it was in black-and-white.

Some people might think my parents are crazy for doing what they did — up and leaving their jobs to build a campground in the Middle of Nowhere, USA. But they had a plan. They knew that a decade later, hundreds, maybe thousands of people would travel to this exact spot to be a part of something that hasn't happened in mainland America for over seventy-five years and won't happen again for a hundred more. And this flock, this *throng* of people, would need a comfortable, safe place to stay, wouldn't they? With hot springs and hot coffee and clean bathrooms and their choice of tents or cabins, and no televisions to remind them of anywhere other than here.

My parents knew that, for one day, our two-square-mile campground would be the only patch of land in the entire country to lie smack dab in the path of the Great Eclipse when it passes overhead. In precisely twenty-two days and some hours from now, the sun will get erased from the sky, the planets will come out to greet us, the birds will stop singing, and a glowing halo of light will flutter like angels' wings above our heads.

Except, of course, if it rains.

BREE

1

I was switched at birth.

There's no other explanation for how I wound up in this family. My physicist parents are certified geniuses with, like, a zillion IQ between them and all these grants to study things like dark matter and antimatter, which are apparently very different things. My eleven-year-old sister Melanie gets straight A's, does cartwheels in public, and actually enjoys watching science documentaries on PBS with my parents. I prefer MTV to PBS, and to me, dark matter and antimatter really means *don't matter*. But as smart as they are, my family members are all rather plain-looking. Not ugly or anything even close, but just sort of plain. Average. Like soft-serve vanilla ice cream in a cup, not even a cone.

I am not plain or average or — god forbid — vanilla. I am peanut butter rocky road with multicolored sprinkles, hot fudge, and a cherry on top. Not that I would ever EAT such a thing, because it would go right to my thighs.

I don't mean to sound stuck-up, but I happen to be very attractive. My whole life strangers have stopped my mom on the street to say what a beautiful daughter she has. And they aren't talking about Melanie. Granted, you can't help the looks you're born with. I can't help that I'm the tallest girl in my grade, or that I never get pimples, or that my eyes are as blue as Cameron Diaz's. But I make sure to do everything I can to stay beautiful. Every morning I brush my dark brown hair a hundred times until it shines like silk, and if any nails are chipped I fix them with the manicure kit I bought last year at Things of Beauty in the mall. Every night before bed I do fifty sit-ups. I drink bottled water because you only look good on the outside if you're healthy on the inside. My friends and I keep up with all the latest trends, and we share clothes and even shoes sometimes. I worked extremely hard to become one of the most popular girls in my grade, and I work hard at staying there.

Today is the last day of school, and I can't wait for summer. Even though I'm only thirteen and a half, I'm going to be working at Let's Make Up in the mall. I'm only allowed to work two hours a day until I'm fourteen, but that's okay. My official title is "junior consultant" and it's a very important position. When you're a teenager and shopping for a new eyeliner or lip gloss, you don't want an old lady telling you what you need. You want someone you can identify with. And if a customer happens to think they can look like me just by buying our makeup, then so be it. They buy the makeup, they look better, I get a bonus, and I spend it next door at Hollister. Everybody wins!

My parents, of course, don't see it that way, which harkens back to the whole switched-at-birth theory. They don't understand that while I might not share their goal of discovering what kind of tiny invisible particles the universe is really made of, I still have goals. I plan to work at the mall, get discovered by one of the scouts looking for kids with modeling potential, be on the cover of *Seventeen* BEFORE I'm seventeen, and then make enough money as a supermodel to retire when I'm twenty-five and my beauty is fading. Melanie has accused me of being high-maintenance, but I don't think that's true. I just like things to be orderly and pretty, and I'm happy to give those less fortunate than me tips on how to improve themselves. I like to keep my life uncomplicated. Complicated people get wrinkles before their time.

We all have things to offer the world. My beauty is what I have to give.

And the best thing about being beautiful?

No one (except maybe my deluded parents who don't understand that modeling is a perfectly respectable career choice) expects me to be anything else.

JACK

1

My father has no head.

Well, of course he HAS one, but I've never seen it. All I've seen is about a hundred photos of the rest of his body. A big, roundish guy in suits, shorts, and once even a bear costume. I found the pictures in a shoe box in the back of my mother's closet when I was snooping for Christmas gifts a few years ago. I can just imagine her sitting on the floor of her bedroom, angrily snipping off the heads. I snooped some more in case there was another box with only the heads, but there wasn't. She must have thrown them away.

My mother never talks about my father, who left before I was born. I stopped asking when I realized all it did was make her upset. She said that anyone who would leave his pregnant wife and four-year-old son to go "find himself" didn't deserve another thought. It sure was a terrible thing to do. But it seems to me that my mother is better off alone than with a guy who has no head and ditched his whole family.

Still, I wonder about him. Even in the bear costume, I can tell I inherited his build. Big and wide, and good for one thing only — playing football. And if I was even REMOTELY good at playing football, I'd be all set. But I can't run across the room without getting winded or a cramp in my side. My second-grade gym teacher told me I had two left feet. For a week after that I would only wear left-footed shoes because I thought he meant it literally. My brother Mike has two normal feet, and no problem running across a field. In fact, he's the star first baseman on the high school baseball team. Luckily he's four years older than me, so we won't ever have to be in the same school again. No way can I compete with him in anything. I gave up trying a long time ago. I also gave up trying to pay attention in class. And trying to get people to like me. It's just too much effort. When they look at me, the other kids just see a big pudgy kid who sits in the back of every class drawing in his art book, or on his desk if the teacher confiscated the book. I don't belong to any clubs or after-school activities either. But not paying attention in class came back to bite me on the butt this year. Failing science class gave me a one-way ticket to summer school. It's humiliating. Having to sit in a stifling hot room with a bunch of my fellow rejects learning for the millionth time what the different types of rocks are called. What a total waste of time. All I want to do is be left alone so I can read (fantasy and SF), draw (aliens, monsters, and wizards), and conserve my energy so when everyone else is sleeping and dreaming their normal dreams, I can do something that most other people can't.

I can fly.

ALLY

2

Now that the big day is within sight, we all have to step up our chores to get the campground in order. The eclipse chasers are going to start trickling in over the next few weeks, and Dad wants to be sure not a single tree root is sticking up. With all the looking up at the sky these people will be doing, someone has to make sure they don't trip. That someone, according to my dad, is me. I may be small, but I'm strong. I have a reputation as the best dirt-smoother in the family. I don't take much pride in that achievement. My dad could do it, but as the handyman and all-around-maintenance guy, he's always busy fixing fences and drain pipes. Mom has her hands full as the office manager, taking reservations, placing ads for the campground. Kenny can't do it because he gets too distracted whenever he spots a bug in the upturned soil. He stops and examines the bug from every angle. It takes him a whole day to do what I can do in an hour. So it falls to me.

I'm starting with the labyrinth, since that way I also get to daydream while I work. Yes, we have a labyrinth. We built it a few years ago, and it took all summer. Mom read in a book that if you're going to open a campground in the middle of nowhere, you have to offer the guests unusual activities to keep them occupied. After all, there's only so much swimming in the lake, fishing, hiking, playing on the playground, and roasting hot dogs and s'mores one can stand. Although I personally never get sick of s'mores.

At first I thought Mom was talking about building a maze, and I got all excited because I pictured these big green hedges and it being all sort of Victorian and fairy tale–ish. But she explained that a labyrinth and a maze are two very different things. A maze is like a game: you can't see where you're going and the entrance and exit are two different places. A labyrinth is an ancient series of spiraling circles created on the ground with stones that you walk through. You're supposed to ponder some big question like what you should be when you grow up, or if a tree falls in the woods and no one is around to hear it, does it still make a sound? (I say no, because a sound is only invisible waves in the air until it hits someone's ear, but Kenny says yes because the resulting crash would still cause vibrations, and the earth itself would "hear" it.) *Anyway,* when you reach the middle, you're supposed to get your answer. So far I haven't had too many big questions to ponder, but I find that my daydreams are really vivid when I'm walking it. Almost like visions. It's pretty cool. Kenny was really disappointed that it wasn't going to be a maze. Every now and then I find a stuffed dinosaur or some mythological beast like a gryphon or a scary plastic minotaur in the center, and I have to bring it back to his room.

Besides the labyrinth, we created five other Unusuals. Campers can pan for gold (also known as gold-colored plastic nuggets) in a small stream that runs alongside the campground. They can paint whatever they want on the wall of the Art House, and when that gets filled up, we'll start on the floor and the ceiling. The Art House is the only cabin we don't rent out because Kenny swears it's haunted, but I've never seen any ghosts. He claims it's haunted by the ghost of the great Galileo himself (Galileo was our old cat who died when Kenny was four, not the famous scientist, although the cat was named after the scientist, obviously). When Kenny was five, he came running into the kitchen screaming and waving his arms, "Great Galileo's Ghost, it's hot out!" The phrase has become our family's way of swearing without actually swearing.

In the back room of the Art House is Alien Central, where campers can monitor the computer that sweeps the sky for alien radio transmissions all day and all night. We're part of an organization called the Search for Extraterrestrial Intelligence (SETI). Our computer is one of millions that analyze radio signals as they come in from outer space. It's a very popular Unusual. Everyone wants to be the one in front of the computer when the first alien signal comes in.

Besides finding aliens, people can walk through the Sun Garden and tell the time by the shadow they cast on the ground. It took us one whole winter to make the giant sundial out of mosaic tile and concrete. Up the hill from the Pavilion with all the picnic tables and grills, we have the Star Garden, where guests can try out a bunch of different telescopes and binoculars that astronomers have donated to my parents over the years. Our campground is pretty famous within the astronomy community. We have Star Parties each year where people come from all over the country to stargaze together, since the skies up here are so dark and wide. My whole family is trained on how to use the equipment, but most of the guests request me. I know the difference between a reflective scope and a refractive scope, and the names of most of the craters on the moon. I can point the campers in the direction of newborn stars in the Orion Nebula or a dust storm on Mars as easily as telling them which way to the restrooms. And if we're lucky enough to see the dancing lights of the Aurora Borealis, I'm out there with hot chocolate and warm blankets. If pressed, I can explain that the reds and oranges and greens that billow down from the sky are different types of gas atoms and molecules colliding with solar particles. But mostly I just like to enjoy the show.

No other campground in America has six Unusuals. Most don't even have one. They require a bit of up-keep, but we don't mind.

"Make sure you pack the dirt down tight, Ally," Dad warns, as though this is my first time doing this. I know he's just tense because in all the years we've been here, we've never had more than two hundred campers at once. And now we'll have over a thousand. Pretty big difference.

"And after you're done, please check on the other Unusuals, and no skipping the Art House like last time."

"But Dad, that spider was as big as my face. Bigger, even. It could have eaten me in one bite."

From behind me I hear Kenny laugh. But there's no meanness in his laugh; there never is. Kenny is one of those rare people who are all goodness. That's not to say he doesn't do the typical annoying little brother stuff like grab the last buckwheat pancake off my plate or stick a wet finger in my ear. But he's also really smart and pretty funny. If I had to pick anyone to grow up with in the middle of nowhere, he'd be the one.

Kenny joins us and says, "You can sleep outside half the night, but a little old spider freaks you out? All sorts of things could be crawling on you. A lot bigger than that spider, I bet. I'll show you my chart at lunch."

"First of all," I reply, "this was no little spider. It had a *presence*. It had a *soul*. A *mean* soul, intent on eating me. And second, I am not sleeping when I'm out there on my lawn chair. I am intently *stargazing*. And third, I don't ever want to see that creepy chart of yours again. I had nightmares for weeks the last time you left it open on the kitchen table."

Kenny is determined to get his name in the history books by finding a bug that hasn't been discovered before. He keeps a huge sketchpad with drawings of every creepy crawler he's come across since he was five. He then compares the drawings to pictures of bugs in the encyclopedia-like volume *The Complete Bug-Hunters' Guide to Insect Life in America, from Ants to Zarthopods.* The title alone is enough to curl my toes. I can deal fine with your regular garden variety bug. It's just when one has an overabundance of legs, or is of a size more commonly associated with a household pet, that I get freaked out.

I prefer looking up, rather than down, and have a different plan to secure my immortality.

I'm going to discover a comet.

According to the rules of comet-finding, my comet will be named after me. Even if I'd wanted to name it something else, I wouldn't be allowed. Every time it circles around the sun and approaches Earth, excited onlookers will exclaim, "There goes Comet Summers, isn't it bright? Isn't it amazing?" My grandpa had hoped to find a comet or an asteroid but never did. His eyesight wasn't so good, and even powerful binoculars didn't help after a while. If I find an asteroid

I'm going to name it after him, because you can't name an asteroid after yourself. Don't ask me why — that's just the way it is.

"C'mon, Ally," Kenny says, picking up one of the long flat brooms. "I'll help you."

"Don't forget to fill out the logbooks," my father says over his shoulder as he walks away. "Things are going to get crazy soon, and you need to keep organized."

Kenny whispers, "You know he's saying that because he and Mom were arguing last night and he wants to keep the peace. She's the only one who checks those boring logbooks."

"Mom and Dad were arguing?" I'd heard them whispering loudly to each other, only to stop when I walked in the room, but I didn't think much of it. I figure they don't get much privacy and it's not my business if they don't want me to hear something. I bend down to snip at some roots while Kenny starts his slow smoothing process. It would go faster without his help, but he's usually good company.

"I did hear one other thing," he says, even though I hadn't asked. "But it didn't really make sense. I probably heard it wrong."

I pick up a twig off the path and toss it into the woods that surround the labyrinth. "What did you hear?"

"I'm sure it doesn't mean anything. Never mind." He begins smoothing faster, not even looking for bugs.

Something is up. I reach out and put my hand on the broom to stop it. "Just tell me," I say firmly.

"Okay, okay. I heard Dad say, 'But Ally wears a meteorite around her neck. The kids might not understand.'"

My brows crinkle. "*What* kids? Why wouldn't someone understand my necklace?"

He shrugs. "That's it, that's all he said." He goes back to brushing the dirt path. "I told you it didn't mean anything. I probably heard him wrong anyway."

"I guess," I say, picking up my own broom and entering the first circle. I reach up with my other hand and clutch the pouch around my neck, feeling the familiar lump inside. As always, it makes me think of Grandpa. He is the reason the Moon Shadow Campground exists. He started my mom on her love of the stars, she got my dad hooked, and the rest is history. And it was all because of a rock.

When my grandfather was ten years old, a rock fell from the sky and grazed his left ear. He was lying on the grass at the time, staring up at the stars. Convinced that a piece of the moon had broken off and landed on Earth, he ran inside to show his mother. She was more concerned with the trickle of blood that was sliding down his ear onto his neck. She wouldn't even look at the shiny black rock until she had dabbed some whiskey on the cut.

At first his mother was convinced the rock had been

thrown by a mischievous neighbor boy named Hank, but an investigation determined that Hank was "indisposed" at that time, which was the polite way of saying that Hank had eaten some bad carp that he had fished illegally from the river behind the glue factory and had been stuck on the toilet since dinner.

The next day my grandfather's father brought the rock to work with him at the factory and on his way stopped at the local library, where apparently all the smartest people in town worked. The head librarian took one glance at it and announced that my grandfather had indeed been struck by an object that had been hurled out of the heavens — a meteorite. Now my grandfather's father, he was a nice guy, played ball with his son, went to church on Sundays, but he never did have much aptitude for science. Noticing his blank expression, the librarian explained that a meteorite was what happened when a meteoroid broke through the earth's atmosphere, but didn't burn up like it was supposed to. The meteorite, she explained, was made of iron, and was probably a tiny chunk of an asteroid. The librarian made some calls, and found out that as long as the meteorite wasn't found on government land, like a national park or the White House lawn or something, the person whose property it lands on is the rightful owner.

That weekend my grandfather's parents took him to the five and dime store, where my grandfather picked out a small blue pouch about the size of a deck of cards. His mother punched holes in it and looped a leather string through them. My grandfather dropped the meteorite in the pouch, tied it closed, and slipped it over his head, where it remained for the rest of his life. Well, he took it off for showers and swimming, of course. And when he slept. And anytime he had to wear a suit. Oh, and to wash the pouch occasionally. But other than that, it thumped on his chest in tune to the beating of his heart. Or so he claimed.

As a kid, he showed the rock (and the scar on his ear) to anyone who would listen, and explained that the odds of getting hit by a meteorite are a trillion to one. While I would have thought this would make him really popular, it didn't. It did make him really interested in space though, and in the way that all the planets and stars and galaxies are kept in a delicate balance. He worried that because a piece of an asteroid had landed on Earth, the balance of the universe was disrupted. He became obsessed with trying to even things out by bringing a part of the earth up to the sky. He figured spotting a new asteroid and having it named after him would even things out. But just in case he never found one, he had a backup plan. When I was one year old, he put a pen in my hand and guided me to sign my name on a piece of paper. I'm sure it wasn't legible, but that signature was scanned into a computer and put on a disk along with

Grandpa's and my parents' and a half a million others, and that disk is a billion miles away, circling Saturn right now in the *Cassini* spacecraft.

By the time he died, I had already inherited Grandpa's love of the stars. Then I inherited the meteorite, too.

I haven't noticed if it has negatively affected my popularity status or not.

But why would my parents be arguing about my necklace? I'm now standing in the center of the labyrinth, where everything is supposed to be clear. But it's not. I can't wait till tonight so I can talk this over with Eta and Glenn and Peggy, my three best friends. I just wish they could talk back.

But that's what happens when you all live on different planets.

BREE

2

Melanie sticks her head in my room. "Are you ready, Bree?"

"Five more minutes." I squeeze past her and duck into the bathroom. She follows me and hops up onto the counter to watch me put on my makeup. I never mind when she does this. I figure as her older sister, it's my job to educate her in the ways of the world. She's only eleven and doesn't wear makeup yet (although a little blush wouldn't hurt), but our mother's certainly not going to teach her. Mom loves to tell us how she hasn't worn makeup since her wedding. I guess scientists don't need to look good.

When I get to the part with the eyeliner, Melanie scrunches up her face as usual. "Doesn't that hurt?" she asks.

I shake my head. "It doesn't hurt today, it didn't hurt yesterday — when you also asked me — and it won't hurt tomorrow." I finish lining my eyes, smudge 'em a little, and turn to her. "See how my eyes look even bigger now?"

She nods slowly, but then says, "And big eyes are good? Why?"

This girl is hopeless. "They just are," I tell her. "Who would want small eyes?"

"Not me?" Melanie asks.

"Exactly. Now let's go."

My best friend Claire and I are going to a free lecture at the community center called "Breaking into Modeling." My parents would never let me go, so I haven't told them about it. They think I'm taking Melanie to the library, which I am, but only because it happens to be inside the community center. Melanie has been checking out books lately about kids whose families move. She even requests them from other libraries. She actually believes that my parents will eventually get the big grant that they've been waiting for, and then we'll have to move so they can do their research. Our parents have been warning us about it for three years now, and there's no sign of any grant. I panicked for a few weeks, but now it's like that old story about the boy who cried wolf. I think Melanie uses it as an excuse not to have to work on being popular right here and now. Plus, I think they've given up on that one and have some other project in mind. I may be the dumbest in the family, but I know people's patterns of behavior. The excited whispers when they think we're asleep, the late-night phone calls, the computers and printers going at all hours. It always leads up to some big new project. When you have parents who are scientists, you get used to them being in their own worlds. It's no big deal. I have more important things to worry about. Besides my job this summer, I have lots of plans. There are pictures of models to clip from magazines for my Wish Book, boys to follow around in the mall, and sleepovers with Claire and the rest of the A-Clique.

It's one of those perfect summer days, with no humidity to swell up my hair. I take a deep, happy breath of the clean air as we head into town. A good hair day is worth its weight in gold. When we've gone a few blocks, Melanie says, "I had one of them again last night, didn't I?"

She's talking about night terrors. They're like nightmares, except she's not dreaming at the time. It's like some weird screaming state that you can't wake her out of. Then she doesn't remember much in the morning. Mom and Dad have done a lot of research on it but haven't found a cure. The doctors say people usually outgrow it. It's weird that a kid who is so relentlessly happy all the time screams in her sleep.

"Yeah, around midnight. I found you in the corner of the living room and brought you back to bed."

"Thanks."

I'd been finding Melanie in corners of our house since she was four. This is why whenever Claire and I have sleepovers, they're always at her house. Claire

☆

has been my best friend since that time in second grade when her nanny forgot to pick her up after dance class and I found her crying into her tutu. But we both know that if one of us is going to make it as a model, it will be me. Claire isn't very tall, and she has a crooked nose, which she's going to get fixed as her sweet sixteen present. She always forgets to use conditioner, and really, that's the most important part of washing your hair. She's the most popular girl in our grade though, because she's super rich and her mom used to be in horror movies before she met Claire's dad and became respectable.

We meet up with Claire at the corner of Main and Tanglewood, a few blocks from the building. Melanie doesn't bother to ask why Claire's joining us. She's a *go with the flow* kind of girl, which is yet another reason why I know we can't be related by blood. I like to have everything completely planned out. That way I always know what to wear.

"Total ten today," Claire says, falling in step with us.

I'm wearing the white tank dress that shows off my tan. "Thanks," I tell her, "you too!" Really though, she's more like an eight.

Once inside I tell Melanie I'll meet her in the lobby in an hour. She skips off without a backward glance. It is majorly embarrassing having a sister who skips in public. Claire and I hurry into the large room where the meeting is about to start. The air is heavy with perfume. Perfume is the one beauty product I just don't understand. It was invented back when people couldn't take baths so they could cover up their smell. But now all you have to do is use a shampoo that smells good. I make a mental note to tell that to all my customers at the store this summer. A woman at the door hands us index cards and tells us to fill out our name, age, and home phone number.

The small room is packed and we have to squeeze into the back row. I immediately recognize the B-Clique from school sitting right in front of the podium. Figures they'd be here. They're pretty enough, but if they were so great, they'd be in the A-Clique. There are even some people in the audience who are at least thirty. Don't they know their modeling days are long behind them? A woman who looks like she just stepped out of the pages of *Vogue* gets up and says, "Modeling is fifty percent looks, fifty percent attitude, and one hundred percent awesome!" We all clap. She continues, "It's also a lot of hard work. You can't go out with your friends every night and dance till dawn, then try to rely on makeup to cover those puffy eyes. You can only drink coffee or soda through a straw. People don't hire models with brown teeth."

Two heavyset women next to me start grumbling. "I'm not drinking my coffee outuva straw!" The other nods, and they get up noisily and bang through the back door. Like they would have had a chance anyway.

A lot of the *Vogue*-lady's speech is about signing with a reputable modeling agency, and other things my parents won't even consider until after high school. I've told them repeatedly that most supermodels start by fourteen or fifteen, but being the brainiacs that they are, they refuse to discuss anything that would ruin my education. But she also tells us how we're supposed to walk (one foot directly in front of the other, heel to toe, like walking on a high beam), how to hold ourselves (eyes looking forward, neck long, back straight), and what to think about while our pictures are being taken (exude a "cool sense of peace and confidence"). The last thing she says is, "Now look around this room. The odds are that only one of you will make it."

I could SWEAR she winked at me when she said that!

"Keep in mind," she continues, "there are other perfectly wonderful careers out there where you can make a ton of money, see the world, and have fabulous friends." She smiles broadly as she says this, but it's pretty clear she doesn't believe it. Neither do I.

We walk out of the room slowly, heel to toe, heads high, smiles bright, all cool peacefulness and confidence. "This is harder than it looks," Claire says out of the corner of her mouth. I would nod, but our heads are supposed to be stationary at all times. As we enter the lobby I almost collide with a man awkwardly holding up a big blueprint with one hand. "It's not going to work," he yells into a cell phone. The blueprint flaps angrily and interrupts my cool peacefulness.

☆

To my horror, I catch sight of Melanie doing cartwheels across the far end of the lobby. That girl will be the death of my social life. I untangle myself, ignore the guy's rude grunt, and lead her out of the community center by the elbow. Claire hurries after us, used to Melanie's weird behavior by now. "You can't do cartwheels in public," I whisper loudly. "Don't you want to have friends?"

"I have plenty of friends," she says, smiling that easy grin of hers.

I sigh. "Don't you want to have friends whose idea of a good time isn't solving quadratic equations and then having Scrabble tournaments?"

Melanie opens her mouth to respond, but right then our parents pull up in their embarrassing beat-up brown van. They use it to haul their equipment, even though I have begged them to get a car I wouldn't be mortified to be seen climbing in or out of.

"Hop in, girls," Dad says cheerily, leaning his head out the window as the engine idles loudly. That van does everything loudly.

Melanie runs toward the car, but Claire and I take a step back. The B-Clique girls who were at the seminar might be watching, and even though I'm pretty sure my position in the A-Clique is secure, people have been demoted for much less. Emily Flanders got booted all the way from A to C because she wore white pants after Labor Day.

I look from side to side. The coast seems clear, but

I'm not taking any chances. "I'll see you at home later," I call from the safety of the sidewalk.

Mom leans across Dad and says, "Get in the car, Bree. We need to talk."

"I can't," I tell them. "Claire and I have plans. Important plans." We had been planning on going back to her house and practicing our new walk. Her house is, like, mansion-huge, perfect for walking down pretend runways.

Claire takes a step away from me. "It's okay, Bree. I'll text you later."

Before I can protest further, Claire takes off down the block, putting as much distance as possible between her and the van, which is now spewing out black exhaust. Can't blame her, I suppose. I'd do the same thing if it were me.

With one last backward glance, I hurry into the van and shut the door quickly behind me. In order to fit on the seat I have to push aside one of the many cardboard boxes filled with copies of Mom and Dad's book, *Dark Matters,* which they store in the van for when they do speaking engagements. I glance in the back to see why the boxes aren't in their usual spot and discover the back is filled with folding tables and poster boards.

"What are those for?" Melanie asks, following my gaze. It always surprises me that she is interested in what my parents do. They and I have an unspoken agreement: I don't pry into their lives, they don't pry into mine. Works out just fine.

My parents share a glance as Dad pulls up to a red light. Then Mom says, "That's what we need to talk to you girls about." Another glance. I swear my dad's eyes are twinkling. I'm starting to get nervous. Mom continues, "We're having a garage sale. In two days."

I relax into the seat. My parents get excited about the strangest things. "What's the big deal?" I ask. "We've had garage sales before."

"This one is going to be a little bigger," Dad says after a pause. Before I can ask what he means, he pulls the van into the park near our house and turns off the engine. It bangs and sputters before quieting. I cringe.

"Are we going on the merry-go-round?" Melanie asks, bouncing up and down in her seat like a little kid. I roll my eyes.

"Let's go sit in the gazebo," Mom suggests, only it's more like a command. I can always count on her not to make us sit on the grass. She's very squeamish about bugs. I don't like them either, but for me it's about the dirt. I'm very anti-dirt. Especially in white.

Melanie jumps out of the car and I reluctantly follow. How did my first day of summer vacation turn into Family Day? Mom has a thick blanket tucked under her arm, which she spreads out on the floor of the gazebo. She gestures for us to sit.

Mom takes a deep breath and says, "Your father and I have some big news."

"I knew it!" Melanie yells, and pops up. "We're moving! It's finally happening."

I hear the words coming out of her mouth, but they honestly don't register. A really cute guy with the broadest shoulders I've ever seen has started jogging on the path around the gazebo. He'd be a total ten if his shorts weren't quite so short. They're so last summer.

Dad puts his arm around Melanie's shoulder and squeezes. "Yes! And the best part is, we're going to be staying at a campground. Managing the place, in fact, for the next three years while we're doing our research nearby. You'll love it there. You'll learn tons of things you could never learn here in the suburbs. It's going to be wonderful."

Something about a campground trickles into my brain. "Huh?" I ask, turning my head back to the group. "Did I miss something? Are we going on vacation? Because my job starts next week and I —"

Melanie plops down next to me. "Bree! Didn't you hear? We're moving! To a campground! Isn't it great? You used to love camping when we were little, remember? You won that nature trophy in camp and —"

If I wasn't already on the ground I swear I would seriously faint. I yell so loudly my voice echoes in my head. "We're WHAT???"

JACK

2

"Are you gonna stay in there all night?" Mike calls up to me from the bottom of the tree. I wish I actually *could* stay up here all night. Mom never lets me sleep in the treehouse. She thinks I'll sleepwalk right out into the air.

I pretend I don't hear him over the loud chirping of the crickets. I focus on my book. I have two pages left of a Ray Bradbury short story. It's about this girl who lives in a world where the sun almost never shines. She hasn't seen it in five years. Then these bullies lock her in a closet when the sun is about to come out. I have to find out if they let her out in time to see it.

"Jack!" Mike calls up again. "I can see you up there!"

For the zillionth time I bemoan the lack of privacy. SD2 (Stepdad number two) left before we built a door to the treehouse, so there's just an open hole where anyone can look in. I know my way around a toolbox, but I can't build things from scratch. SD3 was more of a deep thinker. He couldn't tell a hammer from a nail, but I can thank him for teaching me how to wake up in my dreams without waking up for real. He called it *lucid dreaming*. It's because of him that I can fly. He taught me how to tell the difference between the real world and when you're dreaming. And when you learn to recognize the difference, you can control your dreams. You can do all sorts of things, but I like to fly. When I'm flying, I don't weigh anything at all.

So far there's been no SD4. I wonder what he'll be like, if there is one.

"Just ten more minutes!" I call down. "Hold your horses."

I turn back to the book. The girl misses the sun. I can't believe it. I feel so angry and sad for her. I wish I could write stories like that, where you feel something after you finish reading them. I'm no good at writing though, but I'm really good at drawing spaceships and little green men. Not that I let anyone see them. If Mom knew I could draw she'd sign me up for art classes to "build my confidence" or "raise my self-esteem" or one of the other phrases I've overheard the guidance counselors say to her over the years.

I close the book and stick it in the corner next to my stash of Ranch-flavored Doritos and Orange Crush. Mom doesn't let me eat junk food since the doctor said I should watch my weight. But she never comes up here. Fear of heights, which works out well for me.

I'm about to pop the top off a can of soda when I

hear Mike climbing the rickety stairs to the treehouse. I'm surprised he hasn't given up bugging me. Usually at this time his girlfriend Suzy is over and they're in his room "studying." Of course he'd be dating the prettiest girl in school. Who else? I'll probably never get to "study" with a girl.

The stairs give a final creak as Mike reaches the top. "Yo. I'm giving you a heads-up here. One of your teachers is on the phone. So whatever you did, you might want to think of a good excuse before you go back into the house."

I sit up at this news, almost hitting my head on one of the hard wooden beams. My mind races with things I could have done wrong. Yesterday was the last day of school. Did I skip gym? Well, sure, but it was the last day. A lot of kids skipped. Did I pick up my report card? Yup. My homeroom teacher handed it to me, and I chucked it in the garbage can on my way out. Then when I remembered how mad Mom was last time I did that, I went back in and dug it out. Ray Smitty had already thrown gum on it. Did I leave an old tuna sandwich wedged in the corner of my locker? No, but I know the kid who did. Did someone see me drawing that spaceship on my desk? I don't think so. I had my Earth Science notebook up the whole time. Plus it was in pencil, so it's not really a big deal.

So why was one of my teachers calling me?

I scramble down the ladder, narrowly avoiding the bottom step, which has a large crack running through it. It's going to break under my weight any day now. I find Mom in the kitchen, holding the cordless phone toward me. Surprisingly, she doesn't look mad. There's a mixture of amusement and surprise on her face. Weird.

"It's your science teacher," she says. "He has a question to ask you."

Okay, so if it's Mr. Silver that means it's about the spaceship after all. I wonder what the punishment is for drawing on school property. He already failed me, dooming me to summer school — what more can he do? Although to be fair, he really did give me a lot of chances to bring my grades up. If only I'd remembered to include Saturn in my model of the solar system, I might have squeaked by with a D. If only science wasn't right after lunch. I get so tired after lunch. When I don't make a move to take the phone, Mom pushes it into my hand. Bracing for the worst, I say, "Hello?"

"Hello, Jack," Mr. Silver says.

It's very surreal hearing a teacher's voice on the other end of my phone when school is out for summer. Well, out for the kids who actually paid attention in class. Maybe I fell asleep in the treehouse and am dreaming this whole thing. I push my feet into the ground, but can't lift into the air. Okay, so I'm not dreaming.

"Jack," he continues, "I have an offer for you. I'd like you to participate in a very special scientific project this summer."

Oh, NOW I know what's going on. Before he can say any more I jump in. "Mr. Silver, this is Jack *Rosten*. You're looking for Jack *Rosen*." Rosen gets straight A's in science. Teachers confuse us all the time. But only our names. That's the only thing that's similar between us. I'm about to hang up the phone when he laughs.

"I assure you, I know who I called. Would you like to listen to my proposal? If you're not interested, no hard feelings."

"I'm listening," I say, only half meaning it. I'm already thinking about getting back to my book. Plus I'm still pretty sure he has the wrong guy.

"I'd like to offer you the chance to come with me on a two-week eclipse tour that I'm leading this summer," he says. "You'd be my right-hand man. The kid who was supposed to come broke his wrist skateboarding. You don't skateboard, do you, Jack?"

I don't answer. Anyone who knows me knows I'm not about to get on a skateboard. He continues as though I've responded, as though I'm possibly going to say yes to whatever it is he's talking about.

"Good," he says. "Because this is a very important job. No room for broken bones. And I hope you don't mind roughing it. Camping for two weeks isn't for the faint of heart. I'm also going to need your help setting up the equipment, monitoring the telescopes, making sure the rest of the participants have what they need, things like that. I can't pay you, but it's free room and board."

What is this guy TALKING about? "Um, what are you talking about?" I ask.

He laughs again. "Let me make myself clearer. I'm inviting you to join me and thirty others, for a two-week eclipse tour up north. I'll be doing some scientific experiments during that time, and at the end is the big solar eclipse we talked about in class."

I remember him talking a few weeks ago about some eclipse. He seemed really excited about it. I don't remember any details though, since we weren't going to be tested on it.

"And you know the best part?" he asks.

I can't imagine why he's asking me, of all people, to do this. Maybe he lost a bet with the other teachers so he has to pick the most loser-ish kid. "What?"

"The *best* part," he says dramatically, "is that if you participate in the program, and write a short paper at the end, you'll get out of summer school."

I blink.

"Think about it," he continues. "Two weeks in the wilderness, camping under the stars. And then witnessing firsthand a total eclipse of the sun, the most amazing spectacle in the entire solar system."

My heart starts racing. All I can think is, *no summer school!* I glance up at my mother, who smiles hesitantly. "It's up to you," she says in a loud whisper.

I turn back to the phone. "Just so I heard you right, if I do this, I don't have to go to summer school? You're sure?"

"I'm sure."

My mind races with the other things Mr. Silver said. Camping. I like camping. I used to be a Boy Scout until I was nine. That was the summer the kids joked about who they would eat if they were trapped in the wilderness. Guess who they said would feed the most people? I quit after that. Witnessing an eclipse? So it gets dark in the middle of the day. It gets dark every single night. Not sure what the big deal is. But who am I to say no to a chance to be outside for two whole weeks without Mom or Mike bugging me? And if it will keep me from summer school, heck, it's a pretty easy decision.

"When do we leave?" I ask.

"Well, that's the thing," he says, hesitating for the first time. "The bus leaves from the town hall parking lot tomorrow morning at nine."

"Tomorrow morning?" I repeat. Mom hears me and kicks into gear. She reaches up and starts taking cans of food out of the cabinets.

"I'm real sorry for the last-minute notice," he says. "I can give your mom a list of things to pack for you."

"Can I just ask you one more thing?"

"Ask away."

"Why me? Lots of kids would be better at something like this than me."

"How do you know that? I happen to think you're the guy for the job, that's all."

I find it hard to believe I'm the guy for ANY job. I

just hope when he sees me he doesn't realize he's got the wrong kid after all. I give Mom the phone to get the packing list.

Mike follows me down the hall to my room. "So what was that all about?" he asks.

"My science teacher wants me to go on some eclipse trip with him," I say with a shrug. "No big deal." I say it like it doesn't matter, but it kind of IS a big deal. One minute the summer is one way, and the next it's a whole other way.

"Sounds like a big deal to me," Mike says, watching me as I try to yank my duffel bag from the back of my closet. It's buried under my winter sweaters and a box of old toys. "Who else is going?"

I stop pulling on the duffel's handle. "I don't know," I admit. "I didn't get a chance to ask."

"What if it's you and the teacher and, like, fifty old people?"

"It doesn't matter." I give the bag another yank, freeing it. I plan on keeping to myself as much as possible anyway.

"Whatever you say." Mike glances at his watch. "It's gonna be quiet around here without your stupid Game Boy beeping and buzzing all day long. Why do you still play with that thing? Do they even make games for it anymore?"

I grin. "Is insulting my GBA your way of saying you'll miss me?" Mike pushes me around and all, but he's always looked out for me. I unzip my bag, grimacing a little at the musty odor. I haven't used it since the Boy Scouts voted me Best Dinner Option. "I'm sure Suzy will keep you company," I point out. "Shouldn't she be here by now?"

"What's it to you?" he asks, his voice suddenly hardening.

"Nothing, jeez."

"Whatever," he says, and stomps off down the hall.

I shrug. I have bigger concerns than whether Mike and his girlfriend are on the rocks. Like whether I have enough batteries for my Game Boy to last two weeks.

Mom hurries into the room, waving a piece of notebook paper. She rattles off the list so quickly the words blend together. "Long pants, shorts, t-shirts, long-sleeved shirts, hiking boots, umbrella, heavy jacket, hooded sweatshirts, sneakers, a bathing suit, underwear, socks, detergent, backpack, notebook, pens, pencils, ruler, calculator, flashlight, bath stuff, first aid kit, compass, pocket knife, bug repellent, sunblock, toolbox, sleeping bag, water purifier, snacks for the bus, canteen, and a camera." She lays the paper on my bed and then plops down next to it. "It's going to be a long night," she says. "You're sure you want to do this, right? You've never been away from home this long."

"I'm sure."

"Good," she says, jumping up and pulling open my top drawer. "I think you'll get a lot out of it. Going away with a big tour group is a very social experience." She starts tossing socks onto the bed.

I sigh. It always comes around to me being social. Or not social enough, to be specific.

I pause from throwing my socks into the duffel to look at her. I forget sometimes how young she is because she's really tired from all her jobs, and from taking care of us. She had Mike right after high school, so she's a really young mom compared to other kids' moms at school. Not having me around to worry about for two weeks will give her a break, even though she'd never admit it. Maybe she'll find SD4.

I leave Mom to work on the packing while I go out to the treehouse. It's almost fully dark out now and I can see a few stars. It's weird to think I'm going to be staring up at them every night, and studying them or whatever I'm supposed to be doing. I usually avoid looking up at them at all. The stars just make me feel even more insignificant than I already feel.

I hurry up the ladder and grab my stash of junk food, my book, my flashlight, and my dream journal. I hide the journal up here because I don't want Mike to read it and make fun of me. Writing down my dreams makes it easier for me to recognize them when they're happening. I can see patterns. SD3 said I'm a natural at it. No one else ever said I'm a natural at anything. I don't know why he left. I don't know why any of them left. SD3 had tried to interest Mike in the whole lucid dream thing, but Mike was too busy with his sports. It was our previous stepdad, SD2, who had taught Mike how to play baseball. Mostly what I remember about SD2 is that he smelled like onions and peppermint. Personally, I'd rather be able to fly than be a first baseman.

I shine the flashlight around the treehouse to make sure I'm not leaving anything important. I'm about to click it off when I see a pinkish-brown stuffed ear sticking out from the corner. I quickly grab the bunny and tuck him under my arm with the rest of the things to bring with me. If anyone at the campground asks, I'll say I've never seen the old, ratty stuffed bunny before. I sure as heck won't tell them that it used to belong to my dad when he was a baby and that he left it in my crib when he took off. And I definitely won't tell them that I say good night to it every night before I go to sleep.

It's just too pathetic.

ALLY

3

I close the logbook and place it on the desk in Mom's office. It had taken all day and most of the evening to get the Unusuals ready. I'm exhausted, but it's been dark for an hour already and I'm itching to see Eta, Glenn, and Peggy. I need to talk to them about what my dad said about my necklace. Whenever I crossed paths with my parents today, I felt like they were always about to say something, and then changed their minds. Kenny thinks I'm just being paranoid. Kenny knows a lot of big words for a ten-year-old.

On my way out, I glance up at the huge calendar taped to the wall. It's easy to forget what day it is, living out here. The first big group of eclipse chasers is due to arrive in three days. Then each day leading up to the one circled in red marker has more and more arrivals. We've been living toward that red day for as long as I can remember. I can't even believe it's almost here. I take one last glance at the calendar and then lean in closer. Tomorrow is June twenty-fifth? That means my friend Ryan and his grandparents are coming! They usually don't come until the middle of August, for our annual Star Party. In all the excitement about the eclipse, I'd forgotten about Ryan! His grandparents have been bringing him here for the Perseids meteor shower ever since I was six and he was seven. His grandfather and mine were best friends — they met in the army when they were eighteen. Ryan is the only one who knows that I have friends on other planets. Last year I confided in him that on my seventh birthday, my grandfather pointed to the constellation Cassiopeia and showed me how the bright stars spell out the letter M. He said the star at the end is named Eta Cassiopeia, and that it was the same kind of star as the sun. He said that meant there could be a planet around it just like Earth, with another little girl on it just like me. And that little girl could be looking up at the stars herself, wondering if anyone's looking back. I decided to call that girl Eta, since that's the name of her star. Peggy came later when I found out that scientists had already discovered the first planet around a star other than our own sun. The star is called 51 Pegasi, but whoever heard of a girl named Pegasi? Peggy is much better.

I told Ryan that I talk to Eta and Peggy sometimes, like they're real people. He didn't laugh or anything mean like that. He didn't even ask if they talk back. (They don't.) Instead he told me about a star called Gliese 581, which has a bunch of planets around it.

43

☽

That night we found Gliese on my starmap in the con-stellation Libra, and then looked for it using the big-gest telescope we could find in the Star Garden. I told Ryan that since he was the one who knew about the planets, he should get to name the person living on one of them. He came up with Glenn. It's really cool to know that while I'm looking up at Glenn's planet, so is Ryan, even though he lives hundreds of miles away.

The tiredness slides off as I run at top speed out of the office toward the Star Garden. On the way I pass Ralph and Jimmy, the two handymen/security guards who work here every summer. They're outside of the storeroom, unloading crates of water and boxes of fro-zen hot dogs and burgers in the reddish glow of the streetlight. I like having them here; it makes me feel even safer than I usually feel. One year it was Ralph's quick reflexes that kept a big black bear from getting into the storage room and eating the campers' food. He likes to say he wrestled him with his bare hands, but really he just banged his toolbox against a metal pole, and it scared the bear away. This year with all the eclipse chasers coming, Dad had to hire a lot more people, including people to stock and run the dining hall for the guests who signed up for the meal plan.

"Hey, Alpha Girl!" Ralph calls to me as I start up the hill. "Where ya going in such a hurry? The eclipse isn't for another two weeks!"

Ralph likes to tease. I don't mind. Alpha Girl kind of sounds like a superhero name. The Adventures of

Alpha Girl! Visiting the stars in one giant leap! Plus it's much better than Kenny's old nickname for me: Astrodork.

"Can't tell you!" I call over my shoulder. "Secret Alpha Girl business."

"Aw, leave the girl alone," Jimmy says. "She's probably hurrying off to meet her boyfriend." Then they both guffaw like that's the funniest thing they ever heard. I guess it is pretty funny considering there are no boys my age within an hour's drive. But once Ryan gets here tomorrow, I'll have someone to hang out with who's only a year older than me. Not that he's my boyfriend. I've never thought of him that way. I've never thought of anyone that way.

My three favorite telescopes are lined up in a row, with my stool in front of them, just as I'd left them this afternoon when I cleaned all the optics. I like to look at my three friends at the same time instead of moving one scope between the three of them. Once all the guests start arriving, I'll be lucky to get any telescope time at all.

I sit down in front of the first telescope, an eight-inch Newtonian Reflector, and look up. Even though I can easily find Cassiopeia by just looking for the M-shaped stars, I prefer to do it the way Dad taught me. First I look for the Big Dipper. That's the easiest group of stars to find in the sky. Then I follow the two stars on the edge of the dipper and they lead me to Polaris, the North Star. I love Polaris, because it's the only star that doesn't move. As long as you're north of the Equator, if you can find Polaris, you can tell where you are on the earth. Standing below it makes me feel like I'm right where I'm supposed to be. I keep going in a straight line from Polaris directly to Cassiopeia, and to Eta. "Hi, Eta!" I say out loud. Then I move on to Peggy and Glenn, in the constellations Pegasus and Libra. Libra is a hard one to find, even though I've done it so many times. I usually go to Virgo first, and then scan to the east until I've found it. Once I have them all, I look at each one and give a little wave. I tell them about what Kenny overheard, and about how my parents are acting a little strange. I tell them I'm excited to see Ryan tomorrow, and that I'm a little nervous about what things will be like here when all the people start arriving. They twinkle at me, and I feel that same contentment and peace I always feel when I look at the stars. Like they're protecting me, shielding me from harm. The vastness of space always puts my problems in perspective.

By the time I get back into the house, everyone is asleep. I'm not the only one who worked really hard today. I fall back onto my bed and stare up at the glow-in-the-dark stickers of the solar system on the ceiling. Dad put them up when we moved here to help me adjust to life under the stars. I don't remember ever going to sleep without stars — real or fake — overhead.

I must have fallen asleep because the next thing I

know the sun is hitting my closed eyelids and my nose is oddly cold.

I open my eyes to find a grinning Kenny, clad in his favorite pajamas (green, with giant grasshoppers on them), pressing a purple ice pop against my nose.

"Why, Kenny?" I croak.

"Why what?" he asks innocently.

I roll over and sit up, taking the ice pop from his hand. My mouth feels icky and dry, and the ice pop looks very refreshing. I stick it in my mouth before I have a chance to wonder where the ice pop might have been prior to its arrival on my nose. It is indeed refreshing. I hear Dad and Jimmy outside my window in a heated debate about whether or not we have enough toilet paper for the guests. Dad is saying that as long as everyone uses no more than three squares per bathroom visit, we'll be fine. Jimmy argues that no one uses just three squares. Dad says, "Well, they should!" Then Jimmy suggests they post a sign up in the bathrooms telling people about the three square limit. And Dad says, "Yes, let's do that." Then Jimmy says, "I was kidding, man. We can't do that!"

"What time is it?" I ask Kenny, hopping off the bed.

He points to the watch still on my wrist. I realize I'm still in the same clothes from yesterday. It's a few minutes before nine. Ryan's grandparents always leave their house before dawn and arrive promptly at nine. Good thing I'm already dressed. I shove on my sneakers and slide the rest of the ice pop into my mouth before tossing the stick into my trash can. I shiver a bit as the cold ice hits my teeth.

"Can I come with you?" Kenny asks eagerly. He looks forward to Ryan's visit as much as I do.

"If you can keep up," I reply, running out of the room. The pouch bounces hard against my chest and I tuck it under my shirt. I don't stop running until I'm halfway down the road that leads from the main house to the front gate. It's the only road on the property that's paved, and it always feels weird to have my feet on such solid ground. Ryan's grandfather's car pulls through as I round the corner. Right on time! Ryan and I always race each other from the gate to their cabin when they first arrive. I've been running a lot this past year, and I'm ready to finally beat him.

His grandfather gives a little honk and pulls up alongside me. Then he slowly gets out of the car, stretches, and rustles my hair. Mr. Flynn is the opposite of my grandfather in the looks department. Grandpa was tall and thin, and Mr. Flynn is short and wide. Grandpa used to joke they looked like Abbott and Costello, who I think are some TV actors, but I'm not sure.

While Mr. Flynn signs in with Ralph at the gatehouse, I lean into the car, expecting to see Ryan's grandmother in the passenger seat. Instead, I see Ryan, taking off a pair of headphones and shoving them in his backpack. I glance into the backseat, but she's not there either.

"Hey, Ally!" Ryan says. "How's it going?"

His voice is deeper than I remember. "It's going good. Where's your grandmother? Is everything okay?"

He unfolds himself from the seat and climbs out. He must have grown a foot! And his blond hair is cut so it spikes up a bit in the front.

"She's fine," he says. "Just wanted to stay home this time. She's in some bridge tournament or something."

My jaw falls open. "She's missing the eclipse for a bridge tournament?" That didn't sound like her. Mrs. Flynn was always the first one out in the Star Garden each night. I can't imagine her missing the eclipse for anything.

Ryan shrugs. "Women. Who understands 'em?" He closes the car door behind him and leans down to tighten his shoelaces. When he stands back up he says, "Hey, I bet I can tell the last thing you ate!"

Before I can ask what he means, he says, "C'mon, let's race. Maybe this year I'll let you lose by only a few yards."

Leaving me no time to dream up a suitable response, he takes off down the road toward camp. "Hey, no fair!" I yell, hands on my hips.

"Teenage boys," Mr. Flynn says, with a broad grin and a wink. "Who can understand 'em? You want a ride back?"

I shake my head. "I'll see you later." I take off down the road but fail to catch up with Ryan. My swift feet are no match for his long legs. I watch from behind as

49

☽

Kenny, who has changed into shorts, appears on the road. When he sees Ryan racing toward him, he waves his arms in the air. Ryan waves back as he approaches but doesn't stop. When I reach Kenny I can see the disappointment on his face. He doesn't really understand that Ryan is too old to hang out with him.

By the time I reach the campgrounds, Ryan is sitting on the large rock at the entrance, grinning.

"Not nice," I admonish, breathing heavily.

He elbows me playfully. "Sorry, Al. Just trying to keep you on your toes. So how's life out here in the boonies?"

I lean up against the rock. "The same. It's good. Going to be crazy for the next few weeks though. But it's really exciting. So you wanna go to Alien Central now?" That's always Ryan's first stop when he arrives.

He shakes his head. "Gotta take a shower."

"In the middle of the day?"

He laughs. "People shower at all times of the day, Ally. I'll meet you after, 'kay?"

"Okay."

Mr. Flynn pulls into the parking lot. Kenny hops out of the front seat, carrying Ryan's backpack. He hands it over and says, "Hey, dude, what's the four-one-one?"

I stifle a laugh. Kenny picks up slang from the campers and loves to try it out on new people.

Ryan and I share a smile, and then he clasps Kenny

on the shoulder. "Not much to report, little man. How's life by you?"

"Two thumbs up," Kenny replies, beaming at the attention.

My dad comes out of the office building and gives Mr. Flynn a big hug. My dad is a hugger. My mom calls him a *tree hugger*. Even though the expression means someone who tries to save the environment, he actually DOES hug trees sometimes. "Isn't anyone going to show the Flynns to their cabin?" Dad asks, pointedly looking at me.

"I was just about to, Dad," I say as Kenny grabs Mr. Flynn's suitcase and starts dragging it across the dirt. I try to lift Ryan's duffel out of the trunk, but I can't even budge it.

"What's in here, bricks?"

Ryan laughs and pulls it out of the trunk. "It's my weight set. I have to get strong so I can play football in high school next year."

I let that sink in as Ryan, Kenny, and I start out on the path to the cabins. Ryan's grandpa stays behind to talk to Dad.

"You start high school next year? Already?"

"Yup. Ninth grade. If you were in a real school you'd be going into eighth."

I stop walking and Kenny almost bumps into me. That's true! I haven't thought of what grade I was in for a long time.

"And I'd be going into sixth!" Kenny says with a hint of pride.

"That's right, little man," Ryan says.

This conversation is making me uneasy. I'm not sure what an eighth grader is supposed to feel like, but I don't think I feel like one. I ponder this while Kenny tells Ryan about all the activities leading up to the eclipse.

"And there'll be famous scientists coming from all over the country and we'll learn how to make our own eclipse glasses and Ally's gonna lead a class on the constellations every night, aren't you, Ally? She knows them better than anyone!"

Ryan smiles and I blush. Kenny's my biggest fan.

We reach the cabin and drop the suitcases inside. The overhead fan does a good job of keeping the cabin cool. Ryan pulls the string on it a few times and it goes even faster. The weather doesn't faze me and my family the way it does the guests. Some of the cabins even have air conditioners in their windows.

"Do you want to visit the Unusuals?" I ask Ryan. "After you shower, I mean."

"Sure," he says, unzipping his duffel. "I'll meet you at the stream in, like, an hour? I'm feeling lucky today. Gonna find me a whole lotta plastic gold!"

"Sounds good," I say, heading for the door. Kenny doesn't follow. He's watching Ryan pull out his hand weights. "C'mon Kenny, leave Ryan alone."

"It's okay," Ryan says. "He can stay."

I pause for a second. Does that mean I can stay too? But Ryan has his back to me and is showing Kenny how to do a bicep curl. That's fine. I have a ton of chores to do anyway. I hurry back down the path and into the office. Mom is on the phone and typing at her computer at the same time. She gives a little head nod when she sees me, then keeps talking.

"I told you, sir, only six people can fit comfortably in a cabin. But your party is welcome to join the campers in the field. . . . Yes, there are bathrooms, and you're welcome to use the kitchen facilities. . . . Okay, I'll switch you over." She clicks over to another screen and starts typing. People have been altering their reservations all month. Mom takes it all in stride. She's starting to look a little frazzled though.

She hangs up and says, "The Flynns all checked in?"

I nod. "Did you know Ryan's grandmother isn't here?"

"Uh-huh," she says, scrawling a note on her pad. "I think she's not feeling too well these days."

This was a surprise. "But Ryan told me she had a bridge tournament, that's all."

Mom puts down her pencil. "I guess they didn't want to worry him. Best not to say anything, okay?"

I pick up my logbook and say a soft goodbye as I leave the room. I feel sorry for Ryan, not only because his grandmother might be sick, but because no one told him. One thing about my family is that we don't keep things from each other. Not the big things, anyway.

"Hey, Ally," Mom calls out to me.

I stick my head in the room. "Yeah?"

"Nine o'clock tonight at the dining pavilion. Family meeting."

"Okay." Then I add, "Is this about my necklace?"

"What?" she asks, genuinely not seeming to know what I'm talking about.

"Never mind," I say as the phone begins to ring. She reaches for it and as she picks it up she makes a circling gesture around her mouth.

"Huh?" I whisper.

She says hello into the phone but keeps making the gesture and pointing to me. I duck out of the room and into the small bathroom in the hall. In the oval mirror above the sink I see a ring of purple around my mouth. Ugh! The ice pop! My tongue darts out to lick it off. Mmm, still tastes like grape. I do a quick scan of the rest of my face and find a little more purple on the tip of my nose. I never realized it before, but my face is really quite round. I don't know if that's a good thing. The sun is round though, and I do like the sun.

"Don't forget to put out the towels," Mom calls out to me.

"Have I ever?"

One of my jobs is to make sure all the cabins and

tents have the supplies they need for the next day's arrivals. Running back and forth to the supply room takes longer than I expect, and I haven't even done half of them. I don't want to keep Ryan waiting too long, though. By the time I get down to the stream Kenny and Ryan are already sitting on the bank, dipping their pans into the water. I hear Ryan say, "So, you expecting any hotties this summer?"

"It gets hot every summer," Kenny says, reaching around to scratch his back with his free hand. "And you gotta watch out for the skeeters."

Ryan laughs. "No, I mean hotties, like hot chicks. You know, *girls*."

"Ooohhh! I'm not sure. We're gonna have tons of people though. You should ask Ally, maybe she'll know."

"That's okay," Ryan says. "Girls don't like being asked about other girls."

I can't seem to make myself come closer. After a minute Kenny asks, "Is Ally a hottie?"

"Ally's just Ally," Ryan says. "She's not really like the other girls I know."

I back up a few feet and then move my sneaker around in the gravel a bit so they hear me coming. They both turn around.

"Hey, Al!" Ryan calls out. He lifts up his pan and watches the water drain through the tiny holes. Four gold nuggets remain. "See? Told ya I'm feeling lucky!"

Kenny watches me carefully as I select a pan from the pile by the shed and join them. It's Kenny's job to stock the shallow stream with nuggets, and as soon as I dip my pan I can tell he's put too many in there. Normally I would say something, but my throat is a little tight. I don't think I've ever heard someone talk about me behind my back before. It feels weird. We pan for about twenty more minutes, and then take a tour of all the Unusuals. By the time we get to the Sun Garden, I'm feeling like myself again. We clown around by pushing each other out of the way to see who casts the best shadow. I leave Ryan and Kenny in Alien Central while I go finish stocking the tents.

Ryan's grandpa is a really good cook and he makes a big batch of chili for everyone for dinner. Mom and Dad keep dashing off to answer calls, or to check people in. Nine o'clock comes and goes with only Kenny and me waiting in the pavilion for our family meeting. Kenny falls asleep on one of the benches and almost rolls right off. I escort him back to the house and up to his room. On my way back down, I find Mom rummaging through papers in her filing cabinet, pencils stuck behind both ears. I point to the clock, which now reads 9:45.

Her eyes widen when she sees the time. "I'm sorry, honey," she says, closing the metal drawer. "Tomorrow morning, I promise."

I sit out on the front porch and look up. For a minute I'm tempted to get Ryan so we can say good night to

56

Glenn together, but when he left dinner he said he was going to work out. I don't want to bother him.

"Good night, Glenn," I whisper. "Night, Eta and Peggy." I close my eyes, picturing them, countless light-years away, laying their heads on their pillows. I wonder if they HAVE heads. And pillows.

I wonder if they're hotties. Not that I have the slightest idea what makes someone a hottie or even if it's a good thing to be.

Or why, according to Ryan, I'm not one.

BREE

3

I can't even speak as my parents fill in the details of our move. Literally, all of the muscles that are supposed to move my mouth have gone slack. Unfamiliar words are flying at me. Homeschool-in-a-box. Alien House. Unusuals. Solar Eclipse. What do these words even MEAN? I would be more than happy never to find out.

I'm on my feet now, staring up into my father's face. "Please, please tell me you're kidding. You're not really taking me out of school, away from my friends and my new job and everything that matters to me, to go live somewhere where aliens have their own HOUSES? Tell me this is a joke. I'm begging you."

"Honey, you knew this was a possibility. You just didn't want to believe it. I know it sounds extreme, but —"

"Extreme?" I repeat. "It sounds insane!"

"I think it sounds awesome!" Melanie says, jumping up and throwing her arms around Dad.

I whirl around to face her. "You don't mind leaving everything you've ever known behind?"

She shakes her head. "You guys will all be there, so what's the big deal?"

I feel like my head is about to explode. "The big deal is that we'll be living in the middle of nowhere! There will be NOTHING around us for miles and miles. No people. No restaurants. No stores. No movie theaters. NOTHING. Who lives like that?"

Melanie shrugs. "It sounds like an adventure."

"That's the spirit, honey," Mom says.

I feel like throwing up. Literally, I may lose my breakfast bar right here and now. All my dreams are flying past me. *Whoosh!* There goes the one where I decide which of the A-Clique boys I want to date this summer. *Whoosh!* There goes the one where I get discovered at the mall and become a bigger supermodel than Kate Moss. *Whoosh!* There goes the one where I get voted Prom Princess in high school.

I get down on my knees and clasp my palms together. "Please, please, let me stay with Claire while you guys are gone. Mrs. Rockport loves me and they have plenty of room. I'll come visit every school holiday. Well, Thanksgiving and Christmas, because Mrs. Rockport already invited me to Florida with them next spring break."

"Hey, drama queen," Dad says, crossing his arms. "We're not leaving you a thousand miles away from us, so forget about it."

The guy with the broad shoulders jogs by again and I suddenly feel the need to be running, too. How could they tell me we're moving in like, a *week,* and I'm just supposed to be like, oh, okay, great! "I'm going to Claire's," I announce as I run out of the gazebo. "I'll see you at Thanksgiving!"

"Claire lives three miles from here," Mom yells after me.

I don't answer. I just keep moving. After about a mile, I'm vaguely aware that they're following me in the van (okay, I'm highly aware of it because no other car in town bangs and hisses as it goes down the road), but I pretend not to notice. I have to stop every few blocks so that I don't pass out, but I'm determined to get there. All those step aerobics classes must have done some good because even though it hurts to breathe, at least I'm still moving. When I'm two blocks away I call Claire and tell her to leave the front door open. She asks why. Panting, I reply, "Parents . . . moving . . . campground . . . no . . . life . . . not . . . going . . . live . . . you?"

"Your parents are moving to a campground where you'd have no life so you're not going and you want to live with me?" she asks.

And that's why Claire is my best friend.

When I get to her front door a few minutes later, she's waiting for me. She steps aside. I run in and collapse on the white leather couch. I'm panting worse than Claire's dog Maizy, who's watching me warily from across the room.

"My mother said of course you can stay with us," Claire says, kneeling next to the couch. "You can't move away from here — that's crazy. What would I do without you?"

"Water," I croak.

She hurries into the kitchen and comes back with a bottle of Evian. It's bubbly, and it hurts a little going down. The doorbell rings and I freeze. "Don't open it! It's THEM."

We huddle together on the couch as the bell rings again. Finally Mrs. Rockport comes out to answer it. Claire tries to stop her, but her mom says, "There's no excuse for bad manners," and swings open the door.

"Hello, Elizabeth," I hear my mother say.

"Hello, Sandy," Claire's mother replies. "You look — I mean — it's marvelous to see you."

"You too," Mom says. I can hear the forced cheerfulness in her voice. "Is it okay if I come in? I really need to talk to Bree."

"Of course," Claire's mom says, even though Claire is glaring at her.

I bury my face in the couch. It occurs to me too late that my makeup is probably smeared all over it.

"Bree," Mom says, resting her hand on my back. "I know you don't want to do this. I understand what a big sacrifice this is for you, I truly do. But I promise, this will be a wonderful experience. The three years will just fly by."

"Three YEARS?" Claire says. "You'll miss most of high school! How will you get into college?"

"Yeah, Mom!" I say, flipping over like a fish. "You don't want to risk me not getting into a good college. That's all you and Dad talk about!"

"First of all, that's not true. And second, colleges look very favorably on homeschooling, and —"

"*Homeschooling?*" Claire shrieks. Across the room I hear her mom gasp too. "Bree," Claire says firmly, "you CANNOT do homeschooling! That's only for spelling bee champions. Not for future Prom Princesses!"

"Tell me about it!" I wail. "Mrs. Rockport, do something!"

Claire's mom steps forward and clears her throat. "Um, three years you say? That's a bit longer than Claire had indicated."

"Mom!" Claire cries. "Bree's my best friend. You have to let her stay!"

Her mother doesn't say anything, but mine does. "Girls, I'm sorry, but we're moving as a family. And right now we have to get home and start sorting through our things. I'm sure the two of you will keep in touch. Nothing has to change."

Everything will change. I'll talk to trees for company, and Claire will become best friends with Lara Rudy, who's been trying to worm her way between us since the fourth grade. My hair will lose all its sheen by being subjected to harsh outdoor conditions. I'll lose my sense of style and start wearing pink with red and last season's shoes. Meanwhile, Claire will discover deep conditioning treatments and get her nose fixed and she'll be chosen Prom Princess instead of me.

I throw my arms around her and we both burst into tears. I can see the mothers rolling their eyes at each other, which makes me cry even harder.

"I'll spend every day until you leave with you," Claire promises, her mascara halfway down her face. Mrs. Rockport clears her throat. "Actually, Claire, we're leaving tomorrow for your grandmother's seventy-fifth birthday party in Boca. Remember? We'll be gone for a week."

This makes us cry all over again. I cling to her, hoping it will make the chilling fear go away.

"Wait here," Claire says, pulling away. "I want to give you something." She runs upstairs while I shoot my mom such a look that she turns away and feigns interest in the gold silk drapes.

Claire runs back down and hands me her modeling scrapbook. I look up at her in surprise. "You're giving me your Book? But you'll need it."

"I'll start another one," she says, sniffling and rubbing her eyes. "You're the one who inspired me in the first place. You should have it. It will help you remember me." She bursts into tears again and I hug her with the Book clutched tight to my chest.

"Okay, girls," my mother says, gently prying us apart. "This isn't going to get easier if you drag it on. You'll still visit each other, I promise. This isn't forever."

I wipe my eyes and drag my hand under my nose, sniffling. I shouldn't expect Mom to understand. Dad is, like, her only friend. How will I know who I am if I'm not Claire's best friend and co-leader of the A-Clique? My whole life has been about being at the top of the social hierarchy. And I got there in spite of my family's nerdosity. Now they want me to abandon that and, what, wallow in obscurity during the prime of my life?

After one last crying session complete with promises to write every day, I let Mom lead me out the door and back to the van. I don't think I have any more tears left in me. Dad and Melanie try to be nice on the way home by offering to help me go through my stuff for the garage sale, but I ignore them. They're too cheery and it's making me feel worse. Mom and Dad talk excitedly about how beautiful the campsite is. Unspoiled land, a big lake with fish and frogs, babbling stream with gold nuggets. Mom says witnessing an eclipse is something people wait their whole lifetime for, but they're rarely in the right place at the right time. I don't understand how you can have an eclipse in one place and not in another, since there's only one sun, but I don't want to encourage them by asking questions about it. She babbles on about how it's going to be so exciting to watch the eclipse with people from all over the world. Wow, staring at the sun with a bunch of strangers. For that I have to give up my job at Let's Make Up? A lot of other kids wanted that job.

"Aren't you not supposed to look at the sun?" I ask, hunched down in my seat. "Didn't I learn that in kindergarten?"

"We'll have special glasses," Dad replies. "The lens filters out the amount of sun that hits your eye. Don't worry."

Right, like THAT'S my biggest worry!

When we get home I go straight to my room, lock the door, and throw myself on the bed. Staring up at the poster of Orlando Bloom on the ceiling, I wonder how I'm going to get through this. I'm not the spend-time-on-my-own kinda girl. It's like that old saying about a tree falling in the woods. If no one hears it, does it still make a sound? If I'm so beautiful but no one sees me, am I still beautiful?

Mom knocks on my door and when I don't answer, she says, "I'm leaving some empty boxes outside your door. Anything you think you can part with can go in them. The garage sale is on Saturday, and the rest we'll donate. Be generous. We won't have room for storage up there."

"I can't part with anything!" I yell.

"I'm sure that's not true," she calls back. "All your magazines are a fire hazard, and they'll have to go."

All my *Vogues* and *Vanity Fairs*? All my *Entertainment*

Weeklys? "They're only a fire hazard if someone lights them on fire!" I squeeze my eyes shut tight against the tears.

Mom ignores my very logical argument and says, "Any item of clothing you haven't worn in two years goes in there since you'll have outgrown them."

I'm already the tallest girl in the eighth grade. Chances are I'm not growing much more. It took years of saving my allowance and birthday money to build up my wardrobe, and all the belts and shoes and bags and jewelry to go with them. "I better keep everything," I argue. "You know, for Melanie."

Silence from the other side of the door. We both know Melanie would never wear my clothes. It wouldn't kill the kid to wear something other than old jeans and t-shirts once in a while.

After another hour of feeling hideously sorry for myself, I bring the boxes into my room. Melanie has already filled one up and placed it outside her door. I'm sure no one expects me to donate anything since they're always saying how materialistic I am. Well I'll prove them wrong! I pull down everything from my shelves, the trophies from summer camp that everyone wins even if you're the worst athlete there, the dried-out arts and crafts projects, my old collection of four-leaf clovers, trophies and dusty candles and seashells and broken toys. I toss them all into the biggest box and push it into the hall without a second glance.

☆

I don't know why I've kept that stuff so long anyway. None of it says anything about who I am today.

It takes two hours, but I manage to cut out all the pictures from my magazine collection that I want to keep. Clearly I'll have plenty of time to tape them into my Book once we get to Purgatory, which is how I've begun to think of the campground. We learned in English class that Purgatory is the place where souls go to wait before being sent on to their final destination. That's like me. My life is being put on hold for three whole years. It's so unfair.

I continue tearing through my room, pulling clothes out of drawers and off hangers. Who knew I had so many shoes? But when I'm done going through all my clothes, I'm still left with not being able to part with most of it. I start to go through my CD collection and then realize all of them are loaded on my iPod. I pile them neatly in a box and slide it next to the other one outside my door. Melanie still only has the one box. Granted, she had a lot less stuff than me to begin with, but whose fault is that? Not mine.

I don't say a word at dinner. Dad had picked up pizza, which is apparently something else that I won't have for three years since not even Domino's delivers to Purgatory. Melanie chatters on about how excited she is to learn how to use a telescope and to hike through the trails and it's all I can do to keep from crying again.

☆

The garage sale is horrible. I watch from my bedroom window as our furniture and dishes and silverware get snatched up by strangers. It's not like it was even that nice to begin with, since Mom and Dad were never big on buying fancy things. But still, it was *ours*. Who knows what the furniture in our new house will look like? Supposedly the people who are there now are leaving most of it for us. I watch as the pimply guy from the local record store buys up all my CDs for one dollar each. I'm sure he'll sell them for a hefty profit. Someone even buys my old soccer trophy from camp! What's wrong with these people?

When the last bookshelf has been carted away, Mom and Dad count the money at our kitchen table, which is practically the only thing they didn't sell. When all the crumpled bills are sorted into piles, they do a little dance around the kitchen.

"Now we can buy that new spectrometer," Mom says gleefully.

"Not to mention pay our bills and moving costs," Dad says, twirling her around. "We should have done this years ago!"

I don't point out that had we done this years ago, we'd have no where to sit or put our stuff and nothing to cut our food with. Mom gets on the phone with the people who will be renting our house, and Dad goes out to the driveway to tinker with the van. He's going to leave a few days early with all their research equipment and meet us at the closest airport, which is still four hours away from Purgatory. He asked if I wanted to drive with him, but since I'm currently not speaking to anyone, I don't think I'd be very good company. Plus there's no way that van isn't going to break down on the road, and I don't need to be a part of that.

The next few days pass in a haze. I feel like a zombie in my own life. The house is bare. All our stuff, including my clothes and Mel's precious books, has been sent ahead. Dad is gone. Melanie is so excited to fly that she is able to talk of nothing else. Claire is still in Florida, but the rest of the A-Cliquers come to pay their last respects. Lara Rudy asks if I'm taking my pink Abercrombie t-shirt with the lace on the bottom. I had actually packed it in the one small bag Mom is letting us each bring on the plane. I figure if I give it to her, maybe she won't try to steal Claire from me. So I dig into my bag and hand it to her. She squeals and runs into the bathroom to put it on. Lara's only a 7.5 on her best day, so at least the shirt won't look better on her than it did on me.

Waking up on the last day in our house is the hardest. I don't want to get out of bed. Melanie runs in and jumps on the bed. "Get up, get up, it's time to go!" Then she hops off and skips across the room. Honestly, the girl is more like five than eleven. I make it downstairs in time to hear my mom say into the phone, "Thank you again, but as I've said, it's not going to be possible. We're moving quite far away. Thank you for your interest in Bree." Then she hangs up and seems surprised to see me standing there.

"What was that about? Who was on the phone?"

She looks like she'd rather not say, but I don't budge. "That was someone from some class they said you went to on modeling?"

I redden, then press on. "And?"

"They were just calling to offer you a place in a course they're giving."

"Really?" I KNEW that woman had noticed me!

"Don't get too excited," Mom says, putting out the last of the bagels. "I'm sure they call everyone who attended. It's probably a scam."

I open my mouth to argue, but what if she's right? I can't even ask Claire if she got the call, because if she didn't, it would be awkward.

"Can I still do it?" I ask, holding my breath.

"What do you think?" Mom says.

"I think this whole thing bites!" I say, and storm out. My iPod remains on from the moment we leave the house to the moment the flight attendant says to turn off all electrical devices. I'm squished between Mom and Melanie, who is chomping loudly on honey-roasted peanuts and pointing out each type of cloud as we fly overhead. When we first came on the plane we had to walk through first class and it was soooo nice. Roomy leather seats. Foot rests. And a cute guy in a college t-shirt checked me out. I might be the best-dressed person on the plane in my strappy sandals and pink cami and wraparound skirt. Everyone else looks like slobs in sweats or jeans or shorts. I firmly believe one should always look their best, no matter what the circumstances are. If I wasn't being sent to Purgatory, I might have flirted with College T-shirt Guy.

Melanie keeps poking me and reading passages from a book about eclipses. "Listen to this one," she says, not waiting for a response. "In the middle of watching a solar eclipse, this woman says, 'If it could be repeated every day for a year, I would never budge from where I stood.' That must mean it's pretty amazing."

"Trust me," I say, closing my eyes, "I'll be able to budge."

Dad is waiting for us in baggage claim when we arrive. He looks tired, but he perks up when he sees us. Melanie goes running into his arms. I grunt a hello. I look for College T-shirt Guy when we land, but I don't see him. Flirting would at least be something to do. Even the airport is in the middle of nowhere. Cornfields and distant mountains and cows. It feels strange to see Dad's van parked in front of such an unfamiliar place. It bucks and grunts as he turns the key, but it feels a little like home.

After a few hours we arrive in a little town that as far as I can tell consists of two streets with a diner, a video store, a Laundromat, and a tiny market. We pull into the diner. I'm surprised to see the parking lot is full.

"We're about fifty miles from the Moon Shadow," Dad says as a little bell rings to announce our arrival inside.

"What's the Moon Shadow?" I ask hoarsely. Then I clamp my mouth shut, remembering my vow of silence.

"That's the name of the campsite," Melanie says, bouncing on her heels. "Because during a solar eclipse the moon's shadow covers the earth. Isn't it a great name?"

"Fab," I mutter.

A waitress appears and leads us to the one empty booth. I bet they don't even have bottled water here. I'll die of thirst before I drink a soda. I can't help wondering who all these people are. Some old, some young, some even speaking foreign languages. They can't possibly all live out here. As if reading my thoughts, she waves her arm around the room and says, "Eclipse chasers. Come a few weeks early. I 'spect you all doing the same?"

Melanie and I slide into the booth as Dad says, "Actually we're here to take over the Moon Shadow Campground."

The woman hands me a plastic menu and then pauses. "Really now? I didn't know the Summers family was leaving. Where they goin' then?"

"We're not sure," Dad says, looking to Mom, who shakes her head.

"The Midwest, I think," she says. "This all happened very suddenly. In fact they're not even expecting us for another week. We figured we'd come a little early so we can learn how things are run before the eclipse."

Another WEEK? We didn't have to be here for another week? I fume into my menu, which is sticky with ketchup.

Once the waitress leaves, Dad nudges me and says, "You might want to try the meat loaf with gravy fries. It gets cold up here in the winter. You need to put some meat on your bones."

I stare at him as if he's just suggested I sprout wings and fly through the air. I can't put meat on my bones and expect to be ready to model when we get back to civilization. Then it hits me. Maybe being in Purgatory is, like, my test. It's not easy being a model. You have to watch what you eat all the time; you have to compete with all the other girls; you have to stand really still while bossy designers nip and tuck clothes around you. Plus you get really jet-lagged flying around the world. If I can handle this, I'll know I have what it takes to put up with all the hardships that go with life as a supermodel. Maybe it won't be so bad. After all, I can appreciate natural beauty. It will give me plenty of time to practice my runway strut. And without the smog from the city, I bet my complexion will be totally clear.

Oh, who am I kidding? It's gonna suck.

JACK

3

The ride to the bus is quiet. I'm in the backseat of Mom's Toyota, staring out the window. Most of the town is still asleep. Mike is in the front seat as usual. You'd think that since we're in the car because of me, he'd let me sit in the front. But no. He never thinks of things like that.

"I'm not pushing you into this, right?" Mom says, glancing at me through the rearview mirror. "It's your choice to go?"

Mom has asked me this three times since Mr. Silver's call. "Yes, Mom, it's my choice. Don't worry, I'll be fine."

"I'm not worried," she says. But she clearly is. I don't have a great track record with school trips. In sixth grade she had to come pick me up from Six Flags because Timmy Johnson bet me I couldn't eat ten hot dogs. I ate eleven, and threw up all over the tilt-a-whirl and half the riders. Then last year my history class went to a museum, and I thought a piece of modern art was a trash can and spit my gum into it. That didn't go over well either. But I'm older and wiser now. I plan on keeping a low profile and staying out of trouble. Plus Timmy Johnson — or anyone else — wouldn't bother to bet me anything now since they don't notice me at all.

We pull into the town hall parking lot and I see the bus idling in front. I feel a little flutter in my stomach, followed by a big flutter. Mom gets out, but I don't move from my seat. I pat the pockets of my jacket to make sure my book and sketch pad and Game Boy are still there. Mr. Silver is standing by the side of the bus, checking people in with a clipboard. Am I crazy to be doing this? What if I'm totally useless and Mr. Silver fires me and Mom has to drive hundreds of miles to pick me up? I don't want to let her down again. I don't want to be grounded again. For me being grounded means I can't go into the treehouse.

Mike gets out of the car, and I have no choice but to follow. He's already grabbed my duffel from the trunk by the time I reach it. He plops it on the ground in front of me. "I have something for you," he says, handing me a red folder. "I thought you might want to learn a thing or two about eclipses before you got there. You know, so you won't feel left out."

I open the folder and flip through the pages. There are three articles: "Elements of a Solar Eclipse," "What to Look for During a Total Solar Eclipse," and "Three Thousand Miles for Three Minutes of Totality." There are diagrams and photographs, too. I couldn't be more surprised. "Where did you get these?"

"I downloaded them early this morning."

We stand there awkwardly for a minute, looking around the parking lot. Mike was right, most of the people taking bags out of their cars are over fifty. But there are a few younger groups, and one family with a kid who looks around six years old. Mom approaches with Mr. Silver. I've never seen him in shorts and a t-shirt before. He looks younger than he does in school, not much older than my mom. I hold my breath. Now he's going to realize he's got the wrong guy. But he just swings my duffel over his shoulder and says, "Ready for the adventure of a lifetime?"

I glance at Mike and he gives me a little shove. "I guess I am," I reply, clutching the folder. Mom gives me a hug and slips five twenty-dollar bills in my hand. "For emergencies," she says. "And snacks."

I wave goodbye to them as I follow Mr. Silver to the bus. He tosses my duffel into the open compartment underneath. Good thing I don't have anything breakable in there. He's still checking people in, and tells me to go find a seat anywhere I like. I step onto the bus and feel a blast of air conditioning hit my face. The aisle isn't very wide, and I have to be careful not to jostle anyone on my way down. Whacking an old guy with my elbow wouldn't be a good start to the trip. I catch bits and pieces of words that make no sense to me. Words like *Baily's Beads, Corona, Shadow*

Bands, Diamond Ring. Is someone proposing on the trip? I look where the voice is coming from, but it's an old man in thick glasses. He doesn't seem like a likely candidate to get married any time soon.

Most of the back of the bus is empty. I settle into the window seat in the very last row and flip open the folder. I only get two paragraphs into the first article when I sense movement toward my end of the bus. An old woman in a pink sweat suit is heading determinedly down the aisle. *Please don't sit here,* I silently beg. I'm sure she's a nice enough lady, but I really don't want to have to make small talk with a stranger for fourteen hours. *Please be heading for the bathroom.*

So of course she sits down next to me. She looks even older than the rest, with the brightest white hair I've ever seen. You could see her hair from space, I bet. I can't imagine why she would have walked all the way down the aisle when there were plenty of open seats up front. She smiles at me, so I smile back. I hope she can't sense my disappointment at not getting to sit alone. She settles into her seat, lifts a huge container of red licorice out of her enormous pocketbook, and offers me a piece.

"Um, thanks," I say, peeling one off the top.

"What's that you're reading?" she asks, tilting her head toward my folder.

I glance down at my lap. "Some articles about eclipses. I'm, uh, trying to learn stuff before we get there."

She nibbles at her licorice and says, "You don't need

to read any articles. You got a living, breathing eclipse expert right here."

I nod. "I know. He's my science teacher at school."

She laughs and then starts coughing. It goes on so long I start to worry. I wonder if resuscitating old people is on my list of official responsibilities. I move my licorice to the other side of me so she doesn't cough on it.

"Not Silver," she says. "Me! This is my sixth eclipse. I've traveled the world for 'em. Saved all my money to do it, too. Worth every penny and then some. I've got almost half an hour of totality — that's total darkness, you know — under my belt. If I *wore* a belt, that is. Never could understand the fascination with belts. Let's tie something really tight around our waists. Cut off our circulation. That's smart! The things people do for fashion. Doesn't make any kind of sense."

When I'm pretty sure she's done ranting about belts, I say, "Well, I don't know why women wear belts, but guys need them or else our pants would fall down."

Her brows rise under her white hair. "Is that so? I never knew that."

I nod.

"So what can I tell you about eclipses in exchange for that tidbit of knowledge?"

The bus is starting to pull out of the lot now, and I can see Mom and Mike standing by the car, watching. The windows are tinted and I know they can't see me, but my hand goes up to wave anyway. Yesterday if someone had told me I'd be here now, talking about belts and eclipses with a little old lady in a pink sweat suit while eating licorice, I'd have thought they were crazy. But here I am.

"Well," I say, swallowing the last bit of licorice, "I've only read a little bit so far, so I don't really know what to ask." She looks disappointed, so I think for a second. "But I guess you could tell me why people would spend their life savings to see it get dark for a few minutes. It's dark for, like, twelve hours a day anyway."

She laughs again and I'm afraid it's going to turn into another coughing fit. Fortunately, she catches her breath. "Only a poet can truly describe an eclipse, and I'm sorry to say I'm not a very good one. But comparing what you see during an eclipse to the darkness at night is like comparing an ocean to a teardrop. Do you see what I mean?"

I shake my head.

"Well, it's the same thing, what makes up a teardrop and the ocean, but completely different in magnitude. Yes, it gets dark during an eclipse, and the stars come out in the daytime, and that's all well and good," she explains. "But it's what the SUN does that makes it so special. At night, it's dark because the sun is shining on the other side of the earth, right?"

I know I'm supposed to say yes, but hey, I failed seventh grade science. I nod, figuring that is the safest answer.

She continues. "During an eclipse, it's dark, see, but

79

the sun is still there, right in front of you. Only it's not, because the moon is completely covering it. So all you can see is this perfect circle of white streamers billowing out at you. And it changes everything around you. It changes you, too, on the inside." She lowers her voice. "Some religious folk even say it's the Eye of God. Could be, but all I know is it's something to marvel at for sure." She wipes a tear away from her face and I look away, totally clueless as to what to do.

While she fishes around in her bag, probably for a tissue, I become aware of a clacking sound. It seems to be coming from under the bus. Probably just something in the storage bins rattling around. Hopefully.

Mr. Silver's booming voice suddenly fills the air. "Hello, everyone!" I peer over the seat in front of me and see him standing at the front of the bus, gripping the top of the seat for balance. He's holding a cordless microphone and is wearing a hat that I can only describe as a big stuffed sun. If the kids at school could see him now!

He tips his hat to the group and people laugh. He says, "Hello and welcome to the Eclipse Tour. I recognize some faces from our trip to Tibet a few years back, and many new faces, too. Whether this is your first eclipse or your tenth, I know this will be an experience you'll never forget. Unlike the other trips, this one won't include much sightseeing or fancy meals or visits to local museums. You won't have to pack up your belongings each day to travel to the next location. This is a quieter trip, but no less extraordinary. We'll set up camp and explore the heavens under one of the darkest skies in the states. We'll learn how to tell Andromeda from the Great Bear. We'll search for faint fuzzies — those distant deep sky objects — with a variety of telescopes and binoculars. And during the day we'll search for intelligent life on other planets, we'll walk a labyrinth, and contemplate the beauty of nature from a kayak in the middle of a pristine lake. And then what happens at the end?"

He pauses here, and cups his hand over his ear. In unison, everyone (except me) shouts, "The eclipse!"

"That's right!" he says, laughing. "We're going to be on the only spot of American soil to witness all of nature holding its breath. Of course we'll be holding our breath along with it!"

Everyone cheers.

"Raise your hands if this is your first eclipse."

I raise my hand a few inches, even though no one can see me in the back row. About half the group raises their hands, too. This makes me feel better. I'm not the only clueless one.

"A special welcome to the newbies!" Mr. Silver calls out. "Where are you all from?"

Voices call out from all over the bus. "New York City! Memphis! Dallas! Seattle!"

I'm shocked. All these people came together in MY hometown to take a fourteen-hour bus ride?

"Who can tell me why they call a total solar eclipse

Nature's Greatest Coincidence?" Mr. Silver grins as hands shoot up all around the bus. We're barely out of town and already I feel like I'm back at school, not knowing the correct answers.

Mr. Silver calls on a lady in the front and waves her up to the microphone. He places the sun hat on her head and says, "Whoever has the hat, has our attention, folks." She giggles, adjusting it on her head. Then she says, "The only reason we can see an eclipse is because the moon and the sun happen to look the exact same size from earth. But really, the moon is 400 times smaller. It's just that coincidentally, the sun is 400 times as far away as the moon, so they look the same size to us. If the moon were even a few miles smaller across, it wouldn't hide the face of the sun when it passed in front of it."

Mr. Silver lifts the hat off her head and puts it back on his own. "Thank you for that concise overview, uh —"

"Rebecca," the woman says, leaning into the mike.

"Thank you, Rebecca!" Everyone claps and Rebecca makes a little curtsy before carefully making her way back to her seat.

I still hear that clacking sound. Every once in a while a quick *hiss* joins in. Pink Sweat Suit Lady doesn't seem to notice. Although she's so old she could be hard of hearing. None of the other adults notice either so I guess it's just a normal bus noise and I'm being paranoid.

"I'm going to let you all relax in a minute, but I just want to introduce my assistant on this trip — Jack Rosten. Where are ya, Jack?"

My face burns when I hear my name. "Uh, I'm back here," I say, lifting my hand.

"Stand up, Jack," Mr. Silver booms. "Let everyone see who ya are."

I stand up awkwardly in my seat, and the folder goes flying onto the head of the person in front of me. Very coordinated.

"Jack here is going to be my right-hand man. Anything you need and I'm not around, you can ask him. Right, Jack?"

I smile weakly as everyone cranes their necks to look at me. The last time I was the center of attention like this was when I was a stalk of broccoli in the third grade play and forgot my one line. It was something about how broccoli is an important antioxidant or something like that. The whole audience stared at me until finally the carrot stepped forward to deliver her line about carrots being good for the eyes.

"Pssst, I think you can sit down now," whispers Pink Sweat Suit Lady, tugging gently on my sleeve.

I quickly sit. The guy in front of me slips my folder through the seats and I take it.

"I didn't know you were such an important figure," she says, offering me another piece of licorice. I'm too shaken up to take it. How am I supposed to be this guy's right-hand man when I don't know anything

83

about anything? I'm starting to think I made a big mistake. At least at summer school all I'd have to do is sit there.

Mr. Silver is talking again. "Now everyone lean back and enjoy the countryside. We'll stop for lunch in a few hours."

The chatter picks up again and then eventually people either drift off to sleep or start reading. It doesn't take long for corn and wheat fields to replace the strip malls and office buildings. I bury myself in reading the articles. All the words I had heard when I first got on the bus are explained in there. I guess it sounds interesting, but I honestly still don't see what the big deal is. I take out my sketchpad and a thin charcoal pencil and start drawing. Mr. Silver becomes a tall, thin alien in a sun-hat. Instead of standing in front of a bus, the alien is at the front of a spaceship. A pudgy wizard in a high pointy hat stands next to him. I'm the wizard.

I thought Pink Sweat Suit Lady was sleeping, but she leans over and looks at my picture before I have time to jerk it away. "Remarkable likeness," she jokes. "You must really be interested in outer space."

I shake my head. "Why would you say that?"

She scrunches her brows at me. "Well, besides the fact that you're the assistant eclipse tour leader, you're drawing pictures of aliens."

Okay, so she has a point. How can I explain that I

never really thought of my aliens as living on other worlds, like they could possibly exist? I just think of them in some alternate reality, the same as wizards and monsters.

"My name's Stella," she says, extending a frail hand.

I reach out to shake it, afraid to hurt her. Her shake is surprisingly strong and firm.

"My son and his wife are up front," she tells me. "His wife doesn't like it when I'm in the way too much. So I try to stay out of the way. You know that old saying, 'your daughter's your daughter all of your life, your son is your son till he gets a wife'?"

I shake my head.

"Yeah, well, it's true. So be good to your momma while you're young." Then she pulls two long knitting needles out of her bag. A skinny red scarf is attached, clearly a work in progress. Stella starts knitting so quickly I can barely see the tips of the needles darting in and out of the yarn. I close my eyes and wonder again how I got here.

I must have fallen asleep, but the clanking and hissing awakens me. Most people are sleeping, too. Stella isn't in her seat. I see the restroom door says occupied, so she must be there. I lift up the armrest between our seats and slide out. We're going pretty fast, and it's hard to keep my balance, but I manage to make it to the front without too many "sorry's" and "excuse me's."

I kneel next to Mr. Silver, who is going through some

papers. "I think there's something wrong with the bus," I whisper, so as not to alarm anyone nearby.

"What do you mean?" he asks.

"There's a clanking and a hissing."

"Can you describe the clanking and the hissing?"

"Well, the clanking sort of sounds like a clank, and the hiss is well, a hissing sound."

"I was kidding, Jack," Mr. Silver says, laying his papers on the empty seat next to him. "Lighten up, kid, or it's going to be a long two weeks."

Sometimes I'm not sure when people are joking. One of my many deficiencies.

"We're going to pull off for lunch soon, and I'll have the driver check it out then, okay?"

I nod. I'm starting to get a little nauseated facing backward, so I make my way down to my seat. Stella is back, her face buried in a book. As I get closer I realize with horror that it's MY book she's holding. Not the short story book — my sketch pad! I never, ever let anyone look through it. My first reaction is to grab it from her hands, and it takes a lot of self-control not to. I watch her expression as she turns each page slowly. She almost looks, well, *pleased*.

I clear my throat. Or I try to. It comes out more like a gargle.

She looks up, then hoists herself out of her seat so I can squeeze by. "Well, my young friend. You are quite talented."

I don't answer, I just take the pad from her hands and sit. She picks up her needles again.

A few minutes later, the bus pulls off the highway and into a McDonald's restaurant that says WE WELCOME BUSES on a big sign out front. The bus clanks and hisses to a stop. Everyone files out, and I'm the last one off. I linger to watch the bus driver unscrew a panel in the back, right under my seat. He tinkers in there for a few minutes and then goes back into the bus. He returns with a full toolkit. I want to watch, but the smell of hamburgers wafts through the air, and my stomach growls in response. I'm no match for the pull of the burger.

When I get inside the restaurant I immediately flash back to the middle school cafeteria. I always hated walking in and not knowing where I should sit. Last year I wound up sitting with a few other kids who didn't have a place to sit. It was better than sitting alone, but it's tiring pretending I wouldn't rather be asked to sit somewhere. I get in line behind the young family with the little boy. The father recognizes me from the bus and puts out his hand.

"Hi, Jack," he says warmly. "I'm David. This is my wife Hayley and our son, Pete. It's our first eclipse."

"Mine too," I say, shaking all their hands, even Pete's.

"How did you wind up here?" he asks as Hayley orders their meal.

I almost tell him it was this or summer school, but

instead I just say, "Mr. Silver is my science teacher. He invited me."

"Wow," David says. "I can't imagine having someone like him as a teacher. What's he like in the classroom?"

I shrug. "Just like a teacher I guess. Talks a lot . . . gives tests . . . chalk on his pants."

David glances admiringly over toward where Mr. Silver is eating with a group of eclipse chasers. "Really? He's so famous and all, I would have thought he'd be really amazing."

"Huh? Famous?"

"Well, he leads these eclipse tours all over the world. They always fill up years ahead of time. Plus he's written a book on backyard astronomy that many people believe is the best around. So I'd say he's pretty famous." He picks up the tray and says, "See you later."

I'm speechless.

"Welcome to McDonald's, may I take your order?"

"Huh?"

The teenage girl pops her gum and says, "Welcome to Mc —"

"I got it," I reply, and order the first thing my eyes land on, a double cheeseburger Mighty Kids Meal. While I wait for the food I stare across the restaurant at Mr. Silver. I might not listen much in class, but I'm pretty sure he never told us he wrote books. The people at his table are hanging onto his every word. I'm still staring as the bus driver hurries in and whispers something in Mr. Silver's ear. He stands and follows him out. I ask the girl to make my order to-go, and she puts it in a bag.

I hurry out after them. The driver is now under the bus, with only his legs sticking out. Mr. Silver sees me and says, "There he is, the hero of the day."

"Me?"

"I knew bringing you along would pay off. I just didn't realize how soon! The driver has to replace a faulty crankshaft. If he had driven on it much longer, the whole engine could have gone. We would have broken down in the middle of the highway."

I'm filled with an unfamiliar feeling. Something like pride?

Of course later Mr. Silver embarrasses me by announcing to the bus that I single-handedly saved us from certain doom. Everyone claps for me, and Stella gives me her whole container of licorice. Except for peeking in my sketchbook, she's turned out to be a pretty good traveling companion.

After two brief breaks at rest stops, and endless miles of cornfields, we pull into a motel. It has two floors and is so nondescript that it blends into the gray twilight. I've never stayed in a hotel or motel before. Whenever we go on a family trip, which isn't very often, we always stay with relatives or friends of Mom's. Mr. Silver waves for me to join him and asks everyone else to wait in their seats. I can't say I'm getting used to everyone looking at me as I walk down the long aisle, but at least my face has stopped burning.

I accompany him to the front desk, where they hand us a list of restaurants that deliver food, and a whole batch of envelopes, each with a last name or two on it. He assigns me the job of reading out the names and distributing the envelopes. Of course I mangle half the names, but eventually all the envelopes are gone except for Mr. Silver's and one marked ADAMS. I guess that was the kid I replaced. I slide a plastic card out of the envelope and turn it over in my hand a few times.

"What's this for?" I ask Mr. Silver, risking sounding stupid.

"It's your room key. You slide it in and the door clicks open. I'm right down the hall, so if you need anything, come get me. We should exchange cell numbers, too."

"Um, I don't have a cell."

"Oh. Well, we won't get any reception once we're at the Moon Shadow anyway."

"The Moon Shadow? Isn't that a Cat Stevens song?" SD3 used to play Cat Stevens all the time.

"Indeed it is. But it's also the name of the campground," he says, reaching under the bus for the only other bag besides mine. "Hey, tonight if you're not too tired, I'd like to go over the project I'll be needing your help with."

"There's more than just the eclipse?"

He nods. "Yes. This is unrelated. I'm on a team to find exoplanets, and we need to coordinate our efforts perfectly with the other members of the team, stationed at various coordinates around the world. We'll only have a small window of time to do the experiment, a few days before the eclipse."

I stare at him blankly.

He sighs. "I'll explain on the bus tomorrow instead."

I make my way up to my room, which is on the second floor all the way at the end. By the time I get there I'm dripping with sweat. I think Mom must have tossed some of those cans of food in my bag even though I told her not to. David from the McDonalds walks by with an empty ice bucket. I ask him if he knows what an exoplanet is.

"Sure," he says. "It's what they call a planet around a star other than the sun. You know, like in other solar systems."

"Oh, right," I say, as though I'd known but forgotten.

"See ya," he says, and heads off to the ice machine, whistling. He seems so at ease with himself. So not like me, sweaty and unable to get the door open. I turn the card every different way until finally a little green light comes on and I hear a click.

My room is just like I've seen in the movies. Worn-out blue carpet, stained orange bedspread, faded painting of a boat riding a wave. It smells like cigar smoke and feet.

It's actually pretty cool.

I snack until midnight on pretzel rods and orange soda from the vending machines and watch an *Outer Limits* marathon on the Sci-Fi channel. The marathon might have been a bad idea, because as soon as I turn off the lamp, I hear all sorts of creepy noises. I try pulling the blanket over my head, but the sheet and blanket are tucked in so tight on the bottom that they don't budge. When the digital clock displays 1:00 AM, I finally push the battered armchair in front of the door and play with my Game Boy until my fingers start to cramp up. At three AM I tune the television to something less likely to give me nightmares — the all-night shopping channel. All I want to do is fall asleep so I can fly, but sleep just won't come.

I wake up a few hours later unsure if I actually purchased a Super Fantastic Egg Blaster for two monthly payments of $14.95 or if I dreamt it. I'm pretty sure I dreamt it, since the last time I looked, I don't own a credit card. We don't have to be back on the bus till nine, but I want to make sure I get the muffins and juice that come with the room. I'm about to go down to the lobby to get it when there's a knock on my door. I open it to find a guy in his fifties who I'd seen a few times during the trip.

Skipping any pleasantries, he says, "You were sitting next to my mother, Stella? On the bus?"

"Yes, Stella," I repeat. I *knew* I shouldn't have accepted that whole container of licorice. I ate half of it when I couldn't sleep, but there's still a decent amount left. I grab it off the dresser and hand it to him. "Here you go," I say. "Sorry about that."

He looks down at the container in his hands and pushes it back at me. "No, you don't understand." He takes a step back, looks around, and says, "She's missing."

ALLY

4

When I get down to the kitchen, Kenny is alone at the table, one of his bug books open in front of him. He is munching on a Pop-Tart while turning the pages.

"Where are Mom and Dad?" I ask, sitting down across from him. I align the Golden Grahams box so that it blocks my view of the book.

"Dad had to go into town," he answers, his mouth full of crumbs. "Mom's down at the RV park. One came in really early this morning."

"So much for our family meeting," I say, making a bowl of cereal. "Did they say anything to you about it?"

Kenny shakes his head. "Here," he says, handing me an orange plastic spoon. "This was in the cereal box. It's supposed to change colors in milk."

I dip the spoon into my bowl. It instantly turns green. "Cool."

The screen door bangs open and Ryan walks in. I like that he doesn't feel he has to knock.

"Ready to search for aliens?" he asks.

I hurriedly finish off my cereal and place the bowl in the sink. I expect Kenny to jump up, too, but he reaches for his third Pop-Tart instead. "You're not coming?"

"Gotta help Ralph in the kitchen. I'm behind from yesterday."

I'll take dirt-smoothing over kitchen duty any day. Kenny doesn't seem to mind though. Over the last few months he's even learned how to cook. Wait till he has to make eggs for five hundred hungry campers!

"I just need to grab my sneakers. Come up with me."

Ryan takes a swig of orange juice directly from the carton and then follows me to my room. We used to have sleepovers up here when we were little. Ryan sits backward on my desk chair and smiles. "One great thing about coming here," he says, "is that nothing ever changes. It's like whenever I come back here, no time has passed at all."

I look around. True, I don't change my room much. The blue blanket with the sun on it is the same one I've had my whole life. Same stuffed panda. Same lamp with the torn yellow shade. Same small wooden desk with my school notebooks on it. The books on my shelves change, though. And the poster on the back of my door is new. I point it out to Ryan, who leans forward for a closer look. If you didn't know better, the big poster would look like a chart of fuzzy dots with little red check marks next to some of them.

"The Messier objects," he says, impressed. "You're looking for them?"

"Yup. I haven't found too many yet though. Some cool galaxies and globular clusters will be in view over the next few weeks. You can help look, if you want." I grab my sneakers from the closet. "Isn't it amazing how we could never travel to other galaxies in a hundred lifetimes, but with a telescope we can be there instantly?" He nods, takes a last glance at the chart, and follows me out.

"The Moon Shadow is hosting a Messier Marathon next March," I tell him as we head outside. "So I just wanted to get a head start. Plus, I need to know all of them eventually. You know, for the whole comet thing."

"What do the Messier objects have to do with finding a comet?"

"They have a lot to do with it," I explain. "The Messier objects started as a list of faint objects in the sky that AREN'T comets, so if you find them, you won't mistake them for one."

"Right," he says. "I forgot about that."

"Maybe you and your grandparents can come up for it. It's the only night of the year when all the objects are visible. We'll get to stay up all night. It'll be really fun."

"I don't think I can," Ryan says. "We have this school talent show thing at the end of March. Me and my buddies are in a band."

First his grandmother is going to miss the eclipse, then Ryan skips the Messier Marathon for a talent show? People have strange priorities.

The steady hum of the old computer greets us as we walk into Alien Central. We pull the two wooden chairs closer to the desk to examine the screen. The upper left corner shows us that the current batch of data, called a work unit, is 82 percent analyzed so far. The upper right corner lists all the information about where in space the signal originated, and also shows how many work units our computer has analyzed so far. The coolest thing is that it also shows the constellation it's currently searching. Right now it's working on a section of Libra.

The part I like the best is in the lower half of the screen where a big grid shows blocks of vibrant colors spiking up and dropping. The different colors stand for the different frequencies coming through. Usually the patterns just reflect the sounds of cosmic noise given off by different stars and satellites and space itself. But any unusual change in the pattern could possibly mean the computer is receiving a signal from an intelligent life form.

"Wouldn't it be great," Ryan says, leaning forward in his chair, "if this was the year we actually found something?"

I laugh. "You've said that every year since you came here!"

"Well, I'm not as lucky as you to have this every day."

"You could put it on your home computer if you wanted."

Ryan shakes his head. "My father won't let me. He's all paranoid about running programs that send information back to the source."

In all the years Ryan has been coming here, I've never met his dad. He doesn't sound like a nice person.

"Plus," he adds almost as an afterthought, "my friends would think I'm a geek if they knew I was interested in this kind of stuff."

"Really? Why are they your friends then?"

"Never thought about it. They've just always been my friends. It's not like I chose them exactly."

"People don't choose their friends?"

He shrugs. "Not really. It's usually people you live near, or kids in your classes. You're stuck with each other, so you become friends. You know, like we did."

"Oh." I stare down at my hands.

"That didn't come out right," he says quickly. "I just mean that I showed up here, and we were sort of put together by our grandfathers and so we became friends."

I pick my words carefully. "So we're not friends because we like each other? Because we like hanging out together?"

"Of course we are. But that comes after."

"Oh," I say again. It feels different being with Ryan this year and I can't pinpoint why. I wonder if he feels it too. We sit quietly and watch the waves of color cross the screen. It's almost hypnotic. I'm startled out of my trance by a loud rumbling out front. A huge RV is turning the corner toward the cabin. They must have taken a wrong turn on their way to the RV park on the other side of the lake. We put all the RVs as far away from the main camp as possible so the noise and exhaust doesn't bother other campers. It's also closest to the playground, and a lot of the RVers have kids.

"Be right back," I tell Ryan. "Don't find any aliens without me." The screen door bangs behind me as I go out onto the dirt road to wave down the RV. The driver sees me and stops. A middle-aged guy with a Mets baseball cap gets out, clutching one of the paper maps he would have been given at check-in. He is followed by a tired-looking woman holding a cell phone. "Hello?" she says repeatedly into it. "Can you hear me now?"

"I'm sorry," I tell her. "We don't get cell phone signals up here."

She flips the phone closed. "I was just trying to call the front desk. We can't find where we're supposed to go."

"I'll show you." I walk over to the map the man is holding out, and start pointing out where we're standing, and how to get to the RV park. As I trace the path with my finger, two little boys step out of the RV. They are pale with bright red hair. I've never seen identical twins before, and can't help but stare. They are wearing the same outfit — blue jeans and yellow t-shirts with a cartoon character on them. It looks like a train with a face.

Both look at me with interest, then one of them says, "Mommy, I've gotta go potty."

The mother smiles apologetically at me. "We're still working on the whole toilet-training thing."

I smile weakly in response, not sure what else to do. I remember when my mom was toilet training Kenny, she just used to let him run around the campground without his diaper. It only took a few days. But that was back when no one else lived here. The woman takes her son back inside, and the other follows closely at her heels.

"No one was at the office when we pulled in," the man says, tucking the map into his pocket. "The guy at the gate checked us in, but I'm waiting on a fax from my business partner, and it's supposed to come to the main office."

"I'll check on it," I tell him. "When it arrives I'll be sure someone brings it out to you."

He nods, and climbs back in. I hold my breath as the exhaust wafts past me. Back in the cabin, I tell Ryan I have to go. "No one's manning the office, so I have to —"

He suddenly stands up, knocking over his chair and

cutting off what I was saying. My first thought is that he's seen the huge soul-eating bug that I found in the Art House last week. I immediately jump back and press myself against the wall. The bug must have snuck over to this side of the cabin, even though once glance tells me the door is still closed. I KNEW that thing had superpowers! But Ryan's pointing wildly at the computer screen, not at the ground.

"What is it? You're freaking me out." I hope people still say "freaking out."

"The pattern!" he yells. "It spiked! Look!" He jabs at the screen, sending little prisms in all directions.

He's right! The red section of the graph is spiking really high, then low, then high again, in a pattern I've never seen before. We turn to stare at each other, eyes wide.

"Great Galileo's Ghost!" I shout.

"What do we do?" Ryan asks.

"I'm not sure. We never thought we'd really find anything." Alien Central is really Kenny's domain. He should be here. Dad said he has walkie-talkies to give us so we can all find each other easily once things get crazy, but he didn't hand them out yet. "Hey, you know what I just realized?"

"That we could be the first people to discover life on another planet?"

"No! I mean, yes, but something else. That signal came from the constellation Libra, right?"

"Yeah?"

101

☽

"That's where Glenn's planet is!"

"Huh?"

"Glenn! From Gleise!"

He recovers quickly. "Oh, right! Cool!"

"Don't you look for him anymore?"

"Um, well, with all the light pollution it's getting harder to see many stars in the suburbs."

"Oh." I try not to show my disappointment. All this time I thought Ryan was looking up at Glenn, too.

Then Ryan says, "But if our signal is The One, then EVERYBODY will be looking up at Glenn!"

He's right! I feel instantly better.

The screen door bangs open and we both whirl around. "What's going on?" Kenny asks. "I heard you three cabins away."

"Look!" I point to the screen. Kenny goes closer and then yells, "Great Galileo's Ghost! We have to call them."

"Call who?" Ryan asks. "The aliens?"

Kenny looks at Ryan like HE'S an alien. "The SETI people! We have to call them!" He looks at me expectantly. Kenny's the idea man, and that makes me the one who actually DOES anything. I upright Ryan's chair from the floor and move it in front of the desk. Hands shaking, I stick in a disk and save the portion of the work unit that has been processed so far. Then I click back to the results screen and onto the home page. "I can't find a contact number."

Kenny starts pacing, rubbing his chin just like Dad does when he's frustrated. "How about an e-mail?" he asks. I keep looking and finally find a way to contact volunteers through a live chat. I click on that and wait for someone to turn up. I'm a pretty patient person, but as the seconds tick by I'm starting to get agitated. Finally someone's name pops up on the screen and the words "Can I help you?" appear in a little box on the left side.

I type as fast as I can. "Yes! Hi! We think we've found a signal. What do we do?"

The three of us beam at each other while we wait for a reply. A few seconds later: "You don't do anything. We get a large number of errant signals a month. When your work unit is complete, it will upload automatically. If we find a signal that merits looking into, we will contact you with the information we have on record."

Our collective bubble bursts. "That's it?" Kenny says, sagging into the other chair. Ryan nudges my shoulder. "Ask how long it takes."

I type the question, and the reply says, "Could be a few weeks."

"Okay," I type, slower this time. "Thanks."

"Well that's that," I say, staring at the patterns, which have returned to normal. "I guess we wait."

No one says anything for a minute, then Kenny says, "Pretty cool!" and Ryan and I say, "Yeah it is!"

☽

and we start laughing because it IS pretty cool. It's REALLY, REALLY cool! Then I remember I was on my way to the office and I leave them high-fiving and whooping.

I hope Mom and Dad are back because it's getting pretty busy already. More arrivals are making their way to their cabins as I hurry down the road. I can feel the grin from finding a possible signal still splitting my face. When I round the corner toward the office, I see a girl about my age sitting on the stoop, her chin in her hands. She doesn't look happy. I hope she and her family haven't been waiting long.

"Can I help you?" I ask her as I approach. I stop a few feet away and stare. She is the prettiest girl I've ever seen outside of magazines. She has blazing blue eyes and long brown hair that shimmers where the sun hits it.

"Not unless you can get me a different set of parents," she says firmly. She gestures with her thumb to her parents and a younger girl. The others are talking excitedly, and turning in circles to point at different things. I'm about to interrupt when the younger girl suddenly does a back flip. In midair! Just standing there! My jaw falls open. Behind me, the girl on the stoop sighs loudly.

"That was really cool," I call out to the younger girl.

"Thanks!" she replies, chewing happily on her ponytail.

I go over to the parents. "Are you trying to check in?

My mom just got caught up somewhere, but I can help you."

To my surprise, they both reach out and hug me!

"You must be Ally!" the mother says. "We've heard a lot about you."

"Um, you have?"

They pull away and I stand stiff. I can't remember when the last time people I hadn't met before hugged me. Never?

"It's US!" they exclaim, their eyes shining. "The Holdens!"

"Um, okay." Mom sometimes gets chatty with the people she makes reservations for, but she must have really bonded with these people. "Let's go in." I turn and hurry past the girl on the stoop and push open the screen door. I grab the clipboard with the daily arrivals off the desk and scan the list.

"I'm sorry," I say, looking up. "I don't see your name here."

They laugh. "We're a few days early," the father says. "We just couldn't wait to get settled in our new home."

I smile. It's nice when people come to think of the Moon Shadow as their home away from home. "Well, I'm sure it won't be a problem."

"This office," the mother says, "it's attached to the main house, right?"

I nod, looking around for Mom's reservation book. She must have it with her.

"We'd love to see the rooms later, if that's okay," the mom continues. "Just to peek."

I'm taken aback. No one has asked to see our house before. I don't know how to respond. The girl on the stoop calls into the room. "Don't forget you said I get first pick of rooms, not Melanie! You promised!"

Her parents roll their eyes at each other. "We didn't forget, Bree."

"Do you know if our boxes arrived yet?" the father asks. "They were supposed to get here yesterday. About twenty of them?"

I shake my head. This conversation is starting to make less and less sense. No one has ever had boxes sent here before, let alone twenty. "I don't think so. The mail is really slow here." The door squeaks open behind me and Mom rushes in, sweaty and harried. I feel a flood of relief. She can sort this out. I really want to tell her about the SETI readings, but these people are obviously confused.

"Mom, these are the Holdens. They're checking in, but they're a few days early. And they're looking for some boxes they had sent ahead?"

Her face drains of color. She stares at them in horror. A little prickle is starting to creep up my neck. Who *are* these people? The girl from the stoop comes in and leans against the wall.

I clear my throat. "Um, Mom? What's going on?"

She recovers and, with obvious effort, forces a smile. "I wasn't expecting you yet. We didn't get to, I mean, we haven't explained yet, I mean . . ." She trails off and just sort of sags a little, her smile dropping away.

"Mom? Is everything okay?" The prickles are picking up in intensity.

She stands there for a minute, then takes a deep breath. Reaching over to me, she takes my hands in hers. "Honey, we should have told you by now but there was never a good time. These are the Holdens." She gestures at the group, but I don't take my eyes from her face. "They are here to take over the Moon Shadow after the eclipse."

My jaw falls open. I couldn't be more surprised if she told me NASA called to say the eclipse has been cancelled. My knees buckle. My mother tightens her grip on my hands. "WHAT? What are you talking about?"

"Oh, wow," the girl leaning against the wall says. "And I thought MY parents snuck this on us! But at least we had *some* warning."

"Shh, Bree!" her mother says, herding them all out the door.

"Mom?" My voice shakes uncontrollably.

Still holding my hands tight, she says, "Honey, your dad is going back to work in Chicago, and we're going with him. You knew we weren't planning on staying here forever, right?"

It takes a minute for her words to sink in. "*What?* No, I didn't! This is our home. This is all Kenny's ever known. You can't do this."

Her eyes fill with tears. "It's time, Ally. You and Kenny need to learn to live in the world. We can't keep you tucked away forever. You need to meet other kids your age. You need to have experiences that you can't have here."

"But lots of people come through here," I argue, my heart pounding in my ears. "And maybe we can travel more, see more places. We don't have to MOVE."

She lets go of my hands and I rock back a little on my heels. "We do, honey. The Holdens are here to take over, at least for a few years."

I feel my hopes rise a smidge, grasping onto any small scrap. "Then we can come back?"

She shakes her head. "No, then it will be up to them to find replacements. It won't be hard to do. It didn't take us long to find them."

Her words are starting to sink in. My brain is whirling, my stomach is churning. All these thoughts are going through my head. Why didn't they tell us? Where are we going to live? How am I going to leave here? This place is more than just where we live. It's a part of us. And we're a part of it. I'm too stunned to cry.

"I better get out to them," Mom says, gesturing toward the front porch. "We'll have that family meeting tonight and explain everything. I wish we had done it already, then you wouldn't be caught off guard like this. We knew how you'd react, and didn't want it to ruin all the eclipse excitement for you. I'm so sorry. We put it off too long."

"But where are we moving?"

"Back where you were born. Near Chicago."

I search my brain to bring up any memories of a time before here. All I can bring up are tall buildings that blot out the sky. And a crowded, noisy department store that smells like too much perfume. It's not much, but it's enough to know I don't want to live there.

"Don't tell Kenny," she continues. "Let me and your father do it."

I shake away the blur of noise, colors, people, and smells. Why would anyone want to be there, when they can be here, where the air is clean and you can breathe? "Do you have to tell him tonight? He's in such a good mood. I was too." I almost don't want to share the news with her after what they did, but she'll find out eventually. "We found a possible signal today. In Alien Central."

"You did? That's wonderful! What happens now?"

"They said they'd let us know if the signal is real or not."

"Well, that's very exciting," she says.

I don't answer. It's hard to feel excited about anything right now. I cross my arms tight, trying to hold myself together.

"I'm really sorry, honey," she says, stroking my hair. "This will be a good thing, you'll see. I do think we need to tell Kenny tonight though, so try to steer clear of him if you can."

One look at my face and Kenny would know something was very wrong. I've never been good at hiding my feelings. I've never had to.

Before Mom can say anything else, Mrs. Holden comes back into the office with her older daughter, who has a name I've never heard of before, rhymes with *knee*?

"We're sorry to bother you," she says. "But my daughter is anxious to find out about those boxes. She'd like to change her clothes." The woman says the last part apologetically, with a "you know teenagers" kind of grimace.

I take in the short, wavy skirt, the sandals, the hot pink tank top. Definitely not the usual camping attire. She looks like she stepped out of the pages of *Teen* magazine. One of our guests left a copy here a few years ago. When I looked at it, I felt like those girls were a different species from me. The pretty girl pulls at the top with obvious disgust. "I've been wearing these clothes all day," she complains. "The taxi, the airport, the plane, the van, the diner, and now this place with all the dirt flying everywhere. A shower wouldn't hurt either. I feel totally gross. How can you stand it, Mom?"

Her mother leans her head in toward my mother's and says, "Bree isn't taking the move so well. You have to forgive her."

Bree's lips form a straight line and she glares at her mother. I actually feel sorry for the girl. She apparently didn't ask for this any more than I did.

"Ally," my mother says, "perhaps you'd be kind enough to take Bree up to your room? She can use your shower, and I'm sure you have some clothes you can lend her."

Doesn't she see that Bree is about a foot taller than me? And thinner? And somehow I don't think she's going to be too excited about my clothes. Bree starts to say something, but her mother shushes her and says to me, "That would be very kind. Thank you, Ally."

I didn't realize I had agreed to anything. The two mothers turn toward the bulletin board to look at the chart of available high-end cabins, ignoring us both. I can't believe that in the span of half an hour I went from jumping for joy over the possibility of discovering that we are not alone in the universe, to feeling like all the air has been sucked out of my body. I know I should cry, should be screaming to the rafters at the unfairness of it all, but I'm just numb. It feels so unreal.

I turn on my heel and Bree follows me. We don't speak as I lead her around to the front of the house. As we're about to enter, Ryan approaches from the other side. "Hey, Ally!" he says, heading toward us. He stops short when he sees Bree. I swear his mouth drops open a bit. Bree just stands there, lids half closed like she's bored, while he looks her up and down. I guess Bree is what a hottie looks like. She probably doesn't realize how pretty she is. Ryan doesn't even notice that my hand is shaking so hard on the door-knob that the whole door rattles on its hinges.

"I'll see you at dinner, Ryan, okay?" Not waiting for an answer, I herd Bree inside and upstairs. Kenny must still be at Alien Central. If I see him I'm going to have to run the other way.

When we get to my room she takes it in with one glance, then throws herself down on my bed. Good thing I had actually made the bed today. This morn-ing seems like a lifetime ago. "You're SO lucky you're getting out of here," she says, staring at the ceiling. "It's like you're getting sprung from jail. I can't even BELIEVE this is my life now."

I can't believe I heard her correctly. I can feel the heat rise to my face. "*Jail?* I'm lucky to be *leaving*? You're lucky to be *coming*! The Moon Shadow is the best place on the planet to live. And I can't believe this is your life now, either. This is supposed to be MY life."

She bolts upright. "I totally don't want your life. Trust me on that one. I don't mean to be rude or any-thing, but you're crazy! Why would anyone want to live out here? There's nothing to do."

"I don't mean to be rude either," I reply, choosing my words carefully, "but there's EVERYTHING to do here. Everything that matters, anyway."

Bree stares at me for so long I start to feel uncomfort-

112

able. In my own room! I turn away and start pulling things out of my drawers that might fit her. Everything looks drab and ragged next to her clothes. I never noticed my clothes were so dull before.

"Look," Bree says, her voice a little less cold. "You obviously like this place, for reasons I can't personally imagine. I really, really don't want to live here. Maybe we can work together."

I close my drawer and turn to face her. "What do you mean?"

She sits up on the bed. "Like we can make a plan. You know, to get our parents to change their minds. Like they did in *The Parent Trap*."

"The what?"

She looks at me like I'm from outer space. "The Disney movie?"

I shake my head.

She sighs. "It's this movie about these two twins who were separated at birth, each to live with one parent. They meet up at summer camp and decide to scheme to get their parents back together. Don't you get cable up here?"

"We don't have a television."

Her eyes become huge. She groans and flops forward on the bed again, pressing her face into my blanket.

"And, um, I don't know if you've noticed, but we're not twins."

"I've noticed," Bree says, her voice muffled. "That's not the point. Are you in, or not?"

"Do you really think it would work?"

"It HAS to work," she says, pushing herself up. "It just HAS to. I will shrivel up and die if I have to live here. No offense."

"Uh-huh." Clearly I'm going to have to let remarks like that go if we're going to be working together. "Okay," I tell her. "Let's do it."

"Good!" she says. She whips out a cell phone, presses some keys, and stares at the screen. "Wait, why isn't my text going through?"

"No reception up here."

"What?" she practically shrieks. "How will I call anyone? How will I text my friends?"

I shrug and leave to get her a towel from the hall closet. I don't understand how "texting" works or why someone would want to do it. But I don't want her to think I'm even more out of the loop than I obviously am. I grab the softest towel from the hall closet. I should tell her that she can bathe in the hot springs behind the house if she wants, instead of the boring shower. She'd probably jump at the chance, because who wouldn't? It's always warm, and there's lots of privacy. But I don't want to share the hot springs with her. In fact, I don't really want to share anything with her. This makes me feel guilty, because Mom and Dad taught us that the planet and everything on it (and above it, like the stars, and below it, like the springs) is meant to be shared. But still!

When I come back to the room Bree is facedown on

114

the bed again, her body shaking with tiny sobs. I tip-toe back out and close the door. I wish I could understand why someone wouldn't want to live here, but I can't. A flood of images makes me lean back onto the door for support. The labyrinth with its graceful, peaceful circles, the Art House where hundreds of guests over the years have painted their life stories on the walls, the Sun Garden with its magical way of turning shafts of light into time. And then it hits me with such force that I almost can't breathe — I won't be able to see the constellations in the city! The light pollution will blot out almost everything. Instead of the full glory of Orion, with his sword and his shield, all I'll be able to see are the three stars of his belt. I might not even see the Big Dipper or the North Star. Without the North Star, how will I know where I am? Stickers of the solar system on my ceiling aren't going to cut it.

I drop the towel on the bathroom counter, hold tight to the pouch around my neck, and weep.

BREE

4

I was wrong. This place isn't Purgatory. It's the *other* place. The hot one with the pitchforks and the flames and the ragged clothes. I already have three bites on each ankle. Once I took my shower (which turned lukewarm only minutes after stepping in), I went back to Ally's room and have refused to leave it. Believe me, there's not much to look at, and I've looked at everything. Many times. If anyone asked me, I could probably tell them the shapes of all those blobs on the poster on her door. According to the poster, which I've now read at least fifty times, the blobs are galaxies and clusters and nebulae out in space somewhere. I've heard of galaxies of course, but have no idea what the others are, and I don't want to know. Anything science-related belongs to the rest of my family. They don't think about how to dress (although they really should), and I don't think about anything scientific. It's just how it is.

It had taken a while to find something of Ally's that

I could wear. Everything was so . . . *bland*. It looked like it had all been washed together so many times it had blended into one shade of grayish-blue. Everything was loose fitting, and I finally selected a pair of shorts (which are probably long on her but are short on me) and the t-shirt with the most color left in it.

I feel like I'm wearing pajamas.

I do my daily fifty sit-ups, wishing with every one that I was lying on the soft pink carpet in my bedroom instead of Ally's unforgiving wooden floor.

My stomach tells me it's dinnertime, but I still can't make myself leave the room. As long as I stay in here, I can pretend I'm in a classmate's bedroom back at home. Some unfortunate girl who just moved to town and didn't know how to decorate. I'm here because we got stuck doing a history project together. Any minute her mother will bring us milk and cookies and I'll politely tell her I don't eat cookies.

But when a knock does come on the door, it's Ally. She sticks her head in and says, "Can I come in?"

"It's your room."

Ally comes in and sits at her desk chair. Her eyes are puffy. For some reason that makes me feel a little better. Not that I want someone else to suffer, of course. But it makes me feel better that I'm not the only one who's miserable. She glances at my outfit, but doesn't say anything. She seems like a nice enough kid. Totally backwoods though, like, I doubt she's ever been to a mall in her life. If her wardrobe wasn't so totally out of style, and if she brushed her hair and wore some lip gloss, she might even be pretty. I can't even give her a rating though, because she's at such a disadvantage here.

"Why don't we go down to dinner in the pavilion," she says. "We're having a barbecue for the first bus-load of eclipse chasers. You must be hungry."

I shake my head stubbornly. "I don't want to see my parents. And who, or what, are eclipse chasers?"

Ally raises her brows but says, "Eclipse chasers are people who travel around the world to see eclipses. There's about one a year, somewhere in the world. But sometimes they're in really hard-to-reach places, like a mountaintop, or in the middle of oceans, or by the South Pole or something."

"Or in the middle of nowhere like this place?"

"Believe it or not, this place is pretty easy to get to compared to most of them. That's why we're so busy. If you were in the next town over, you wouldn't be able to see it. I mean, you'd see something, like a partial eclipse, but that's not any good because you can't even look at it directly. The path of the rest of the eclipse is all up in Canada. Aren't you excited to see it?"

I shrug. I hadn't given it much thought. Like, none. "If our plan works, I might not even be here for it."

She gasps. "You'd leave here BEFORE the eclipse? But it . . . it's the most amazing thing you'll ever see."

I cross my arms. "The most amazing thing I'll ever

118

☆

see is that horrible van of my dad's pulling into my old driveway back home."

She shakes her head at me. I honestly don't care if she doesn't understand. I'm not here to make friends. I've had a chance to think about the plan over the last few hours, and I have some good ideas. "Look, let's just go to dinner and we'll sit by ourselves and work on our plan."

She nods. "That's fine. I don't want to sit with my family either."

"Okay then. And we've got to come up with two different plans of attack — one for your parents to convince them to stay, and one for mine to convince them to leave. They both have to change their minds or else it won't work since they have a written agreement."

"They do?" Ally asks, clearly not happy about this formality.

I nod. "My dad showed it to us back home. Full of boring lawyer-type clauses. You really had no idea about any of this?"

Ally shakes her head miserably. "I knew something was up, because my parents were acting a little weird. But I never, ever would have guessed this. I know you hate it here, but I love it. I barely remember living anywhere else. And Kenny was born here. How come your sister seems so happy to be here?"

How could I explain Melanie? "My sister thinks everything is a game. She's really smart, in school and stuff, but when it comes to real life she just doesn't think about things."

"I wish I didn't have to think about real life right now," Ally says wistfully.

"You won't have that choice when you get to be my age."

Ally puts her hands on her hips. "I AM your age. Well, practically. I'll be thirteen in two months."

"Really? I thought you were younger. Sorry."

Ally sighs. "It's okay."

"Maybe if you wore a little makeup . . ."

"Makeup? Why?"

Wow, this girl and Melanie would get along really well. "Um, because makeup makes people look better? And older, too."

She looks at me intently, like she's actually thinking about it. Then she says, "Should we really be talking about makeup at a time like this?"

I swing my legs off the bed, ready for action. "You're right. We need a notebook and a pen. If anyone asks what we're doing, you can say you're drawing a diagram of the place for me." I head for the door. It feels better having a purpose.

"Don't you want to change?" Ally says, pulling out long pants and a nondescript blue jacket.

"Why? It's still hot out, right?"

She tosses me the jacket and pants. "Trust me, you'll want these. It gets really buggy at dusk."

"Great," I mutter, pulling at my shorts. Ally turns

⭐

around quickly to face the other way. I'm so used to trying on clothes with my friends, crammed into one tiny dressing room, that I don't think twice about changing in front of people. The memory of the laughs we used to have in those dressing rooms makes my eyes sting with tears. I refuse to cry anymore though. Especially in front of Ally, who is being very brave for someone in her position. As much as I would rather live in my old town, I wouldn't want to enter middle school on the bottom of the social ladder, which is clearly where Ally will be if we don't change things.

I pull on the pants, slip on the jacket, and feel even less like myself than I did before. "Hey," I say to Ally as she goes to open the door. "Why didn't *you* change?" She's still wearing the bland wrinkled shorts and bland wrinkled t-shirt that I first saw her in. "Do you want privacy or something?"

Ally shakes her head. "I'm immune to mosquitoes for some reason. Always have been. I'll be fine."

If it were anyone else I'd think they just didn't want to cover up, but Ally clearly doesn't care what she looks like. I didn't even SEE a brush in her bathroom.

"You'll want these, too," she says, tossing me a pair of sneakers from her closet. "You won't last long in those sandals." She hands me a pair of socks, too. I can't remember the last time I wore socks. They do cover up my bitten-up ankles though. I stare at the old sneakers and then reluctantly put them on too.

☆

They're a little tight, and so dirty I can't even tell what color they used to be.

I feel like I'm wearing a costume, one that doesn't quite fit right. I follow her outside and down the road toward the dining area. Even the air feels different here. Thinner or thicker or something. It's unnerving.

My parents are standing at the entrance to the eating area, which is really nothing more than a whole bunch of picnic tables under a big tin roof.

"I tried to call you," Mom says, "but I couldn't get a signal."

I don't answer.

"Are you feeling better?"

I grunt. Ally steps aside to talk to her friend, the one who checked me out before.

"I like your outfit," Dad says.

"Haha, very funny."

"Seriously," he insists. "You look very natural. Outdoorsy, even."

They are all dressed in their same shorts and t-shirts. Melanie is already scratching at her legs. They still have that same happy glint in their eyes, which drives me crazy. I refrain from suggesting they cover up.

Ally comes back and says a polite hello to my family. Mom asks if she wants to join us for dinner. Ally looks to me, helpless. "Actually Ally and I are going to eat on our own. C'mon, Ally." I pull her away before anyone can argue.

Mom calls out after us, "I'm glad you two are getting along!"

I keep walking until Ally points to a table in the far corner.

"You wait here," she instructs. "I'll get us some burgers." Then she hesitates. "You do eat meat, right?"

"Why wouldn't I?"

She shrugs. "I don't know."

Why do people always assume that skinny people don't eat? "I eat plenty," I insist. And then without knowing why, I add, "I want to be a model one day, so I do have to watch my weight."

She looks curious. "What kind of model?"

"A model, you know. Fashion shows, commercials, magazine ads."

She tilts her head in thought. "You're really pretty and all, but why would you want to do that?"

"Why *wouldn't* I want to do that?" I look her straight in the eye, daring her to put down my career choice, my passion. To her credit, she doesn't look away. At least she said I was pretty. It's been hours since anyone noticed that.

"I'm sorry," she says softly. "I'm just not myself. It's none of my business what you want to do. It's not like it's any stranger than what I want to do."

"Which is what?"

"You'll just think I'm weird."

"Ally, nothing you could say would make me think

123

you are anything BUT weird. So you might as well tell me."

She glares at me, or at least she tries. It looks more like she's trying to hypnotize me. I don't think she has much experience glaring.

"Okay, fine. I want to discover a comet. I'll settle for an asteroid. But they're much more common so it's not as huge a deal as a comet."

I honestly have no response for that. And I usually have a response for everything. "That's, um, interesting," I finally manage. "You can do that for a living?"

She looks surprised at that answer, like she never thought about it before. "I . . . I don't know," she says. "I guess maybe you can't."

Her face kind of sags and I'm afraid she's going to cry. Poor girl. So out of touch with the world. She clutches onto a tattered blue pouch around her neck like it gives her some kind of strength. I'm used to comforting my friends when things go wrong for them — the guy they like likes someone else, bad grade on a test, bad hair day. But I don't have any experience in comforting someone whose world is being turned upside down. If I did, I'd be able to comfort myself. I manage to say, "Um, it's okay, Ally. I'm sure you'll figure something out."

She nods, clearly not convinced. Then she places her notebook on the table and heads toward the barbecue line. I watch her go and catch sight of her friend checking me out again. He's definitely cute. This year's

124
☆

jeans, Abercrombie long-sleeved top. A full-on 9.2. The extra point-two is for the spiky hair. He reminds me of the guys at home, and anything that reminds me of home right now is a good thing. I'm about to do the glance up, smile, look away routine when I remember what I look like right now. No hair dryer for my hair, nail polish already chipped, these shapeless clothes. I quickly pick up Ally's notebook and flip through it. Hopefully he'll think I'm hard at work and won't bother me. At least not until tomorrow after my clothes have shown up.

Ally's notebook is filled with typical school assignment stuff, like vocabulary words and math problems. I flip to the last page, which is where I always write the list of guys I like in my school notebooks. I'm pleasantly surprised to see Ally has a list too! But a closer look tells me it isn't a list of boys' names at all. It's a list of possible names for asteroids! This girl is hopeless! But at least she seems smart. And we're going to need smart right now if our plans are going to work.

My stomach growls again. I check to see where Ally is in the line. You'd think being the owners' daughter she could cut. That busload of people she was talking about must have just arrived because all these old people are walking around the pavilion in kind of a daze, looking crumpled and tired but with a skip in their step. I bet that's what Melanie will look like when she gets old. The thought of getting old sends a shiver

125

☆

down my spine, even in the heat. Ally is finally near the front of the line, but she's stuck talking to her dad and is ignoring the guy holding out the hamburgers to her. I'm tempted to hurry her along, but they look like they're in a heated debate.

I'll just have to start taking notes by myself. I open to a blank page and draw a line down the middle. On one side I write *BREE'S PARENTS* and on the other I write *ALLY'S PARENTS*. I can be a very organized person.

I stare at the empty page, not sure where to begin. Thankfully Ally comes back with the food.

"Sorry about that," she says, her eyes red.

I'm already biting into the burger. Normally I'd take the bun off, but I don't want Ally to comment. I suddenly stop in mid-chew. "Hey, this is a regular hamburger, right? It's not some weird animal like a moose or a buffalo?"

"It's not moose or a buffalo," Ally says. "Why would you ask that? Does it taste bad? My dad hired a whole bunch of new people so we've never had anything like this before. If it tastes bad I'll tell him."

I take another bite and shake my head. Ally doesn't make a move to eat hers. "It's fine," I tell her. "I promise. I've just heard about people like you eating weird animals."

"People like me? You mean people who live in the country?"

126

★

"Um, you don't live in the country, Ally. You live in the WOODS. It's very different."

She crosses her arms over her chest and pouts.

I take another bite. It's actually pretty good. "Aren't you going to eat?"

"I'm not hungry. You know in a few weeks, if the meals aren't good, it will be YOU who'll be the one to tell someone."

I stop mid-chew again. Suddenly I don't feel hungry either. I pick up the pen. "Let's get to work." I show her the columns and ask what her family's weaknesses are.

"Weaknesses?"

"Yeah, you know, fears, dreams, things like that. Things we can prey on."

She sits back. "Well, Kenny is really into bugs. He likes studying them and hopes to discover a new breed. And you know my dream."

I write:

Not many bugs in suburbia. Kenny's dream will die.

Then under my own parents' column I write:

Tons of bugs. Mom will freak. They are everywhere.

Back in Ally's column:

Too much light near the city. Can't see the stars. Ally's dream will die.

She makes a little squeak. "How did you know that? About the light and the stars?"

"On the way up here my parents were ranting and raving about how amazing it's going to be to see all the stars up here. How we'll never believe it's the same sky because there's no light pollution."

Her eyes fill again.

"Sorry, but we've gotta be ruthless here. We're trying to make our parents feel guilty. Guilty and scared. And I'm thinking there are lots of things about your new life that we can scare them with." I chew on the pen for a minute and then write:

DANGERS ALLY AND KENNY WILL FACE:
drugs
gangs
street crime
bullies at school

NEW EXPENSES:
cell phones
whole new wardrobe
allowance
lots of money for lessons

I turn the page toward Ally. "Anything else I should add?"

Ally's expression is frozen. She looks horrified. "Drugs? Street crime?"

I put down the pen. It almost seems cruel to upset her, but she needs to know what she's walking into. "Sorry, but that stuff is everywhere."

"Not here!"

"Well, everywhere else. But don't worry, Ally. You'll be fine. My friend Claire's dad once took a wrong turn and wound up in a really bad neighborhood. He thought these two guys were coming toward his car but it turned out they were just crossing the street. It was really scary. But he was fine."

No response. Just more staring. Some people are hard to get through to. After a minute she jabs at the list and asks, "What lessons are you talking about?"

"Oh, you and Kenny will wind up taking lots of lessons and classes. Everyone does. Things like horseback riding, soccer, art, gymnastics, even Girl Scouts costs money. You'd make a great Girl Scout."

"Aren't Girl Scouts for, well, *girls,* not teenagers?"

"Oops. I keep forgetting you're almost thirteen. Sorry!"

She groans and rests her head on the table.

"How about we move on to my parents?" I suggest. "What are some things that might scare them about living here?"

Through her hair she says, "Tell me something about them." Or at least I think that's what she says.

I'm so used to *avoiding* talking about my family that it takes a minute to gather my thoughts. "Well, you've met Melanie. She's always happy and bouncy. Sometimes she's more like a cartoon character than a kid. She gets really bad nightmares though, so that's rough. She sleepwalks sometimes. And screams."

Ally lifts her head and pushes her hair out of her

129

eyes. "Wow, that's horrible. And it can be really dangerous out here if someone's not paying attention to where they're walking. I can't smooth out EVERY root."

My eyes light up even though I have no idea what she means about roots. I write:

Multiple nighttime hazards for Melanie. Will have to chain her to the bed.

Ally rolls her eyes. "Okay, and what about your parents?"

"They're pretty much workaholics even though they don't make much money. They're both scientists. They got a grant to study something that's supposed to take up a lot of space, you know, in outer space. Like almost all the universe is supposedly made out of it."

Ally's head snaps up. "Dark energy?"

I nod. I should have realized someone whose whole life revolves around waiting for the moon to cross paths with the sun might be familiar with it. "Something like that. Dark matter, not energy. Maybe it's the same thing, I don't know. I don't really pay attention."

"Your parents study one of the biggest mysteries of the universe and you don't pay attention?"

"Hey, I have a life you know. I stay out of their way, and they stay out of mine."

"Not for long," she mutters.

"What's that supposed to mean?"

"Just that if our plan doesn't work, you guys are going to be seeing an awful lot of each other. It's pretty hard to stay out of anyone's way here. There's a lot to be done, and everyone has to work together to keep this place running."

My mouth suddenly feels very dry. I take a swig of the lemonade Ally had brought with the burgers and write:

Must work very hard to run campground. Research will suffer.

"That's a good one," Ally says, finally getting into the spirit. "And you can say the electricity goes out a lot."

Electricity not reliable. You will lose important computer data.

"And homeschooling is expensive. You have to pay for the materials, not like public schools, which are free, right?"

I nod.

Will have to pay through the nose for your children's education.

"Okay, what else?"

"Oh, I know!" Ally says after a few seconds. "You can tell them that sometimes an inmate from the prison on the other side of the lake escapes!"

I stare at her, wide-eyed, mind racing to every horror movie advertisement I've ever seen. None of them end well for the heroine.

"Just kidding," Ally says with a note of triumph in her voice.

My heart slowly returns to its normal rate. She

smiles for the first time since I've met her. "No in-mates," she says, "I swear. But there *are* bears. And the ghost of our dead cat, Galileo. And the occasional moose. And anything that you see flying around after dark *isn't* a bird — it's a bat. No buffalos though, so that should make you happy."

I'm so relieved that I won't be chased by knife-wielding murderers that I almost don't hear her say the words *bears* and *ghost* and *bat*. Then it registers. I stand up and almost fall backward over the bench. "No way! No way am I living out here. This is crazy!"

"Calm down," she says, grabbing hold of my arm. "I'm sorry, I shouldn't have done that. But you were trying to scare me, too."

Reluctantly, I let her pull me back down. "Why are you so cheery all of a sudden? Cracking jokes, smil-ing. Are you, like, mentally unstable?"

She shakes her head. "No. At least I don't think so. It's just that while you were writing that last thing I realized something. We *can't* move! Because once the word spreads that we had a potential alien signal — which happened this morning before you arrived — everyone will want to talk to my dad. He'll be so busy traveling to conventions and being interviewed for magazine articles, that he won't be ABLE to hold down another job. So even if our plans don't work, we al-ways have THAT to hold over them."

I admire the kid's enthusiasm, I really do. As a for-mer cheerleader, I know what it takes to drum up enthusiasm when you're having a bad day. But somehow I just can't get too excited about her idea. "Um, I don't mean to sound stupid, but how many other people are checking for these alien signals?"

Her smile sags a tiny bit. "Over five million people since the program started in 1999. From 128 countries."

"And how many signals have turned out to be positive so far?"

Her smile fades a bit more. "Well, none."

Neither of us says anything for a minute.

Finally I ask, "How about we focus on the plan?"

She nods, her smile now completely gone. I feel like I'm always bursting Ally's bubble. It's not like I ENJOY doing it. I really don't. I'm about to tell her to forget what I said, that I'm sure her signal is "The One," but she starts shooting out suggestions on how to put our plans into action, so I get busy writing them down. I've gotta hand it to her, she might not have much experience being devious, but the girl has good ideas. We're so engrossed in our plans that when a tray crashes to the ground in the center of the pavilion we both jump. Everyone turns to look, just like in the school cafeteria. I crane my neck, but can't see anyone.

"There's a kid on the ground!" Ally says, jumping up. She runs toward where a crowd is forming. I swing my legs over the bench and run after her. The boy is about six years old and he's just lying there. In fifth grade I saw a kid have a seizure in gym class, and at

☆

first I thought he was just trying to get out of climbing the rope. But the boy on the floor isn't shaking or anything like that, just lying there with his eyelids fluttering. His parents are on either side of him, but I can't hear what they're saying. Before I even think, I'm kneeling down next to him, stroking the kid's hair and telling him it will be all right.

"I've got it," a voice calls out above the crowd. I turn to see a pudgy kid about my age running toward the group. "I'm so sorry," he tells the father as he reaches into a canvas bag and hands him a first-aid kit. The father hurriedly opens the box and pulls out what looks like a magic marker. Everyone watches in silence as he leans over the boy's leg and jabs it against his thigh. Within seconds, literally, the boy is sitting up and asking what happened. His parents give him a hug and his mother starts to cry. The pudgy kid gives me a quick glance, then picks up the kit and puts it in the bag.

"He ate a peanut-butter cookie by mistake," the father explains to the small crowd that still remains. "He's usually so aware of what to avoid." He looks around, probably for the pudgy boy, but he's gone. I start to stand up when I see my parents and Ally gaping at me. I don't want to have to explain why I flung myself to the rough cement floor to cradle the head of some strange boy. So I do the only thing I can think of.

I stand up, dust myself off, and run.

☆

JACK

4

The box of licorice slips out of my hands and narrowly misses landing on my foot. "What do you mean she's *missing*?"

Stella's son jangles the change in his pocket impatiently. "I went to her room to get her for breakfast, and she wasn't there. Simple as that. We looked in the lobby, in the breakfast room, the game room, the bus. My wife suggested you might have seen her, or maybe made plans for breakfast?"

A few thoughts jockey for position in my head, in an order I'm not proud of. First, *there's a game room at this motel?* Second, *I hope nothing bad happened to Stella,* and the third and craziest — *I wonder if this guy is my biological father?* I used to wonder this whenever I'd meet a middle-aged man. I'd size him up against the headless pictures to see if there was a match. I quickly push the first and third thoughts away and focus on the second. "I haven't seen her since we got off the bus yesterday," I tell him. "But I'll help you look." I hurry out the door and close it, realizing a second too late that I left my room key inside.

"Here," the guy says, handing me a business card. "Let's split up. Call me on your cell if you find her."

I glance down at the card. Greg Daniels, Certified Public Accountant. "I don't have a cell," I tell him.

"How can you not have a cell?"

"I'm thirteen. How many important calls do you think I get?"

He sizes me up. "My son's thirteen. His phone doesn't stop ringing."

I stare at him, unable to find a response to that.

"Just call me if you find her," he says, hurrying down the walkway.

Before rushing off anywhere, I decide to think like a detective. I rack my barely-functioning-on-three-hours'-sleep brain for anything Stella might have said that could help point me in the right direction. Nothing comes. What if she got confused and wandered off into the highway and was hit by a car? Or wandered into the fields behind the motel and was eaten by a mountain lion? Maybe she got hungry, went to breakfast, and her son just didn't see her?

I follow signs to the restaurant, a small room off the lobby. I guess it wouldn't hurt to get some food in me that doesn't have high fructose corn syrup as the first ingredient. The place is packed with hungry eclipse chasers, none of whom have seen Stella. David waves me over, and I don't want to be rude so I join them.

David's son, Pete, talks a blue streak. In the time it takes me to wolf down three mini-blueberry muffins and a tall glass of orange juice (two minutes, twenty-six seconds according to the wall clock that I keep glancing at), Pete has brought up everything from the virtues of SpongeBob Squarepants to the magician he's having at his sixth birthday party to whether or not chocolate should be considered a food group. I'm only half listening, because I'm thinking of more and more things that could befall a little old lady in a remote motel.

When Pete pauses to take a breath I explain I'm on a super-important mission and have to go. The bus is supposed to leave in only twenty minutes. Pete asks if he can come with me. I'm about to say *no, I work alone,* when his parents are, like, "Sure, go ahead. Just meet us back at the bus." So off we go.

In the lobby we pass a poster of a small garden. Pete reaches out a little finger and pokes the poster. "Green," he says. I remember seeing the poster when we checked in last night, but now I look closer. The poster is advertising a small garden behind the motel, donated by the local gardening club. Suddenly a tiny thread of something Stella told me comes floating back. I ask at the front desk how to get there and the guy points us down a long hall and says, "Follow the signs to the garden. It ain't much to see." Pete and I hurry through the mazelike halls, stopping at each intersection to read the signs. Finally I push open a heavy door and smell fresh-cut grass.

There, standing on one leg with her arms held out in perfect balance, is Stella, in a yellow sweat suit, doing Tai Chi like she does every morning before breakfast. I'm hugely relieved to see her. I let the dark thoughts dissipate from my mind as she catches sight of me and smiles.

Only fifteen minutes left till we're supposed to be on the bus, but I can't make myself interrupt her. Pete and I sit on a concrete bench and wait. I keep glancing at my watch — an old birthday present from SD3 before he left. I still haven't packed. Stella gracefully goes from one pose to another almost like a dance. I never would have thought she could do that at her age. I sure can't do it at mine. "Mr. Daniels — I mean — your son, is really worried about you," I say when she makes a little bowing gesture and finally ends her routine. "He thought you had disappeared."

"I was right here. He just didn't think to look."

"Does he know you do this each morning?"

She shrugs. "He never asked." She reaches down to pick up her huge pocketbook from the ground. I offer to take it from her and she hands it over.

"Well, he's going to be glad you're found."

"I always knew where I was."

Even though I'm not too fond of the guy, I suddenly find myself taking his side. "He was worried. Maybe you should let people know if you're going to go off, like, from now on."

"Yes, *Dad,*" she says with a wink.

I redden. I guess I did sound like a dad. I've never had anyone to look out for before.

"Who's your friend?" she asks as the three of us head back through the maze of hallways. We only have ten minutes left now.

"I'm Pete Goldberg," he says proudly. "I'm six. I helped find you."

"I wasn't lost, I simply —"

I nudge her on the arm and she sighs and says, "Yes, you did, Pete. You found me."

We head toward Stella's room but run into her son pacing in the lobby. He doesn't even thank me, just starts yelling that she shouldn't wander off like that in a strange place. Now I feel like I should stand up for *her,* but honestly the guy scares me a little. Pete backs away, and I steer him to the check-in desk so I can get an extra key to my room. I hope I don't have to pay for it because I didn't bring my money.

The card turns out to be free, I just have to promise to return both copies later.

I almost trip over the licorice when I step into the room. Pete drops to his knees and grabs two pieces that had fallen onto the carpet when the box fell. Before I can stop him, he sticks them in his mouth. Now I'm an eat-off-the-floor type of guy, too, but who knows what has been on this floor? "Hey, don't you know the two-second rule?"

He shakes his head, chewing happily. I take the second piece out of his other hand. "It means you have two seconds to eat something that has touched the floor before it gets all covered in germs. This has been here for a lot longer than that."

"But I'm allowed to eat licorice, see?" he holds out his arm and pushes up the sleeve of his Disney World sweatshirt. A bracelet dangles from his wrist. I hadn't noticed it before. He brings it up to my face. There are symbols of a peanut and a fish, each with a red line through it. "See? No peanuts, no fish. Nothing about no licorice."

"Okay, well, it'd be really helpful if you threw the rest in the trash so I can finish packing."

Pete dutifully tosses the licorice one by one into the trash, missing every other time. I run around the room making sure I don't leave anything behind. Good thing it's a small room.

When we get down to the bus, Pete's mom is in the front, handing her last suitcase to the bus driver to store underneath. I toss mine in after, and see for the first time that the whole middle compartment is packed full with telescopes. At least I think that's what they are since they're all wrapped up, some in a silver foil-type material, others in blankets or long boxes.

"He wasn't any trouble, was he?" Pete's mom asks, putting her arm around his shoulders.

"I helped solve a mystery!" Pete says. "And I had some licorice!"

"Did you, now?" she says, amused. "Sounds like you had a busy fifteen minutes!" She thanks me for watching him, and they join David on the bus.

"There you are," Mr. Silver says, waving me up the stairs. He makes a little check on his clipboard and then stashes it in his briefcase. I guess I'm the last one.

"I'd like to finish our conversation from yesterday," he says, climbing up behind me. "Why don't you come down to talk to me once we're underway?"

"Okay." I'm glad he didn't ask me to sit up front with him. When I get halfway down the aisle I'm surprised to see Stella sitting next to her son, with the daughter-in-law across the aisle. She rolls her eyes at me and says loudly, "Gotta sit here so the warden can keep an eye on me. Goodness knows what kind of trouble I might get into in the back of the bus!"

"Very funny, Mother," Mr. Daniels says, his lips drawn tight.

I tell Stella I'll see her at the lunch stop and keep making my way back. I get more and more tired with each passing row. After the morning's excitement, the lack of sleep is catching up to me. I settle into the window seat, close my eyes, and the next thing I know I'm on the floor in our den at home. I'm about to reach a new level in *Super Mario Bros. 3* on my Game Boy when the lights on it start going all haywire. Instead of helping Mario to leap over a bottomless pit, every

141

time I press a button a Madonna song starts playing. The fact that I don't KNOW any Madonna songs, coupled with the fact that my game is malfunctioning in this crazy way, alerts me to the fact that I'm dreaming. I know I'm not really at home. I know I'm sleeping on a bus right now surrounded by cornfields and cows. But I've done this enough times that the realization doesn't wake me right up, the way it used to.

Without hesitating, I turn the Game Boy into a hot dog with sauerkraut, ketchup, and mustard. Lucid dream food always tastes better than real food, in the same way that the colors are brighter. Once I scarf down the hot dog, I'm ready to take off. I bend my knees like Superman does before a takeoff, and sort of float up into the air, through the wall, and outside. When I was younger I used to get caught in the wall sometimes. SD3 explained it to me. He said part of my brain still wouldn't accept the fact that a wall in a dream isn't a real wall, and I'd get convinced that I couldn't pass through it. I've had to learn to let go of that or else I get stuck and have to fight my way out, usually waking me.

But now I glide right through, feeling that same freedom and joy that I feel every time I do this. The grass is so much greener than real grass, and without any effort at all, I can make the blue sky orange. Sometimes I'll pretend I'm in a football game and I'm the star player. But mostly I just fly around, watching the landscape change beneath me, and trying to hold onto lucidity. I can usually only make it last a few minutes. I feel it slipping away from me now, like the environment is getting harder to control. I feel the real dream world creeping back over me, so much duller than this.

When I wake up, I'm alone. How much time has passed? I turn toward the window and see we're parked in front of a Burger King. The eclipse chasers are straggling out toward the bus. If this was lunch, I must have been out for hours.

Mr. Silver is the first one back. He heads down the aisle toward me and I remember we were supposed to talk once the bus left the motel. Oops!

He hands me a take-out bag and says, "I thought you might be hungry."

My stomach growls in response. "I'm sorry I fell asleep. I didn't sleep very well last night."

"You looked so peaceful no one wanted to wake you."

I'm thinking more likely no one noticed I was sleeping back here, but I don't argue with him.

"Eat your lunch and then we'll talk, okay?"

What I'd really rather do is eat and then sketch in my book. I nod though, one hand already reaching into the bag. Fries and a Whopper. No drink, but I still have a can of orange soda in my backpack. I eat the burger so quickly I barely taste it. It's good, but pretty bland compared to the dream hot dog. If only dream hot dogs filled me up. I'd take up less space in this seat, that's for sure.

The last fry disappears as the bus pulls out. I wouldn't mind using the bathroom, but Pete broke it yesterday by sticking the toy from his Happy Meal down it. Nothing to do about it but wait till the next rest stop.

I make my way down to the front, wishing I hadn't drunk all that soda. Stella is knitting her red scarf again, and Pete is absorbed in a book. I don't remember if I could even read at that age. Mr. Silver is on his cell phone and motions for me to sit in the empty seat across the aisle.

"We'll need thirty-three pairs," he says into the phone. "Yes, the ones with the alpha-screen." He holds the phone away for a second and says to me, "Those are the ones that let you see sunspots as the moon is crossing."

I nod like I actually understand what he said. I'm getting good at that. Mike's articles helped a little, but I have a hard time picturing anything I haven't seen.

He says a few more things about tents and cabins and ends with, "We should arrive around five. Yes, wishing you clear skies too."

After snapping the phone closed he turns to me with a grin. "Soon you'll be ending your conversations by wishing the other person clear skies."

"I doubt that," I say, but I say it cheerfully so it doesn't sound obnoxious. I figure there's no use pretending I'm going to absorb all this stuff. Mr. Silver *did* have me in class for a whole year, after all. He knows better than that.

"You may want to take notes," he says, handing me a notebook with a yellow cover and a pen that has MOON SHADOW CAMPGROUND printed on it with their phone number. "In fact, throughout the trip you should write down your observations, and then details of the eclipse. For your paper at the end."

"Okay." I open the first page and am pleasantly surprised to see there are no lines. Lined pages always make me think of school. And I don't want to think of school.

"Let me begin by explaining the basis of the experiment you'll be helping me with. As I mentioned, I'm part of a four-person team that works on verifying the existence of exoplanets. You know what those are, right? We talked about it last month in class?"

"Sure, they're planets around stars other than the sun." I say a silent thank-you to David, since I definitely didn't learn it from class.

"Exactly," Mr. Silver says. "I knew you paid more attention than you let on."

I neither confirm nor deny that. He continues. "The rest of my teammates are amateur astronomers, too. We know a lot about astronomy, and we have excellent equipment, but we don't publish papers in scholarly journals, or get funding for our projects. We participate purely for the love of science and because we've proven we're capable. Being chosen for this project is a big honor."

He pauses here, and I wonder if I'm supposed to say anything. "Uh, congratulations?"

He laughs. "Don't congratulate me yet. Save that for if we're successful. What we have to do is very precise, and it's going to be tricky. Using my fourteen-inch scope, which has a special camera attached to it called a charge-coupling device, or CCD, we're going to be doing photometric observations. We're going to measure the change in magnitude of one special star's brightness. The star is over a hundred light-years away, and we're going to detect if it dims by as little as two percent, and for how long. The other folks on my team will be doing the same thing, in different parts of the world. We're all at different longitudes and all our data will be combined to get the full picture. I'll be manning the scope, making sure we've got good tracking on the target star, while you keep track of the photometric measurements so that we can make a light curve. Sound good?"

"Uh-huh." I'm pretty sure he's still speaking English. But I can't be 100 percent certain.

"If the amount of light from our star suddenly decreases," he continues, his voice dropping like he's sharing some big secret, "then we'll know a planet, with an indeterminate mass, has just crossed in front of it. We can't see planets directly because they're incredibly dim in comparison to their parent star."

My palms are starting to sweat a bit. I am so out of my element.

"But the experiment isn't for ten days. So for other duties, just soak in the atmosphere of the Moon Shadow, learn all you can. If a tour member needs something and can't find me, you'll be the backup guy. I'll give you a walkie-talkie when we arrive." He looks pointedly down at my notebook and I realize I haven't taken any notes. I try to scribble down what he said before I forget it, but I'm sure I didn't get everything. Hopefully when we're doing it for real, he'll just tell me to look at a screen and read what it says. I'm pretty sure I can do that much without messing up.

One of the older men is cautiously making his way down the aisle. He stops and holds tight to the back of Mr. Silver's chair.

"Excuse me," he says. "Some of the ladies were wondering if we were going to stop soon for a restroom break."

He winks at me and I smile, grateful that he was asking instead of me.

After the break, I don't try to go back to sleep. Instead I sketch the scene on the bus, with all the people talking and reading and laughing and sleeping. I give them all the heads of aliens instead of people. I feel slightly guilty about that, since everyone so far had been very nice (except maybe Stella's son, who seems uptight in general.) But I don't have any practice at drawing real people.

As the hours go by, the scenery becomes fewer fields and more forests. We finally pull through a carved wooden archway that says MOON SHADOW CAMPGROUND with a carving of the moon crossing in front of the sun. Mr. Silver gets out to show some papers to the guy at the gate and then climbs back on. As the bus slowly winds down the road into the campground, he puts on his yellow sun hat and picks up the microphone.

"Welcome to the Moon Shadow!"

Everyone claps and a few let out whoops.

"We'll be making two stops, first to the cabins for those of you who selected that option, and then at the campsite for those of you who aren't afraid of some real camping! I'll read out the names for the first stop."

Even though I'm not afraid of real camping, I'm hoping he says my name. Two weeks in a tent doesn't sound like much fun. I needn't have worried, Mr. Silver calls my name first. I hear Stella's family and Pete's family called. I count twenty-five others. It seems like most of us went for the cabin option. On the drive we pass wooden signs that announce things like THE PAVILION, THE ART HOUSE, and MINE FOR GOLD HERE. This sure isn't like any campground I've ever been to.

The bus pulls up in front of a large circle of cabins. I

148

can see more rows of cabins behind it, too. As the bus empties out, only five guys in their twenties remain. They are all wearing the same blue t-shirt that says ECLIPSE-CHASERS DO IT BETTER.

I'm not sure what it is they do better, but they seem to be having fun laughing and joking with each other. Usually when I see a group of friends like that I'm glad I don't have to deal with it. I see Mike with his friends and it's, like, someone is always mad at someone else, leaving someone out of something, or stealing someone's girlfriend. Seems like a big hassle to me. But today for some reason it doesn't seem like it would be so bad.

Mr. Silver plops my duffel at my feet and hands me a white plastic box with FIRST AID splashed across the front. Then he digs around his own bag and pulls out a walkie-talkie and a charging device. "Keep the first-aid kit with you in your backpack," he instructs me. "And clip the walkie-talkie onto your waist. We'll use frequency number one, and if that doesn't work, try number two. Keep it charged overnight. Here's the key to your cabin. It's right next to mine if you need anything."

I nod, trying to remember everything.

"See you all at dinner!" he calls out before climbing back on the bus. "Barbecue at the Pavilion!"

I stuff the kit and the walkie-talkie into my backpack and sling my duffel over the other shoulder. A guy in a MOON SHADOW t-shirt shows us which cabins are ours. Mine is one of the first few. As I walk up the stairs I start to feel excited. Besides the motel room last night, I've never had a whole place to myself before. I push open the door to find two cots with thin blue blankets, a wooden dresser, a small writing table, and a tiny bathroom with a toilet and sink, but no shower or tub. I'm feeling pretty stinky after being in the bus all day so I go outside to find the showers. I only get a few feet when a guy about my age comes out of the cabin next to me.

"Hey," he says. "You just checking in?"

I nod. "You know where the showers are?"

He points to a gray building a few yards away. "It's right over there. Hey, I'm about to lift some weights. Wanna spot me?"

I don't know what possesses me, maybe the fact that guys who look like him — clothes with logos, good-looking, at ease in the world — don't usually ask me to do anything with them, but I say, "Okay," and follow him back into his cabin.

His cabin is identical to mine, except strewn with exercise equipment and inside-out clothes. He pushes some hand weights toward me with his toe and says, "You can get started with these while I get set up."

So I do some bicep curls like I've seen guys do in gym class. I must be doing it right because he doesn't comment. He tells me his name is Ryan and that he's here with his grandfather. He says there's a really hot girl here who he wants to impress, so he's stepping up his workouts. He asks if I've got a girlfriend. I laugh.

"Why are you laughing?"

"Who's going to go out with *me*?" I jiggle the pudge around my belly.

He shrugs. "Girls dig confidence. They don't care if you've got rock-hard abs."

"Then why do you bother working out?"

"Hey, it never hurts to have both."

Well, since I don't have any confidence, maybe I really should look into this working-out stuff. I bend down and pick up heavier weights.

"That's the spirit," Ryan says.

After a shower that gets cold too quickly, I throw on jeans and a long-sleeve t-shirt because Ryan told me to cover up from the skeeters at night. Something falls to the floor when I'm going through my bag. I bend down and pick up two pieces of plastic — the keys from the motel. Figures.

I don't even bother locking the door in my haste to get to the Pavilion for dinner. I don't want to miss the food. Working out makes you really hungry! Who knew? I feel good though, and Ryan said I can come back in the morning and we'll work on different muscle groups.

Ryan sees me and waves me over. I feel bad cutting in line, but no one seems to mind. He points to two girls sitting at the farthest picnic table. I can't see them too well from here but they both look pretty. "There she is," he says.

"Which one?"

He looks at me like I'm crazy. "The drop-dead gorgeous one!"

Assuming he means the shorter one on the right, I nod my agreement. I take a dog, a burger, an ear of corn, and two cookies and follow Ryan to a table. He introduces me to his grandfather, and also to a kid named Kenny who looks around ten. Kenny tells me proudly that his family owns the campground. "That's my sister, Ally," he says pointing to the girls at the table. "Over there. Ally's short for Alpha, the brightest star in any constellation."

I'm surprised. Not only that a girl would have a name like Alpha, but that Ryan didn't say the girl he had the crush on lived here. Maybe that's why he was sitting with the girl's brother, as a way to find out more about her.

I'm wolfing down my hot dog, and it feels like the one I ate this morning in my dream was a lifetime away. Then I hear someone drop a tray and then some shouts. I look up to see Pete, of all people, turning red and looking faint. His mom is shouting, "Can you breathe honey, can you breathe?"

Someone yells, "Is he choking? Does anyone know CPR?"

I jump up from my bench just as Mr. Silver reaches

me. "Do you have the kit?" he asks, panic in his voice. "He's having an allergic reaction. There's an EpiPen in there."

I know what this is because Mike is allergic to bees so my mom always has one in the cabinet. But I don't have the kit! I forgot to bring it! "I'll get it," I tell him, and take off at top speed. Running faster than I ever have in my life, I race to the cabin, push open the door, grab the kit and the walkie-talkie (which I had also forgotten) and race back, ignoring the searing cramp in my side.

Apologizing, I hand it to David, who is now on the floor with Pete. He barely looks like he's breathing. The dark-haired girl who was sitting with Kenny's sister is stroking Pete's hair. David grabs the pen, pulls off the top, and jams it against Pete's leg. In a few seconds his color returns to normal and he's sitting up. I take the kit back from David along with the empty pen.

"Wow," says Ryan. "That was crazy."

I don't answer. I'm here two hours and already I messed up. What if Pete had died because I couldn't follow a simple instruction? I run out of the Pavilion before anyone can stop me. Unsure where to go, I take the next path I come to and wind up in something called the Sun Garden. No one is there, which is what I was hoping to find. All around me are sundials, some made of metal, some plastic, some tile. A huge one on the ground is made of colorful mosaic tile. There's no dial part in the middle though. I stand still, not sure

153

what to do when I hear, "You have to stand directly in the middle. It won't work otherwise."

I look up to see Stella, in a white sweat suit now. I don't answer. She walks past me and stands in the center of the sun dial. "See?" She points down at the ground. Her body casts a shadow right where seven o'clock would be. I don't reply.

"They're calling you a hero again," she says, lifting her arms in small circles and watching the patterns they make on the ground. "First you save the bus from breaking down, then the little boy. You've had a busy few days!"

This was too much. "I didn't save him!" I protest.

"You most certainly did! Who knows what would have happened if you weren't there?"

I sit down hard onto a stone bench and put my head in my hands. "But I was supposed to have the kit with me. I could have helped him sooner."

"You were gone and back in practically no time. I've never seen anyone run so fast. You're a hero and don't you forget it."

I shake my head. What was the use in arguing? I've screwed up many times before. I know how it feels. But right then, sitting in that Sun Garden with shadows of light all around me, I make a decision. I'm not going to screw up again. Those days are gone. This is a new place, and I can be a new person here. I *have* to be. People are relying on me. I get to my feet and walk into the sun dial. "Show me where I stand."

ALLY

5

"Let her go," Bree's mom tells me, her hand on my arm. "She doesn't like people questioning her too much."

I don't say anything, but I think there's such a thing as questioning too *little*. Bree had said she and her parents don't really talk.

Her mom continues, "Bree might be a little self-centered, but she has a tender heart. When Melanie has one of her nightmares, Bree is the one who comforts her and brings her back to bed so she won't hurt herself. She's done that since she was four years old."

I don't know what to say. After an awkward minute, she pats me on the back and heads back to her table. I grab my notebook and join the rest of my own family, who are sitting with the boy and his parents now. He's drinking some juice and looks a little worn out, but okay. My mom apologizes for not putting out a sign that said the cookies had peanuts in them, and promises to fix that for the next meal.

Hayley, the boy's mom, says it wasn't my mom's fault, it was *her* fault for not being more cautious and prepared. She says her husband, David, thought *she* had the medicine, and she thought *he* did. They go back and forth many times on whose fault it was or wasn't, until they both start laughing. But the little boy's mom is still sort of crying.

"Pete, have you seen Jack?" David asks suddenly.

"Jack?" my dad repeats.

Pete says, "My friend Jack. The one who saved me."

I realize he must mean the guy who ran up with the first-aid kit. We all look around but don't see him.

"If you're okay now," Mom says to Pete and his parents, "we have a family meeting that's long overdue."

"Can I come?" Pete asks. "Kenny is my friend too. He's going to show me how to find gold!"

"Believe me, Pete," I say, "you don't want to be there for this meeting."

Kenny shoots me a questioning look. We promise to play with him tomorrow and Pete reluctantly lets us go. Almost everyone has finished eating now, and the clean-up crew is starting to empty the large bins of trash. Just having a clean-up crew is taking some getting used to. Not that I'm complaining.

We follow our parents to the other side of the pavilion, near where Bree and I had sat. My parents choose a table that isn't covered by the roof since sound tends to echo under there. They waste no time in telling Kenny that we're leaving the Moon Shadow after the eclipse. His eyes open wide and he fumbles for my hand.

"We'll rent a house at first," Dad explains, "a few towns away from where I grew up. Then we'll look for a house that we all like, in a town with a good school system."

Mom gives Kenny the same reasons for the move that she told me — we need to expand our horizons. We need to be around other kids our age. I stop listening. Kenny grips my hand tighter and tighter but still hasn't said anything.

"Kenny," Mom says, her voice soft and almost pleading, "you haven't met the Holdens yet, but I'm sure both of you will help them make the adjustment. Their youngest daughter, Melanie, will be taking over most of your duties, and Bree will be taking over your sister's."

The image of Bree smoothing out dirt in her high-heel sandals and pink tank top pops into my brain, and I stifle a laugh.

Kenny turns to me and says, "We can't leave here, Ally. This is our home. I don't want to go to Civilization. It's scary out there."

"I know, Kenny. I don't want to go either."

I want to tell him about my plans with Bree, but it'll have to wait till our parents are out of earshot.

Mom and Dad rattle off all the things about the move that will be positive. We'll make lots of friends, will get to do all this cultural stuff like go to museums and libraries and zoos. When we simply sit there, expressionless, they throw in movie theaters and bowling alleys and arcades.

Kenny twitches almost imperceptibly at the mention of arcades, and Mom pounces on it. "There will be so many opportunities for you guys to pursue your interests now. You won't be limited to what we can offer you here."

Kenny turns to me again and says, "Ask them if there will be labyrinths there."

"Probably not," Dad says. "But you can ask us directly, you know."

To me, Kenny says, "Please tell them I'm not talking to them until they change their minds."

"Kenny says he's not talk —"

Dad puts up his hand to stop me. "Yeah, we got it, Ally, thanks." He looks at Mom and they both stand up. "We can talk about this again when you're both acting more civilized."

Without looking back, they head off to the kitchen. When they're out of sight I say, "Bree and I have a plan, Kenny. We're going to make our parents change their minds. Don't worry, okay?" Kenny moves closer to me on the bench, and we sit like that for a long time. His breathing is shallow. We watch the first stars come out, and my eyes sting with tears.

"I'm scared," he whispers.

I squeeze his hand. "Me too."

The next morning I jump out of bed, eager to set the plan into action. I'm not sure what cabin Bree and Melanie were assigned to, so that's the first order of business. When I get out to the hall I'm surprised to see Kenny already dressed, sneakers on and everything.

"I want to help," he says.

I think for a minute. "Okay, go grab your bug book. Bree's mother is afraid of bugs."

He turns toward his room, then suggests, "I can get some real bugs too."

"Okay, grab your sketchbook and some bugs, and we'll meet out in front of the office in ten minutes. Don't let Mom or Dad see you."

He runs off, and I quickly use the bathroom and throw on whatever clothes are on the top of the drawer. I grab a roll as I run through the kitchen and into the office. Mom is at her desk, on the phone. Without meeting her eyes, I scan the wall chart until I find the Holdens' cabins. Not surprisingly, Mom assigned them the nicest ones. They're set a little apart from the others, and have bathrooms and showers inside them.

As I'm waiting, Mr. Flynn strolls over on his morning walk. I haven't had a chance to talk to him since he and Ryan arrived.

"How's Mrs. Flynn?" I ask.

He smiles that easy smile of his and says, "She's doing pretty well. She's sure sorry to miss the eclipse, I can tell you that."

"I'm sure." I don't have the nerve to ask which story is the true one, the bridge tournament, or her failing health.

"How's the comet hunting going?" he asks, changing the subject for me.

"Good, I guess. Last winter I thought I saw one, but it turned out to be the Space Station."

He nods. "Must be pretty tough now, what with those big robot computers they got searching the sky all the time."

This is news to me. "What robot computers?"

"The ones that look for those near-Earth objects, like comets or asteroids that can collide with the earth. Haven't you heard about them?"

I shake my head. My parents are usually really good at keeping us up to date, always supplementing our homeschool material with current events. They must have left this out on purpose.

"They can find these objects easily," he goes on. "In a few years, most all the new ones will be discovered by them, not by people like us. Your grandpa woulda been mighty disappointed."

He must have noticed my own disappointment because he says, "But don't worry none. You'll find your comet one day, mark my words."

"Thanks, Mr. Flynn."

He tips his imaginary hat at me, and continues on his walk. I watch him go, thinking, how many more dreams can get taken away from me? I'm sure Bree's right and it couldn't be my real career, but who am I if I'm not a comet hunter?

Kenny appears holding a shoebox under one arm and the book under the other. I have to pull myself together. I have to make this plan work. If I only have a few more years to potentially find a comet, I need to be under these dark skies. I quickly grasp my meteorite, then let it drop against my chest. "All set?" I ask.

He nods. "Wanna see?"

"Is anything going to jump out at me?"

"Probably not."

I stand back a bit to be on the safe side. Kenny puts down the book and then slowly lifts the lid. I peer in just far enough to see a lot of squirmy legs.

"Nice job."

"Thanks."

We head out to the Holdens' cabins, only I'm not sure which ones are the parents' and which is Bree's. I hope it doesn't come down to us peering in the window. I've never violated a guest's privacy like that. Ryan's cabin isn't far from here. Maybe I should ask him to help us. I tell Kenny I'll be right back and run over there. No one answers when I knock though. We used to have breakfast together every day. So much has changed this year.

Kenny is tapping his foot impatiently when I re-join him.

"This one must be the parents'," he says, pointing down the lane. "I hear computer noises coming out of it." We tip-toe past it, and I lightly knock on the door of the cabin next door. Bree opens it, wearing MY purple striped pajamas!

She sees me staring and says, "Oh yeah, your mom gave us these last night. Hope you don't mind."

Melanie comes to the door in Kenny's red-white-and-blue pajamas that he got last Fourth of July as a gift from Ryan's grandmother. I feel him tense up when he sees them on her, but he quickly recovers.

"I'm Kenny," he says. "And this is a box of bugs." He holds up the box and Bree jumps back. Melanie peers at it, curious.

"Leave that outside," Bree commands. "Then come in before my parents see you."

The girls go into the bathroom to change and I fill Kenny in on the plans. When they come back out, Bree's hair is gleaming and she has makeup on. Except for when we're in town, I almost never see people in makeup. She looks sort of glamorous, sort of fake, at the same time. It takes me a second to notice they're wearing more of our clothes! It's not that I mind shar-ing, it's just one more thing of ours that Mom is taking away without asking.

Kenny is staring at Bree, and she winks. "Never seen a girl in makeup before?"

162

"Ally doesn't wear makeup," he says.

"Well, Ally could stand to wear some." Turning to me she says, "Did you even brush your hair this morning?"

My hand instantly flies up to my head. I almost never think of brushing my hair.

"You don't need to answer," Bree says, tossing me her hairbrush. "It's obvious."

I yank the brush through my hair, wincing as it hits knots. "Why should I brush it?" I ask. "Who cares what my hair looks like?"

Mel and Kenny watch this exchange silently.

"Everyone cares. You're not a kid anymore. There are cute guys here!"

I stop brushing. "There are?"

"That guy, the one I've seen you talking to a few times. Spiky blond hair? Preppy?"

She must mean Ryan. "What about him?"

"Don't you want to look nice for him?"

"Huh?"

She sighs and leans forward, like she's about to address a child. "When a girl likes a boy, she wants to look nice for him. You know that, right?"

I flash back to the morning Ryan arrived. Clothes rumpled from sleeping in them, hair unbrushed, ring of purple popsicle around my mouth. I lay the brush on the floor. No wonder he doesn't think of me as a girl.

"You're not being nice, Bree," Melanie says. "I think Ally's very pretty."

163

☽

Bree grabs the brush and places it carefully on her dresser top. "I never said she wasn't pretty."

"But I don't like Ryan in that way," I tell her, feeling my cheeks heating up. No one's ever talked about me being pretty before. I never give my appearance any thought. Why would I?

"It doesn't matter," Bree says. "You still want him to want you."

"I do? Why?"

But before Bree can reply, Kenny asks, "Can we get on with it please? I have chores to do."

"On with what?" Melanie asks.

Before Kenny can say more, Bree says, "Kenny volunteered to show you how to pan for gold this morning."

Melanie looks surprised. "He did?"

Bree nods and turns Melanie around to face her. I take that second to whisper to Kenny that Melanie doesn't want to move back, so he'll have to keep her occupied for a while so she doesn't foil our plans.

He gets to his feet. "C'mon, Melanie, I'll show you how to fill the stream with gold nuggets. It's gonna be your job soon anyway."

I don't make a move to get up. My stomach has a knot in it that hurts more than brushing my hair did. How am I going to survive in a real school if I can't even brush my hair? If I can't understand the simple rules of boy/girl relationships? I simply can't go, that's all. I jump to my feet. "Okay, let's get started."

Bree nods, and leads the way out of the cabin. She clearly isn't going to mention running off last night, so neither am I.

The first thing we do is sneak behind her parents' cabin. Beeping and printer noises drift out the window screens. I point to where the electricity enters the cabin. All it takes is a little yank, and everything inside goes quiet. Bree and I run around to the front and casually walk by. Bree's dad runs down the front steps. "Ally! I'm so glad you're here. Our power just went out."

I know I'm supposed to say something, but I'm suddenly nervous about lying. I don't have much experience with it. We agreed that I'd do most of the talking with her parents, and she'd talk to mine. That way it would look less obvious. Bree pinches my arm and I force myself to say, "Oh, yes, that happens all the time around here. Especially in the winter months. And in the summer. And I guess in spring and fall, too."

We walk closer to the house. Bree says innocently, "I hope you didn't lose any data." We follow him back inside where Bree's mom is running around the room, testing all the outlets. "We're going to have to start all over," Bree's mom says helplessly.

"It usually comes back on after a few minutes," I assure her. "Usually. But sometimes we have to get someone out here to fix the line and that can take a few days. Or if it's in the winter, a few weeks since the roads can get impassable."

165

☽

We leave them open-mouthed, and run back to the other cabin to get the shoe box and the bug book. We slip back in and sit casually on one of the beds while they tinker with their machines, trying to get them to work again. When their backs are turned, I empty the box on the floor, then push it under the bed.

Two minutes later, Bree's mom screams! She jumps up, slapping her hands on her legs and arms. She points down at a bug about a half-inch big. Bree and I calmly walk over to look at it. Bree gives a little shudder, but only I notice it. "Let me see," I say, lifting the book off the bed. I open it up and pretend to be looking for something. Bree's mom leans in and then grimaces when she sees all the drawings of bugs. "Kenny or I always make sure to have this book with us," I explain. "That way we can tell if a bug is poisonous or not."

Her mom's eyes open wide. "Are there a lot of poisonous bugs around here?"

Wondering how far I dare take this, I say, "Well, besides the occasional scorpion, we'll sometimes get fire ants and black widows. You'll wanna watch out for the brown recluse spiders too. Oh, they're *really* nasty. They'll turn your whole leg gangrene."

Bree's mom is now pale. Her dad says, "I thought scorpions and fire ants were warm-weather creatures."

I shrug. "Must be the gulf stream that brings 'em." I have no idea what that means, but I heard someone say it once. He seems to buy it though.

"C'mon, Ally," Bree says. "Let's go join Kenny and Mel at the stream."

"Speaking of the stream," I say to Bree's parents. "You're gonna find some way to block that off, right? I mean, if you have a child who sleepwalks, a stream is very dangerous. Kids can drown in an inch of water, you know." Bree had supplied me that last fact.

Her parents look at each other.

I continue, on a roll now. "Actually, there are tons of dangers here for someone walking around in the middle of the night. Bears and fallen logs and bee-hives and —"

"Enough," Bree's dad says. "We get the picture. We'll figure something out."

Bree's mom jumps and shrieks again as another bug crosses her path. I hold out the book. "Would you like to borrow this?"

She shakes her head repeatedly. I shrug and tuck it under my arm. Bree tells them she'll see them later, and we walk out of the cabin. Bree stays in front while I go around and plug the electrical socket back in. I hear Bree's dad say, "We're back on!"

We walk quickly back toward the main house. When we're far enough away Bree stops and hugs me. "You were great! You should be an actress someday! Forget about finding comets!"

I laugh. It feels good to laugh again. And this time when Bree stops hugging me I don't stand quite as stiff. I'm getting used to being hugged by virtual strangers.

"You really had me convinced with all that stuff. Like it would really take a few weeks to get the power back on. Classic!"

"Um, I wasn't kidding about that one."

A look of panic flits across Bree's face.

"But don't worry, you can still dry your hair. We have a generator in the main house and in the kitchen at the pavilion."

"And the roads? You really get trapped here for weeks?"

I nod, realizing how it must sound to an outsider. "But it doesn't feel that way, honest. And there's usually really good seeing on winter nights, so we don't mind."

"There's usually *what*?"

I forgot she's a total astronomy newbie. "Good seeing. That's the expression for when the air is really still. It means you can see the stars better. If it's poor seeing, that means the air is hazy and it can be hard to focus your telescope on planets and stuff."

Bree sighs. "Our plan REALLY better work."

We're almost at the office now, and I can hear both of my parents in there, which is what we were hoping for. "Okay, you ready?"

She nods.

We plant ourselves on the top stair of the porch in front of the office, the same place I first saw Bree. Loud enough to be heard clearly through the open door, Bree says, "So do you think you'll go out for softball, or gymnastics?"

"Isn't all that expensive? Like uniforms and stuff?"

"Oh yes! It's all very expensive, but so is living in the 'burbs. My parents had to take out a second mortgage just to pay for all our activities."

Neither of us knew what a second mortgage was, but Bree said she saw it on a commercial about people needing money.

Inside, my parents have stopped talking. "But don't worry," Bree continues, a little louder. "Your parents won't be worrying too much about money. They'll have a lot bigger things to worry about."

"Like what?" I ask, hoping my voice doesn't sound rehearsed.

"Like drugs of course! The drug problem in middle schools today is rampant! You'll be lucky to make it down the hall on your first day without someone asking if you want to buy. And Kenny, holy cow! The elementary schools are even worse!"

"Wow!" I say. "That's terrible!"

"And if you can manage to stay away from the drugs, you'll have to worry about the gangs. Every school has them, and they always pounce on the new kids. How do you feel about tattoos?"

"Tattoos?"

"Sure! All the kids have to get them. Melanie and I have two each. Our parents don't know of course,

☽

because they're dangerous. You could actually die from the dirty needles. But if you don't get them, no one will let you in their clique. You don't want to sit alone in the huge cafeteria every day, do you?"

I shake my head. Bree nudges me with her knee. "No, I do not!" I exclaim.

My parents bang through the door. They look upset. "Oh," I say, pretending to be surprised. "I didn't know you were in there." We'd pretty much reached the end of our banter anyway.

"Bree, do you know where your parents are?" my mom says. "We'd like to have a talk with them."

Bree can't hide her smile. "Last I saw them they were in their cabin, working. I honestly don't know how they're going to keep this place going since they're working all the time. Wouldn't surprise me if they had to close it down."

"Close it down?" my father repeats. "But they can't do that. It's in our agreement."

This girl is good! We hadn't even practiced that last part.

Without another word, my parents stalk off toward the cabins. When they round the bend, Bree and I jump up and I'm the one to hug *her* this time. "You were brilliant!"

"Thank you, thank you very much," Bree says, bowing and curtsying. Her long hair shimmers like the stream does when the sun hits it. Maybe she's right and I should put some effort — any effort — into how I look.

"You were kidding though, right? About all the drugs and tattoos and stuff?"

She laughs. "Yes, I promise."

That's a relief! I don't think I'd be very good with needles.

"What are you guys up to?" a familiar voice asks. I turn to see Ryan, followed a few feet behind by that boy Jack from the pavilion last night.

Ryan is talking to me, but looking at Bree. I'm not surprised. "Bree, this is my friend Ryan, he comes up here every summer for a few weeks."

Bree holds out her hand like she's a grown-up. Ryan eagerly shakes it. I wait for Ryan to introduce Jack, but he's too smitten with Bree. I glance over at Jack, expecting to find him looking at Bree too, but instead he's looking at *me*. When he catches my eye he looks away and kicks at the dirt with his shoe. I don't have much practice identifying teenage boy behavior, but I think that means he's shy. Having grown up welcoming new people to the campground all the time, I've never been shy before. But now I find myself unsure what to say. Finally Bree asks, "Who's your friend?"

"Oh," Ryan says, finally tearing his eyes away from Bree. "Sorry. This is Jack. He's here with an eclipse tour."

Jack takes a step forward, and we all say hi. I find

my voice and say, "That's cool that you're here for the eclipse. Are you excited?"

He opens his mouth to answer, but then seems unsure what to say. After a pause he says, "I guess so. Honestly, I'm not sure. It's a long story."

"Oh." We stand there awkwardly for a minute until Bree suggests we get lunch.

"Great idea!" Ryan says. Without another glance at me and Jack, he lopes his arm casually around Bree's shoulders and they set off for the pavilion. Jack and I follow. His arm, needless to say, stays by his side. To break the ice I ask, "So what's the long story?"

He hesitates, then says, "Well, it was either come here or go to summer school."

I'm about to ask what summer school is when Kenny and Melanie come running up to us. "Ally! Ryan!" Kenny says, not trying to contain his excitement. "We got an e-mail from the SETI people!"

Ryan stops short. "Already? Did you open it?"

Kenny shakes his head. "I was waiting for you guys. C'mon!"

I turn to Jack, "Wanna come?"

"Sure," he says.

We take off running down the road, dust kicking up behind us.

"Ally?" Jack asks as we pass the pavilion, which is filling up with lunch people.

"Yeah?"

"What's a SETI?"

I laugh. "It stands for Search for Extra-Terrestrial Intelligence. It tracks radio signals from outer space."

"Oh," he says.

Newbies are fun. The little red-haired twins and their parents cross in front of us. The twins stop and they wave at Jack. He stops and gives them high fives before catching back up with us. How does he know everyone already? This guy gets around!

Kenny has our work unit up on the screen. The colors are rising and falling like they always do. The task bar reads 97 percent.

"So the work unit hasn't even uploaded to SETI yet?" I say.

Kenny shakes his head. "Probably a few more hours to go."

"So how can they be e-mailing us already if they haven't even reviewed our signal?"

"I don't know," Kenny says.

Bree turns to Jack. "Do you have the slightest idea what they're talking about?"

Jack shakes his head. "I haven't understood most of what anyone's said since I stepped on the bus."

Ryan says, "Can we read it already? The suspense is killing me here."

Kenny clicks over to the e-mail screen and says, "You read it, Ally."

I take a deep breath, and then click it open. "'Dear SETI@home Friend,'" I read.

173

☽

"SETI@home Friend? Not very personal," Ryan mutters.

I continue. "'Over the past few days we've been made aware of irregular signal patterns by many people reviewing work units from the Libra region. If you are receiving this e-mail, it means your work unit was one of the affected ones.'"

I don't like where this is heading. My voice gets softer as I keep reading. "'We are aware of a ground-based radio frequency that has been causing interference in the signal. When we receive your complete unit, we will alert you if the signal was caused by anything other than this interference. Thank you for being a part of our team.'"

"Well," Ryan says. "That's that. I figured it was too good to be true."

Kenny and I don't reply. Besides insuring that my parents would stay here, finding a real signal would have meant that even if I did have to leave, even if I had to go to a school with a thousand other kids, I would have done something really special. Kenny, too.

"C'mon, guys," Ryan says. "Let's go eat."

He and Bree head out. Kenny says, "Are you gonna be all right?"

I nod. "You should go."

Melanie follows him out the door, leaving me and Jack. Jack sits down in the chair next to me. He waits for me to say something.

"Well, I guess I won't be finding any aliens before

we move. Ryan was right of course. It was a huge long shot. But it would have been really cool. And it would have made my grandfather really happy. He founded this place."

"I know," Jack says, surprising me. "I read it on the brochure in my cabin when I couldn't sleep last night."

I laugh. "Then you know about the meteorite that started it all?"

He points at my necklace. "That one, right?"

My hand instantly wraps around it. "Do you want to see it?"

He nods. I slip it off my neck and start untying the string. I haven't shown it to anyone in years. But something about him makes me want to. I pull open the top of the pouch and let the small chunk of iron fall into Jack's open palm.

"It's heavy," he says. "For something so small."

He carefully hands it back to me, and I slip it into the pouch. "Looks like this meteorite is the closest I'm going to get to finding a comet or asteroid. Or life on another planet."

"Not necessarily," Jack says. "What would you say if I told you I know another way?"

BREE

5

With my hair restored to its usual sheen and my makeup on, I feel a little more like myself again. As long as I don't look down at my clothes. Those boxes really better get here today! As I suspected, Ryan is proving a welcome distraction. He talks a lot and at lunch he entertains Kenny and Melanie (who are now glued at the hip) by telling them stories about vampires and werewolves who haunt campgrounds. He better be making those stories up. I keep glancing over to see when Ally's parents are going to come out of Mom and Dad's cabin. I think they'll have to pass this way. I'm still not sure where everything is around here. Hopefully I'll never have to find out.

Melanie jabs me with her pointy little elbow. "What?" I ask, rubbing my arm.

"Ryan's asking you a question."

"Oh, sorry. What was the question?"

"I just asked what you like to do," Ryan says, downing his container of milk. "You know, besides wearing other girls' clothes." He says this with a wink. At least he realizes I wouldn't normally dress this way, which is a point in his favor.

Borrowing clothes makes me think of Claire. I wonder what she's doing right now. She's probably at the mall with Lara Rudy, the best friend stealer! How do I answer his question? I can't very well say, I like to take pictures of myself with my friends and then stick them in a Wish Book alongside real models. So I say, "You know, hang out with my friends, go to the movies, shop at the mall, the usual."

Ryan nods. Kenny says, "That's not the usual around here, that's for sure."

"What's a regular day like here?" Melanie asks.

Leave it to Melanie to ask questions that no one else (okay, me) wants to hear the answers to.

"Well," says Kenny thoughtfully. "It depends. If it's a school day, we do schoolwork in the morning and then do our chores and stuff in the afternoon."

"But it's not like real school," I point out. "You don't have tests and book reports, right?"

"Sure we have tests. My mom makes them up, but they're based on the books she gets for us. Then at the end of the year she has to send stuff to the state, to prove we're learning and everything."

I turn to Mel. "Can you picture Mom as our teacher?"

"She'll be too busy," Mel replies. "We're gonna do the school-in-a-box thing. It's different than regular

☆

homeschooling — it's more on our own. The curriculum arrives in a big box and then we have all year to go through it." She turns back to Kenny and says, "I can't wait."

I roll my eyes at Ryan. "Melanie loves school."

"So do I!" Kenny says. He and Melanie high-five each other. They start to compare their favorite subjects, and I want to scream. I've had enough of Melanie and her excitement over everything. For such a genius, it drives me crazy that she isn't smart enough to see what a bad idea moving here is.

Jack and Ally come into the pavilion, but I don't wave them over. I thought Ally would be really upset about the whole alien thing, but she looks okay. Jack's talking and she's listening intently. Jack's not the kind of kid I would have given a second glance to at school — he's pasty and has clearly eaten a few too many cookies — but he seems to be good for Ally. I bet she's glad I made her brush her hair!

I stand up with my tray and Ryan immediately grabs his and stands up, too. "Do you want a tour of the Moon Shadow?" he asks.

"Okay." Anything to get away from the two uber-geeks.

Kenny and Mel are now testing each other on vocabulary words and don't even notice when we leave. As we walk down the path toward the stream, I wonder if all the people swarming around the campground think me and Ryan are a couple. He's as cute as any of the guys I was considering dating at home, even if he *does* look for aliens in his spare time. I'm cool with him putting his arm around my shoulder, mostly because it would freak out my parents if they saw.

We pass a clearing with a fire pit in the middle of it. A big pile of pointy sticks lay a few feet away. I pick one up and hold it out. "For killing the vampires, I presume?"

"For toasting marshmallows," he says, grinning. "But if you do run across any vampires, you might want to keep one handy. You know, if your family moves here, you'll probably get the fun job of whittling the sticks!"

I quickly toss the stick back into the pile like it burned my hand. "I don't whittle. I'd bleed all over the sticks."

He puts his arm around me. "Don't worry, you'll learn all these things. Ally had to learn everything once, too."

I push his arm off my shoulder. "I'm not Ally," I say. "I can't do all the stuff she can do. And I don't want to learn how."

"Hey, sorry, just trying to help."

"No, I'm sorry," I say contritely. The last thing I want to do is push him away. He's my only link to the real world now. "Let's just talk about something else. Tell me about football tryouts."

His eyes light up as he tells how the coach specifically asked him to try out, and how he's working out really hard. My mind starts to drift, and I'm sort of sorry I asked. I think I'd rather hear about the vampires and werewolves again. I'm saved by Ally and Jack running up to us.

"They're out of the meeting!" Ally says, breathlessly. "They were standing on your parents' porch when we left. Let's go. See you guys later!" She grabs at my sleeve and pulls me away from Ryan. I just have time for a backward wave before we're out of sight.

"Hold up, Ally. Why'd you ditch Jack back there? I thought you guys were getting all hot and heavy."

She stops running. "Hot and heavy?" She asks this like she has no idea what the words mean.

I sigh. "You know, like you guys *liked* each other."

"Oh. He's nice."

"Nice? And . . . ?"

"And what?"

This girl is hopeless. "Never mind. Let's just go."

We keep going and run right into both sets of parents in front of the sign that says LABYRINTH, THIS WAY with an arrow underneath.

"Well?" I ask my parents. Ally shifts her weight from one foot to the other in obvious anticipation.

"What's up, girls?" asks my father. "Having fun exploring?"

I open my mouth to say *no*, but before I do, they look at each other and laugh. It takes a few seconds to realize they're laughing at us. I feel my face darken. Ally stops shifting. "What's so funny?"

☆

Her mother puts her arm around Ally's shoulders. "Honey, we understand what you're trying to do, but you've got to trust us."

Mom says, "We should thank you both, actually. You've raised some very good points. Forewarned is forearmed, as they say."

Ally's eyes fill with tears and mine follow. Ally puts her hands on her hips. "So you don't mind having a tattooed druggie gang member for a daughter?"

"We'll take our chances," says her father. "You're a smart girl, Ally. You'll do just fine at school."

"Don't count on it!" Ally says. I haven't heard her talk like this to her parents before. Maybe I'm rubbing off on her.

Her mom reaches out to hug her, but Ally pulls away and runs back toward their house.

"That didn't go very well," Ally's father says. They all turn to look at me.

I back up. "Don't look at *me*. *My* opinion obviously doesn't count for anything."

I turn on my heel and walk to the cabin. Dad calls after me, but I pretend not to hear. I feel a strange roaring inside my head. I think it's my soul screaming. This is really happening. This place is going to be my home.

The cabin is hot, and I don't feel like waiting till the overhead fan kicks in. I grab my iPod off the dresser and start to leave when I see one of my boxes sitting on my bed. I want to hug it! I tear it open eagerly, and the first thing I see is my Book. I hug it to my chest.

☆

Claire's Book is in here too, along with my curling iron, all my accessories, a pair of flip-flops with jeweled daisies on them, and one V-necked orange shirt. That's it. My eyes sweep the room, but there are no more boxes. I quickly throw off Ally's brown shirt and put on my orange one. I kick off my (her) sneakers and slip on the flip-flops. I yank open the accessories bag and put on every piece of plastic jewelry I own. I clip back my hair with barrettes and put on a new coat of peach-colored lip gloss to match the shirt. I have no choice but to keep on the faded tan shorts with the side pockets. Doesn't Ally know side pockets just make your hips look bigger? No, of course she doesn't.

I clip the iPod to my shorts and stick in the earphones. I love the sound the flip-flops make across the wood floor. If I closed my eyes, I could pretend I'm walking across the stone tiles at Claire's pool. I grab my Book and head out the door. I don't know where I'm going. Just away. I turn on my iPod and set it to random. I turn the volume so high that it blots out the bird calls and shouts of kids and slams of car trunks as more and more people arrive. I have to jump out of the way of a guy lugging a huge telescope across the field. It's not easy to jump in flip-flops. It's actually a little tricky to walk on the dirt road too, but there's no way I'm putting those sneakers back on. Plus I like how my red toenail polish shines against the dull dirt.

I find myself back at the labyrinth sign and figure I

might as well check it out. I carefully make my way down the narrow path and am happy to find no one else there. All I see at first is a big circle of stones in some kind of random pattern. When I get closer I can see the stones form circles spiraling inside each other. In the middle sits a tree stump with what looks like a stuffed purple dinosaur on it. A small wooden sign off to the side has a little diagram with the words HOW TO WALK THE LABYRINTH. I wouldn't have thought it needed instructions. Might as well give it a try. Ally said you feel different after you go through it. I don't know what she meant, but I can't feel any worse than I do right now.

I stand at the entrance, but instead of taking that first step, I turn around and sit on the little bench next to the diagram. I flip open the cover of my Book, and my eyes instantly fill with tears. I remember this first photo. I clipped it out of *Teen* when I was just nine years old. The girl is probably a little older than I am now. At the time she seemed so old to me. She's wearing a green prom dress and a tiara and looks like she's about to go to the party of her life. The next page is of me and Claire in our dance recital outfits. She has a heart-shaped sticker on her cheek, and I have a star-shaped one on mine. I reach out and run my finger over the little stickers.

I feel a touch on my arm and almost jump out of my skin. I whip my head around to find a little old lady in a pink sweat suit and a red scarf. She's saying something to me, but I can't hear a word. I yank out my earphones.

"Sorry to startle you, young lady." She points to the open page. "How adorable! Your little sisters?"

I shake my head. I really don't want to talk to anyone, but how can I be rude to a little old lady? Even if she IS wearing red with pink. "It's me and my best friend. When we were nine."

She nods and waits for me to turn the page. So I do. The next page is a collage of heads. The woman looks at me quizzically.

"It's for the hairstyles," I explain, quickly turning the page. This one is all of feet. Feet in high heels, strappy sandals, flip-flops, sneakers, pumps.

"Let me guess," she says, "you like shoes?"

I've never showed anyone my Book before, besides Claire of course, and I'm starting to feel very exposed, like she's looking inside me. "I'm planning on being a model one day," I explain, closing the Book and placing my hand on top. "This is my inspiration, that's all." I brace for the words that will follow — how it's such a shallow career choice, how I'll always have to worry about my looks. But that lecture doesn't come.

"Ah," the lady says, getting to her feet. "How wonderful to have a goal already. When I was your age I knew nothing about the world or my place in it. I figured I'd be someone's wife, then someone's mother. It never occurred to me to be someone myself. I didn't figure that out till much later. But you've got a head start. Of course, you might still change your mind."

I shake my head. She heads slowly toward the entrance of the labyrinth. "You never know," she says. "Life is short, but it's wide."

With that, she steps easily into the labyrinth. I watch her move through the circles, and it looks almost like a dance. When she gets in the middle she actually *does* start doing a little dance. She must not care at all what people think of her. If I'm dancing alone in the middle of a labyrinth sixty years from now, something in my life will have gone horribly, horribly wrong.

JACK

5

The sharp smell of bug spray floats through the night air. It's almost too dark to see, but I want to finish my book. I haven't done much reading since I've been here. There's so much to see, so much to do. This log isn't very comfortable, but that's mostly due to how sore my legs are. Ryan warned me not to push myself with the weights, but I wanted to keep up with him. The little red-haired twins are circling around Pete, asking him to play with them. All three kids are in their feety pajamas and sneakers.

It seems like the whole campground has come out to hear Ally talk. It's after nine, so it should be starting any minute. On my way here I passed the Star Garden and heard Ally's voice. I was about to go and say hi, but it sounded like she was having a really intense conversation. She was peering through one, then another telescope, talking to someone. Only I didn't see anyone else with her. I crept away so she wouldn't see me. Maybe living out here does something funny to your brain. Not like in a bad way though, because I think Ally's really interesting.

I shiver a little and wonder why they don't start a fire in the fire pit that we're all gathered around. Mr. Silver joins me on the log, along with two of the guys from the trip who are camping in the tents. I close my book, two pages away from the end. Tonight the guys are wearing t-shirts that read MY ECLIPSE IS BETTER THAN YOURS. One of them turns to Mr. Silver and says, "Why don't they light that fire? It's cold out here, dude."

Mr. Silver looks at him like he's insane. "You can't light a fire when you're stargazing! It would ruin everyone's night vision. It takes at least a half hour till you can see all the stars. You take one look into a light like that, and you're done for. Think, man, think!"

The guy shrinks back a bit. I'm VERY glad I wasn't the one who asked. I notice a lot of people have flashlights with red plastic over them and remember one of Mike's articles talking about how red light doesn't affect night vision. I tilt my head back. Mr. Silver is right. I can already see a lot more stars than I could when I first got here, just twenty minutes ago. I pat my regular ol' flashlight in my pocket, glad I didn't use it to read with.

"Hey, everyone," Ally says, stepping into the circle. I know she was upset with her parents earlier because her brother told me. Something about a plan not working out the way she'd hoped. But with everyone's eyes on her, she seems totally together and confident.

Really grown up. I hope Mr. Silver lets me include her in the experiment or else I've gotten her hopes up for nothing. I probably shouldn't have even told her about it before I asked him. I don't have much experience in this sort of thing. I guess this is what I get for not being more social. Somewhere Mom is saying *I told you so*.

"Welcome to the Moon Shadow!" she shouts to the crowd. "One more week till the big day!"

Everyone cheers and whoops. When they quiet down she says, "This is going to be a review for most of you, but for the newbies, after tonight, you're gonna know how to easily navigate the night sky."

I look around the group. She has everyone's full attention. Well, maybe not Bree's. She's sitting in the back row with her earphones in. I watch as her mom reaches over and yanks them out. Bree shoots her a look but tucks them away.

"Has everyone visited our Star Garden?"

Whoops and shouts go up from the audience.

"Well, when you get home, if you don't have access to a telescope, does anyone know what you can use instead?"

"Binoculars?" a brave soul calls out.

Ally nods. "Yes, but that's not what I was thinking of." She gestures to Kenny, who jumps up from his log. He's holding a small object up over his head. It's too dark to see it clearly. It looks like, well, it almost looks like an empty toilet paper roll!

"You can use *this*!" Ally says, taking the object from Kenny. "An empty toilet paper roll!"

Everyone laughs.

"I'm serious," she insists, smiling. "It won't make the stars look closer, but it will make them clearer by helping you isolate them. It also helps bring out the colors of the individual stars."

The younger kids are still laughing. Clearly they think it's the funniest thing they ever heard. It *is* pretty funny. Whoever thought of a toilet paper roll as a telescope? Kenny takes his roll back and sits down. He makes a big show of tucking it carefully into his shirt pocket.

Ally waits patiently until the audience quiets. "There are eighty-eight constellations in the sky," she says, "and everything we can see is contained inside them. Once you know how to find the constellations, you can find anything — the planets of our solar system, distant stars, whole galaxies."

I look up at the sky while she talks and am startled to see how many more stars there are, just a few minutes after I last looked. I've never in my life imagined there were so many. How can anyone make patterns out of zillions of tiny white dots?

I tune back in to hear Ally say, "Space is so incredibly vast. I guess that's why they call it space!"

The audience laughs.

"Everything is so far away, it's easier to measure distance in how fast it takes light to reach us, rather than miles. Light travels six trillion miles over the course of a year. Our own personal star — the sun — is ninety-three million miles away, practically right next door in the scheme of things. Light leaving the sun only takes eight minutes to reach Earth. The next closest star, Proxima Centauri, is four light-years away, which translates to twenty-four *trillion* miles. The farthest you can see with the naked eye is the Andromeda Galaxy, a whopping two-point-seven million light-years away. Anyone out there good with math who wants to figure out how far that is in miles?"

I watch as Ally's brother's hand shoots up, with Bree's sister Melanie right behind him. "You two can do that on your own time." Everyone laughs as the kids lower their hands. "Trust me," she says, "it's really far. And with a telescope you can see much farther than that. Soon there will be a telescope in space that can see back to the beginning of time, somewhere around fourteen billion years ago."

A hush falls over the crowd as that sinks in. I admit, the stars are more interesting than I'd thought. Or maybe Ally's just a really good teacher. I bet I wouldn't have failed science if she had been my teacher.

"Just like Earth," she says, slowly turning around in the center of the circle, "the other planets go around the sun in fixed orbits. That means we can see them easily, in a band of the sky called the Zodiac. Jupiter and Saturn will be out tonight, and anyone who wants to go to the Star Garden afterward can check them out.

They might look tiny through a telescope, but Jupiter would fill the distance between the earth and the moon. And Saturn is actually fluffy, like cotton candy. If there was a bathtub big enough, it would float!"

I glance over at Bree. She actually seems to be paying attention. Melanie is rapt.

"But keep in mind that if our solar system was the size of an apple, our galaxy, the Milky Way, would be the size of North America. And tonight we're going to learn a very basic way to navigate it. If you're ever lost and not sure where you are" — her voice breaks for a second, but then she takes a breath and continues — "if you're lost, all you have to do is find the North Star."

I can't imagine finding one star out of all that mess. There's no way.

"Now you might be thinking there's no way you can find one star out of all the thousands you can see with the naked eye."

Okay, that was weird.

"But trust me, you can. The first thing you need to do is find the Big Dipper, which is part of a constellation called The Big Bear, and one of the most recognizable patterns in the sky. It looks like a ladle. Three stars form the handle, and four stars make up the bowl at the end." She holds up a poster and shines a red flashlight on it. It's a diagram of the Big Dipper. "Try to find it on your own, and then I'll show you."

Murmurs arise as people point and twist their heads around. I've seen it before at home, on Boy Scout camping trips and stuff. But it was easier then since there weren't so many stars. I search all over, but I can't find it. Mr. Silver nudges me and points. I follow his finger but still don't see anything.

"Okay," Ally says, "let's find it together." She whips out a small pen and points it up at the sky. Suddenly a beam of green light shoots into the sky. That's no normal pen! She uses it as a pointer to clearly outline the seven stars that make up the Big Dipper. Once I see it, it seems obvious. It's about halfway up the sky, to our right.

"Can I have a volunteer to help me find which way is north?"

From behind me a small voice starts chanting, "Jack! Jack!" Others join in. It takes a minute for me to realize they're talking about me! I whirl around and see that it was Pete who called out my name. Before I know it, Ally's in front of me, smiling. Mr. Silver nudges me again, and I have no choice but stand up. Great, now I'm going to look like an idiot in front of everyone. I feel like I was just called to the board at school and don't know the answer.

She has me stand in the center of the group, looking up. "First we find the Big Dipper." Thankfully she uses the pointer again because I'm too nervous to find it on my own. Then she points to the two stars that make up the front part of the bowl. "Now, if you look at these two stars and then extend your eye out about five times the distance between the two of them, you'll wind up at the North Star, otherwise known as Polaris." But instead of doing it with her laser pen, she hands the pen to me. "Don't shine it in anyone's eyes," she whispers. "We can't afford a lawsuit." Hand shaking a bit, I take the pen.

"Okay, first go back to where we were." It takes me a few seconds to get it steady, but then I can easily run it along the seven stars. It's such a weird feeling. Almost like I'm touching the stars themselves.

"Now extend it in a straight line and you'll hit the North Star."

I do as she says, moving the laser across the sky. But I've jostled it too much and am no longer in the right place.

"Try again," she says.

I find the Dipper again, and move very slowly this time until I hit the next fairly bright star.

"That's it!" she says.

Everyone claps. Phew, that wasn't so bad. I move to sit down, but she says, "Not so fast. You still need to figure out which way is north. First, find the North Star again."

I start to move the pen, but she takes it from my hand and turns it off. "Find it without this."

I'm about to say I can't, but then I realize that I can. I can actually pick out one star out of what looks like a zillion. I go through the routine again. "Okay, I have it."

"Good. So now wherever you're standing, imagine a

line pointing from you to Polaris. That line points north. It can also tell your latitude. If directly over your head is always ninety degrees, where would you say the star is right now?"

I panic for a second. I only barely squeaked by in math this year. I crane my neck to look directly overhead, and then slowly lower it to the horizon in front of me. The North Star appears to be right in the middle, maybe a little higher, at around 48 degrees. I tell Ally this, and she says, "That's exactly right! If the North Star was directly overhead, you'd be at the North Pole. If it was really near the ground, or the horizon, you'd be standing near the equator. Now don't you feel better knowing you'll always know where you are?"

I nod. More clapping ensues, and then I sit back down on my log. Ally talks for a few more minutes, tracing the shape of the Summer Triangle with her laser pointer. She says how each star of the triangle is in a different constellation and how one of them, Deneb, is so powerful that it gives out more light in a single night than our sun does in a century. She knows so much about things that I never gave a second thought to. But if Mr. Silver says it's okay, I'm going to be able to teach *her* something now. When she's done talking, her dad steps up beside her and says, "Far be it for me to rain on anyone's parade, but the National Weather Center has issued a warning of a strong storm headed our way in a few days. It's already soaked half the

Northwest. It should be here and gone well before the eclipse though, so that's good news. But everyone be careful on the paths, the mud gets slippery in the rain. And those of you in tents might want to make friends real quick with someone in a cabin or an RV."

The lecture breaks up, and all the red flashlights make the air seem otherworldly. I promise one of the t-shirt guys he can have my other bed if or when the storm comes. I want to tell Ally what a great job she did, but there are too many people around her. Mr. Silver hands me my very own red flashlight and we head up toward the hilltop where his experiment will take place. It takes about ten minutes to get there, and we spend the time with him talking and me listening and thinking how dark it is. I don't mind the dark. I've spent a lot of time in my treehouse late at night, but this kind of dark is totally different. Thankfully we've switched over to our regular flashlights, and that makes it much easier to see.

"Now we'll have a two-day window to do this, starting at ten PM the first night, eleven the second. Each team is assigned a block of time since the transit could happen any time during those two days. I'm not even going to consider the possibility of rain, so you set your mind to clear skies."

"Sure thing," I promise, wondering how I'm going to mention Ally.

We get to the top of the hill where his telescope is all ready and waiting. He pulls the silver waterproof cover off and stands back to admire it. "It's a beauty, ain't it?"

"Um, sure. It's really something."

He checks the small computer attached to the side of the telescope and then fiddles with some other piece of equipment, which I assume is the special camera. "Now, Jack, I don't expect you to understand all of this. All you'll have to do is read me the data as it comes up, that's all I ask."

"No problem," I say, more confidently than I feel. "Um, can I ask a favor?"

"Go ahead," he says, busy adjusting something in the viewfinder.

"Ally, the girl who gave the lecture tonight, is it okay if she hangs out with us during, you know, the experiment? She knows a lot about this stuff. I'm sure she wouldn't get in the way or anything."

He looks up with a mischievous grin. "You like this girl?"

How do I answer that question? It's not like a beautiful girl like Ally would be interested in me as anything more than a friend. I'm grateful that she wants to be my friend at all. I decide not to answer. "So can she come?"

"That's fine," he says. "But you can't get distracted. We're both going to need to focus all our attention on what we're doing, because time is going to move quickly."

"I won't, I promise." I'm so relieved he said yes. Now I can't wait to tell Ally.

He surprises me by saying, "Do you want to see Saturn?"

Before tonight I would have said *that's okay*. But after Ally's talk, I'm curious. He takes a few minutes to set it up, then steps aside and says, "Okay. All yours."

Saturn, all mine? A very strange thought.

"Don't jostle the scope or else I'll have to find it again."

Careful not to touch anything, I peer into the eyepiece and see the strangest sight. A little yellowish ball in the sky, with a series of perfect rings around it. My first thought is that it looks fake, like a drawing of Saturn, or a sticker on the end of the telescope. I actually step away and check the lens just to make sure Mr. Silver isn't pulling a trick on me. But no, it really looks like that. I can't tear myself away from the eyepiece. That planet can float in a bathtub? Too soon it starts drifting out of my field of view. When it's gone, I step back, too awed to say anything. I look up at the tiny points of light above me and can't believe the planet I was just looking at is among them. I had no idea telescopes were so powerful, that it could single out one dot of light like that and bring it so close. It was like magic.

Mr. Silver laughs. "I bet you won't forget Saturn in your *next* model of the solar system!"

I shake my head. I won't forget Saturn, period.

Rustling leaves and crunching branches make us both turn around. "Mr. Silver?" a woman's voice asks. It's Ally's mom.

As she gets closer I see her expression is serious. "This fax came for you at the office." She hands him a piece of paper. "I thought you'd want to see it right away."

His brows knit as he begins to read. Then he lets out a small gasp and a groan. His arm with the paper in it drops to his side. "Can you get me a car to the airport tonight?"

Mrs. Summers nods. "We'll work something out. Come down to the office when you're ready." In a softer voice she says, "I hope everything's going to be all right," then hurries back down the hill.

I watch the exchange, wide-eyed.

Mr. Silver is wearing a pained expression when he turns back to me. "My wife is six months pregnant and had a scare. She's in the hospital. She said not to worry, but I have to go make sure she's okay. This is our first baby." He paces back and forth, pulling at his hair. He used to do that in class, too, whenever someone (often me) gave an answer that was unfathomable to him. I didn't even know his wife was pregnant. I didn't even know he HAD a wife. I glance at his left hand, and sure enough, there's a gold wedding band. I've really got to start being more perceptive. My stomach twists at the thought of him leaving.

"Well, it can't be helped," he says. "I'll have to cancel the experiment. I hope I can make it back for the eclipse."

I gape at him. "Cancel it? How can you cancel it?"

"I'll call the lead scientist in Hawaii. He'll have to get someone else."

"But you told me all the data points are programmed into your computer. You said it took weeks. How can someone else catch up?"

He puts his hand to his head. "You're right of course, they can't. He starts pacing again. Then with what sounds like regret, he says, "Greg Daniels knows how the experiment works. He keeps up with all the amateur astronomy research. He'll just have to take over."

"Er, if Mr. Daniels knew how to do it all along, why did you want ME to help?"

"Honestly? I didn't want to have to hang out with the guy!"

As much as I didn't want to do this when he first told me about it, I don't want to hand it over to Stella's not-so-nice son, either. "Can Ally and I still help?"

He nods absently. "Follow me back down to my cabin. I'll give you all the manuals for the equipment, all the instructions on reading and submitting the data. You can go over it with Mr. Daniels in the morning. I was really looking forward to —" His voice breaks and I look down while he collects himself. He rests his hand on the telescope, head bowed. Then he gives me a small smile and says, "You know, Jack, science is all about trial and error. I'm proud of you for being willing to try."

I help him put the thick cover back over the telescope and we head down the hill in silence. It's going to be weird to be here without Mr. Silver. He had stopped seeming like my old teacher and had become more like SD4, even though he doesn't even know my mom. Hanging out with Mr. Daniels isn't going to be much fun. I wonder if Ally hadn't been involved, if I would still have volunteered to help. I'd like to think so, but I don't really know.

When I go to look for Ally in the morning, I can't find her anywhere. She's not at home, or any place I've seen her before. I spot Stella by the stream with Pete and an old man I recognize as Ryan's grandfather. He and Stella are laughing. I wonder why she and her son are so different. "Find any gold today?" I ask them.

Pete holds up a handful. "We're rich! I'm gonna buy a castle when I get home!"

"That's great." I turn to Ryan's grandfather. "Have you seen Ally, by any chance?"

"Try the Art House," he says, pointing toward Alien Central. I figure he's confused about what the buildings are called, but I wish them all happy prospecting, and set off. I open the door of Alien Central, but just the loud hum of the computer greets me. Then I see a door I hadn't noticed the other time I was in here. I knock on it.

"Come in!" Ally calls out.

I push open the door and find myself in a cabin similar to my own, except this one is covered in small paintings, some a few inches, some nearly a foot long, none bigger. They extend all the way up three walls, and in one corner they actually continue onto the ceiling. Ally is sitting cross-legged in the middle of the room, leaning on her hands.

"So this is the Art House?" I ask, although clearly it is.

"Yup. I was just looking at all the things people have painted here over the years. I've seen it nearly every day of my life, although it changes of course when people add things. But still, I've seen it every day, and thought it belonged to me. And all these pictures, all these images, they aren't mine. They belong to the people who made them."

I move a bit closer to one of the walls. It's covered with scenes of parks, stars, animals, fairies, people, planets, everything. "I don't think that's what art is," I say cautiously. "Once it's out there, it's for everyone. Plus, you know, they wouldn't have been able to paint this stuff if they hadn't come here."

She smiles at me. Really smiles, in a way I don't think anyone out of my family has ever smiled at me.

"Do you want to paint something?" Ally gestures to

paint and brushes and jars of water on a small wooden table in the corner.

Her question catches me off guard. I've never painted anything that would be on display before. I think I might like to, though, so I say, "Yes, but not now. I have to tell you something." I fill her in about Mr. Silver saying she could help, and then the part about him having to leave. She starts pacing, just like he did.

"Wow, okay, wow. I didn't want to get my hopes up, and I wish Mr. Silver was going to be there, but thank you for asking him if I can help. That was really nice of you."

I look down at my feet so she doesn't see my cheeks get red.

"C'mon, Jack. We better go find Mr. Daniels and give him everything. There's not much time." She hurries across the room, flicks off the light, and is already out the door and halfway down the road by the time I catch up.

"Hang on, hang on, I know where he is. Mr. Silver slid a note under his cabin door before he left last night. He's supposed to meet me at my cabin in about ten minutes."

"Oh," she says, smiling. "Well that makes it easy, then."

We turn around and hurry in the opposite direction. Ally laughs as we bump into each other trying to keep out of other people's way. My stomach does a little flip. As we pass the Pavilion I look up to see Mr.

Daniels and his wife coming from breakfast. I point him out to Ally, who takes off running before I can warn her that he's not very nice. I run after her, but she's faster.

"Hi, Mr. Daniels!" she says when she reaches them. "Isn't this great? Should we get started?"

"Honey," Mr. Daniels's wife says, tugging on his sleeve. "What is this young lady talking about?"

"I have no idea," Mr. Daniels replies.

"This is Ally Summers," I explain, stepping up beside her. "Her family owns the campground and she knows tons about astronomy. She's going to be helping us with Mr. Silver's project."

Mr. Daniels shakes his head. "You mean she's going to be helping YOU with Mr. Silver's project."

"Um, what?"

"I know how these things go," he says, bending to scratch a nasty-looking mosquito bite on his knee. "The grunts do all the work, and the head guy takes all the credit. I'm not standing out in the middle of the night for hours so some other guy can verify an exoplanet. No thanks."

It takes me a few seconds to let his words sink in. Then I blurt out, "But Mr. Silver's not like that. I'm sure he'd give you the credit, or whatever. He said you were going to do this."

Mr. Daniels shakes his head.

"Can't you just do it, you know, in the name of science?" Ally pleads.

"Sounds like you two've got it all under control," he says, stepping around us. "Come on, honey, let's go pan for some gold."

And with that, they turn and walk away, leaving us staring after them, mouths open.

"Wow," Ally says.

"Wow," I repeat.

"Maybe he's mad because Mr. Silver didn't include him originally?"

"Could be."

"What are we going to do?"

I shake my head. "I have no idea. There's no way I would ever understand how to do the experiment. I guess I'm going to have to find Mr. Silver and tell him."

"Kenny!" Ally suddenly yells out, making me whip my head around, only to realize he's not here.

"We'll ask *Kenny* for help," she says, her usual enthusiasm returning as quickly as it had left. "He's really good at reading manuals and figuring out electronic things."

I'm not sure how Mr. Silver would feel about a ten-year-old working on his project, but it doesn't look like we have any choice. Before she leaves to find him I blurt out, "Hey, I saw Saturn last night."

She stops and smiles up at me. "Pretty cool, right? Those rings are actually individual chunks of ice. The first time I saw it close up I thought it didn't look real."

"Yes! Exactly!"

"I'll meet you in your cabin as soon as I find Kenny, okay?"

Without waiting for an answer, she takes off at a run. Someday I hope to be able to run as effortlessly as her, instead of lumbering along, huffing and puffing. On the way back to my cabin I think about what she said about Saturn not looking real. It's almost like the two of us have seen something that no one else has, even though of course plenty of people have seen it. But it makes me feel good to think that she looked up at it and thought the same thing I did.

Twenty minutes later Ally, Kenny, and Bree's sister, Melanie, arrive at my cabin. Mr. Silver's stuff is piled up in a big cardboard box. Kenny grabs for the logbook, and Melanie snags two of the manuals and opens them with obvious glee.

Ally laughs. "You two are like twins separated at birth."

"Only we're eight months apart," Melanie says, not tearing her eyes from the books.

"Yeah," Ally says dryly. "I didn't mean it literally. Where's Bree?"

"She's hanging out with that guy Ryan," Melanie says, flipping open a notebook. "Last night she said he felt familiar, or something like that. She only says those kinds of things really late at night when she's half asleep."

A flash of something I can't quite figure out crosses Ally's face. I hope she's not upset that Ryan is spending so much time with Bree. I know Ally and him go way back. She told me they were just old friends, but still, it can't be easy watching your friend spend time with someone else. But now that I think of it, Ally's spending kind of a lot of time with me, and I've been exercising with Ryan, so maybe it's okay. Ugh, this social stuff is so hard. It was much easier alone in my treehouse. Lonelier, but easier.

To change the subject, I ask Kenny and Melanie if they think we have a chance to do this.

"We'll go up the hill and check out the equipment," Kenny says. "I bet we can figure it out."

"I told my parents," Melanie says. "They said they could help. Should I ask them to?"

Ally looks down at her sneakers. Kenny busies himself in one of the books. I hide my relieved smile behind a cough. I'm not the only one who doesn't want the grown-ups involved.

"Um, what if we only ask for help if we really need it?" Melanie suggests.

"Yes, sounds good, yup," the three of us say at the same time.

"Okay then," Kenny says, sticking his book back in the box and throwing the top on. "Let's go up the hill and see what we're dealing with." He tries to pick up the box, but his knees buckle.

I make a big show of flexing my arms, and then lift

it easily. It's amazing what a few days of working out have done already. As we head out of the cabin Bree and Ryan walk by. They're walking very close to each other. They look like a real couple.

Ally tells them all about the project and I like knowing that it's because of me she's so excited. "Do you want to help?" she asks them.

"Sure!" Ryan says.

"Count me out," says Bree.

Ryan looks at her and then says, "Sorry, I guess I'm out, then, too. Maybe I'll catch you guys later."

"Oh," Ally says. "Are you sure?"

He nods firmly.

"Okay," she says, clearly disappointed. But her smile comes back quickly. "Have fun."

I didn't think to put the box down while Ally was talking to them and by the time we get to the top of the hill I'm huffing and puffing and letting out the occasional wheeze.

"You know," Ally says, gesturing to the box, "we have carts for that sort of thing."

"That would have been good to know, Alpha Girl."

Kenny laughs. Ally stops walking. "How'd you know about that?"

"Um, I heard one of the security guards call you it. Not that I know what it means." I can hear myself rambling, but I can't stop. "It just seemed like a cool super-hero name, you know, like the Adventures of Alpha Girl."

Ally reddens. "Can we talk about something else, please?" She looks off into the distance. "Like how about those dark clouds? What do we do if it rains?"

Relieved that she's letting me off the hook, I shake my head. "We have two nights to get the readings at specific times, and that's it."

Ally looks at the clouds and frowns. Kenny and Melanie manage to get the cover off the telescope without breaking anything. It all looks more complicated in the daylight. Kenny starts pushing buttons and twisting knobs. Melanie flicks a switch and a small computer display lights up and beeps. She says something in technobabble and Kenny nods and technobabbles back. It sure sounds like they know what they're doing. Hopefully they're not bluffing through it like I would be.

I point to the large blue shed a few yards away. "What's that for?"

"Storage, mostly," Ally says, turning to look at it. "Sometimes people camp up here and leave things. We've found some strange stuff over the years. It all goes in the shed in case the people ever come back."

"Do a lot of people return each year?"

She nods and is about to say something when her voice catches in her throat and she turns away. I know she's thinking about leaving and how hard it will be.

I know because I'm thinking the same thing.

ALLY

6

I hold up the solar filter so everyone can see how I cut it. "Your piece should be three inches wide and long enough to reach your ears. Then you will punch a hole on each end and tie a piece of string through it. Make sure the two strands are long enough to tie in the back of your head. Any questions?"

Hands wave in the air as scraps of the thin silvery-black sheets fly around the pavilion. Each table has a hole-puncher and scissors. At first I had been surprised so many people didn't come prepared with their own glasses. Then I overheard someone say, "You mean it's not dark the whole time?" and I realized most people haven't been preparing for an eclipse for their entire lives like we have. The die-hard eclipse chasers have their own, of course, and many people ordered ahead for them — either the aluminized Mylar ones like we're making now, or goggles with special welder's glass. But for the rest, Dad was smart enough to order material for them to make their own. I had to explain to the group that the retina at the back of your eye doesn't have any pain receptors. That means you won't feel the damage that's being done until it's too late. As soon as I said the words "you can go blind," people rushed up to get their glasses-making materials.

"He stole mine!" one of the little red-haired twins yells.

"No! He stole *mine!*" the other one wails. "Mooooom!!"

Their mother waves them off. "Figure it out, boys."

I love leading the campers in activities like this. Giving the night sky lectures has been one of the only things keeping me from crawling into a hole. Well, that and my new friends. Although I'm not sure I would call Bree a friend, exactly. Sometimes she can be sort of nice, and sometimes she looks right through me. I think she doesn't like me because I'm the one leaving. If anything, it should be the reverse.

An elderly couple comes up to the front wearing their new glasses. "Is this right?"

They look pretty funny. "Yup, looks great."

"Don't want to get blind, ya know. Got new grand-babies at home."

I smile. "I promise, you won't go blind. Just listen for the announcements about when to put them on, and when it's safe to lower them, okay?"

They nod. I walk around the pavilion making sure

everyone has their questions answered. Kenny was supposed to help me, but it's more important for him to be up with Jack. We were up there until it got dark last night, and now they're doing a trial run. I can't believe I'm actually going to see an exoplanet — even indirectly. Comets and asteroids are one thing (well, two!), but an exoplanet? I never even dreamed of it! And we're going to chart it for a real astronomer, all the way in Hawaii! Jack said Mr. Silver told him the guy works at an observatory on the top of a volcano that's, like, the highest spot in the world. Or in America. Something like that. And he needs OUR help!

Thunder rumbles again, still many miles away. We might just make it before the rain comes. The first viewing is about eight hours from now.

Someone tugs on my sleeve. I'm ready to assure the hundredth person that as long as they don't look at the sun without the solar shade, they won't go blind. When I turn around I'm surprised to see Ryan. I've only caught glimpses of him the past few days. He's either jogging or hanging out with Bree. Part of me misses hanging out just the two of us, like in the old days, and part of me is glad we have other people to be with. I've put the non-hottie comment behind me. Maybe if I had wanted to be a hottie in the first place, it would have bothered me more.

"Hey," he says. "I know we haven't seen too much of each other. I'm wondering, um, if you don't mind, could I join you guys? For the planet thing?"

I look up at him in surprise. "Sure! But what about Bree?"

"All her boxes and stuff from home came. She's pretty busy going through everything. She probably wouldn't even notice."

"She must be happy that she can stop wearing my clothes now."

He shrugs. "I think she was getting used to them. She hasn't complained in a day and a half." He winks, then helps me pile up the extra solar filters. "So what's the plan?"

I stash the box of filters outside the kitchen door. "I sent an e-mail to the other members of Mr. Silver's team asking for help. We can check if they wrote back yet." I leave out the part where I didn't write to the main guy in Hawaii because I was afraid he'd cancel the experiment if he knew it was a bunch of kids doing it.

"Race you?" he teases.

"No thanks, cheater." I take one last look around to see if anyone needs help, and then we hurry over to Alien Central. The only e-mail we received told us we had recently won a million dollars and all we had to do was send a check for a thousand and then we could claim it. I hit *delete*.

"You know, it's already the middle of the night in Europe," Ryan says. "They're probably sleeping."

"Probably." For a second it feels like old times, just

me and Ryan, hanging out together like we used to. "Do you want to watch the SETI screen for a while?"

He nods. We pull up the chairs and watch the patterns dance across the screen. It's almost like nothing's changed. Except, of course, everything has.

By eight o'clock, the rolling of the thunder is getting louder as the wind picks up. Almost all the members of Team Exo, which is what we've decided to call ourselves, are gathered on the hilltop. Jack and Kenny are happy that Ryan is here, which I knew they would be. Mom and Dad aren't thrilled about us being up here as the storm approaches, but we have our walkietalkies, and we can take shelter in the shed if necessary until it passes.

Melanie is the last to arrive. She's still wearing Kenny's clothes, which is strange since her boxes must have arrived with Bree's. When she's right next to me though, I realize they aren't Kenny's clothes after all, they're her own. That girl is going to fit in just fine at the Moon Shadow.

Jack has to keep his hands firmly on the telescope or else it will topple over. "It doesn't look good for tonight," he says, frowning.

"It's too early to tell," Ryan says. He has to speak loudly to be heard over the wind. "Sometimes storms out here can blow through pretty quick. Right, Ally?"

I nod as the sky darkens around us. "But this one is taking its time coming, so it will probably take its time leaving."

A strong gust hits us, and Jack's grip tightens. I can tell he's worried. Damaging his teacher's equipment won't look very good.

I pull up my sweatshirt hood right as the first drop of rain splatters on my cheek.

"Help me put the cover on," Jack says to Ryan. He keeps hold of the scope while Ryan wrestles with the thick cover. The drops are coming faster now. I thought we'd have more warning. We should have brought sleeping gear with us.

"We've got to get the equipment out of the rain," Jack calls out, panic in his voice.

"Let's move it to the shed," I reply, shouting now as the thunder booms above us.

It takes all five of us to drag it over there. Silver must have had a cart or wheels, but in his hurry, he never told us how to transport it. We get it to the door of the shed, but it won't fit, not by a long shot. The rain has quickly become a steady downpour. Melanie and I lift the cover and hold it up while Kenny and Jack unscrew the computer component. Ryan, being the acknowledged strongest one here, is holding the scope from falling over. He's starting to breathe heavy. Finally after taking off the computer and the scope's viewfinder, we're able to fit it through the doorframe. It's so bulky that it takes up most of the space in the shed. We all plop down around it like we're sitting around a gleaming silver bonfire. The rain pounds against the walls of the shed and rivulets of water stream down the one window.

"Where's the logbook?" Kenny asks, dumping out his backpack.

"I thought you had it," Jack says.

"It was on the ground by the scope," Melanie says. "Did anyone bring it in?"

We look from one to the other.

"I'll go get it," Melanie says. She pulls her flannel shirt tight around her and runs out before I can stop her. "She shouldn't go out there," I say, jumping to my feet. "We're above the tree line and that lightning is close!" I turn toward the door, but Jack is already chasing her. I try to grab for him, but he's too fast. The rest of us watch as they run across the hilltop, illuminated by flashes of lightning. I can tell they're both trying hard to keep their balance on the slick grass. Melanie is very light on her feet. Jack's slipping and sliding but managing to stay up. A burst of thunder, the loudest yet, roars in the sky and the three of us in the shed jump. Jack is a few feet behind Melanie, scrambling to catch up. He yells for her to turn around, but she either can't hear him or is ignoring him. She bends down and sticks what I figure is the book under her shirt. She pivots to turn back around, but her foot slips and she falls flat on her face. In a second Jack scoops her up and hurries back as fast as he can, which, considering the extra weight, is still pretty fast.

"I'm fine," Melanie insists as Jack sets her down in the shed. Her face and shirt are covered in mud. "See?" She wiggles her ankle. "I can do a back handspring if you don't believe me."

"That won't be necessary," Jack says, wiping the water from his forehead. "You shouldn't have run out like that. It's too dangerous."

Melanie pulls the book out from under her wet shirt. "I'm sorry, I just couldn't leave this out there. Not after all the work we've done. It has the codes for the program."

Kenny kneels down to assess the damage. The thick plastic binder is splattered with mud, but the pages inside are only wet around the outside edges. "It's okay," he announces. "I can still read everything."

I turn to Jack. It was very brave what he did, but still. "You shouldn't have run out there either."

I can't be sure in the dim light, but I think he's blushing. "We're Team Exo!" he says. "We look out for our own."

"Yeah, well, no one else is leaving this shed," I declare. "Until the rain completely stops."

"Or until we build an ark," Ryan says. "I think we're gonna be here awhile."

The sky is completely dark now and the rain sounds like it's picking up, if that's possible. "Okay, let's make a plan," I say, looking around at our wet little group.

"Let's take stock of what we brought with us, and what's here in the shed. Gather anything that looks useful and I'll do an inventory."

Five minutes later I have a big pile to sort through. Three sleeping bags and a blanket, all of which will have to be shaken out since they've been piled in the corner of the shed for months, or even years. "We'll spread two sleeping bags on the ground," I say, "and use the rest as covers. We all have flashlights — five white, three red — and there are two extra here in the shed." I hand the sleeping bags to Kenny and ask him to shake them out as well as he can without knocking into the scope. "In the food category, we have a very healthy variety. One full-size Milky Way, a bag of Fritos, two cans of Orange Crush, and a grape-flavored lollipop."

Everyone laughs when I say "lollipop." Melanie crosses her arms. "I got it from winning a Scrabble tournament at school."

"I love Scrabble!" Kenny says.

"Really?" Melanie says, beaming.

Ryan asks, "You don't have a Scrabble board with you, do you? Like a travel-sized one or anything?"

"No," Kenny says, clearly wishing he had planned ahead.

"Good!" Ryan says.

Melanie kicks him in the shin.

"Moving on," I say. "We have two dry sweatshirts. I think they should go to Jack and Melanie since they're the wettest."

"That one's already mine," Melanie says, reaching for the small yellow one.

"And, uh, that one's mine," Jack says, pointing to the rather large gray one still on my lap.

"Oh. Well, that makes it easy, then!" I toss him the sweatshirt. He turns around to change and I quickly look down at the pile in front of me. "So that leaves us with the random things that were already here in the shed. One toothbrush, a half-filled-in book of Mad Libs, a flip-flop, a sneaker, a hiking boot, a fish hook, a bottle of red nail polish, a matchbook with one match, and two mismatched socks."

"Well," Ryan says, rubbing his hands together, "if we're bored we can always do Mad Libs and paint each other's nails!"

Finished dressing, Jack looks at me and says, "Do you think there's any hope?"

"For Ryan? Nope."

Jack tries to laugh, but I can tell he's stressing out. "I mean for tonight. The experiment."

I know it's not what he wants to hear, but I shake my head. "The storm isn't going anywhere for a while. The thunder and lightning are very close together, that means we're right in the middle of it."

Jack takes a breath and nods in grim acceptance. "Well, no matter what we do, I'm NOT painting my nails!"

"Don't worry," I tell him. "It's not for painting nails. It's for painting the lenses of flashlights red."

"Oh," he says, clearly relieved. "Well, that I would do."

"We should save our flashlight batteries," Kenny suggests. "In case something happens and we really need them."

We agree to leave one running at all times. Otherwise it would be pitch black in here. The moon is less than a quarter full tonight, and behind all those storm clouds, it isn't shedding any light.

"We should call down to Mom and Dad," Kenny says. "To tell them we're staying the night."

"Okay." I hand him the walkie-talkie. He hands it back. I forgot he is still giving them the silent treatment.

After a few beeps, Dad picks up. I ask if we can stay the night, and to let Melanie's parents and Ryan's grandfather know. I glance over at Jack. No one is expecting him back tonight. Without Mr. Silver, he's really on his own. I'll just have to look out for him myself. I have to repeat my request a few times before Dad hears me. The wind howls, and I shiver. Even though I'm cold and wet and disappointed that we can't do the experiment tonight, I'm glad I'm not spending the night in my bed.

Jack gives me a smile as I sit down, almost like he'd heard my thoughts.

"Let's tell ghost stories," Kenny suggests, grabbing the sleeping bags. We lay them out on top of the concrete floor and settle back down.

"I'll start," Ryan says. "Now if anyone gets too

scared, you let me know and I'll stop." This time both Melanie and Kenny kick him in the shins. He takes the one flashlight and shines in under his chin. He looks very eerie. When we were younger, Ryan's grandfather and mine used to compete to see who could tell us the scariest ghost stories. A pang goes through me. I hope Grandpa knows how much I wish he were here.

In a sinister voice, Ryan says, "It was a cold and rainy night. Five kids were stuck in an abandoned shed in the middle of the woods. A man with a hook for a hand was spotted in the area. The children were afraid. They were very, very afraid."

I shiver again, and so does Melanie. We catch sight of each other doing it, and share a smile.

"Hungry and scared, these kids were so far away, no one would ever hear them scream. They kept their ears out for any noises outside, especially the rattling of a hook on the door. They tried to stay awake, but one by one they succumbed to sleep. But they had forgotten something."

We all lean forward. His eyes narrow and he says, "They had forgotten to lock the door!"

At that very second, seriously, that very second, the door of the shed bangs open. We all scream and scramble backward, including Ryan who drops the flashlight.

Outlined in the flashing of the lightning is a figure, but we can't see its features. It sweeps its tangled hair off its face and says, "Hey, guys, room for one more?"

BREE

6

"Why so jumpy?" I ask, stepping out of the rain into the warm, dry shed.

"Bree?" Melanie asks, surprise and relief mixing in her voice. She turns to Ryan and puts her hands on her hips. "Did you guys plan this?"

"Plan what?" I ask, squeezing into the circle between Ally and Ryan. Everyone is staring at me. You'd think they'd seen a ghost.

"Your entrance," Ally says, looking from the door to me and back again. "Ryan was telling a ghost story, and then you . . . right at the . . . oh, never mind. Now that I say it, it sounds kinda dumb."

Melanie jumps up and hugs me.

"What was that for?" I ask, peeling her off of me.

"You came," she says. "I can't believe it."

"How did you get up here?" Ally asks, peering at me closely. "The path must be so slippery. Are you hurt anywhere?"

"And the lightning!" Ryan adds, seeming genuinely concerned. "What were you thinking?"

I don't know how to answer. Yes, it was slippery. And muddy. And really, really dark. Basically it was the scariest thing I've ever done in my life, and I've had my legs waxed by a twelve-year-old (Claire, last year). But I couldn't stay in that cabin alone. Mom and Dad were at the main house, learning about running the campground. I was just sitting there on the floor, surrounded by all my clothes, and it hit me how out-of-place it all was. All those bright colors were a welcome sight, and it felt good to touch fabrics other than boring cotton. But my wardrobe belonged to someone else. Someone who I don't get to be anymore. It was like I was looking at the clothes of a dead person. How can I explain how that felt? The goose bumps that ran down my arms and legs. The sudden tightness in my throat that made me feel like I was choking. How can I explain that after sitting there for an hour, not moving, I got up, carefully packed most of my clothes back into the boxes so they'll be ready for me when I, like Frankenstein, am brought back to life, and then headed up here?

So I shrug and say, "I figured you guys needed me."

They all laugh, which is better than them saying they *don't* need me, which I know is really the case. "So aren't we supposed to be finding a planet or something?"

"Rained out," Kenny says. "We get to try again to-morrow night." He looks longingly at the huge bulky object in the middle of the room, which I figure is the telescope. Drops of water are slipping off the silver cover and forming a puddle underneath it. This is definitely different from sleepovers with my friends. No one's painting anyone's toenails, no pictures of models are being torn from fashion magazines, and I haven't thought of rating anyone even once. Whenever my friends are together it's usually up to me to organize the activities. But now I feel like I interrupted something. "So you were telling ghost stories?"

"Ryan was just telling us about a guy with a hook for a hand who haunts campgrounds," Jack says. "We thought you were him. You didn't see him on your way up, did you?"

A few years ago I might have believed him. Jack seems different than when I first met him a few days ago. He's less shy, and not as pasty. Of course that could just be the lack of light in here.

"You didn't happen to bring any food with you, did you?" he asks.

"Or dry clothes?" Ally adds.

I shake my head. Honestly, I hadn't thought this thing through. I only had a general idea where the shed was from Melanie's description. It wasn't raining like this when I left. I had no idea the path or the hillside would be so treacherous. I actually had my flip-flops on at first and turned back around for sneakers. I'll keep that part to myself.

Jack divides his Milky Way bar into six pieces and

passes them around the circle. I hand mine to Ryan. "Bad for the complexion," I explain.

"But good for the belly," he replies, popping it in his mouth.

One minute everyone (except me) is happily eating their chocolate, the next minute Ally bursts into tears. And not ladylike, glide-silently-down-the-cheek-type tears. Messy, snotty, gulping tears.

At first we're all too stunned to say anything. "Did I miss something?" I ask.

"I don't want to leave the Moon Shadow!" she says between sobs. "I'll never make it out there. I don't want to live somewhere I have to worry about my complexion!"

"Not everyone worries about that," Melanie insists.

"Yes, they do," I say.

Melanie glares at me.

"Well, it's true!"

"I don't want to leave either," Kenny declares.

"Me either," Jack says so quietly I almost didn't hear it.

"And I don't want to stay," I said. "But something tells me you guys already know that."

We all look expectantly at Melanie.

"I'm happy either way. Here, there, it's all okay."

I shake my head. "You're hopeless."

Ally continues to cry. I dig into my pocket for a tissue, but all I find is lipstick and a movie stub. This just makes her cry harder.

Jack passes her a napkin. She takes it and blows her nose. I don't think I've ever in my life blown my nose in front of anyone. It's never pretty, even when *I* do it.

"We've got to help each other," Jack says firmly. "That's all there is to it."

"We already tried," I explain. "We had all these great plans to make our parents change their minds. It didn't work at all."

Ally sniffles loudly. No one says anything for a few minutes as the rain continues to pelt down on the roof.

Eventually Ryan says, "Um, I don't mean to sound obnoxious or anything, but have you all tried just accepting it? You know, making the best of things?"

I give him a glare that would make most boys shudder. "That's easy for you to say. Your biggest problem is what position you'll get on the football team." As soon as it's out of my mouth I wish I hadn't said it. Ryan's been good company these past few days. It's not his fault that he doesn't have any problems.

He breathes in sharply. "Just so you know, my life isn't always easy. How about the fact that I have a dad who I'm pretty sure hates me, and that my grandparents who practically raised me just got a divorce? But I try to make the best of things, and that's all I'm suggesting."

Great. Now I'm the jerk. "I'm sorry. I didn't realize." But in my defense, he had never mentioned his parents to me, or told me much about his grandparents other than to say he came out here with them every summer.

Ally stops sniffling and her swollen eyes open as wide as they can. "Your grandparents got divorced? Can they do that at their age?"

"Of course they can," he replies.

"But why?"

"When I asked, they just said something about drifting apart. But I heard my grandmother on the phone a few weeks ago, and she said she was tired of taking care of someone. She said fifty years was long enough. She lives with her friend Shirley down the block now. Grandpa was pretty down for a while, but I think he's going to be okay. He has a lot of friends from his astronomy club, and I go over to visit a lot."

"I just can't believe it," Ally says. "Why did you tell me that story about the bridge tournament?"

"That's what she asked me to tell everyone. I guess she doesn't want people to judge her. I really felt bad lying to you."

"My mom heard she was sick and that's why she's not here."

He shakes his head. "Nope. She says she's going to travel to the next eclipse somewhere in the Pacific Ocean." He squirms a little on the sleeping bag, obviously uncomfortable talking about it. Turning back to me he says, "But this isn't about me, it's about you guys. Can't you just help each other? You know, tell the other what they'll need to survive in the new place?"

I grunt in reply, but I have to admit it's not the worst idea I ever heard. Ally and Kenny look glum but don't argue. Jack picks at a loose thread in the sleeping bag, like he wants to say something, but can't make himself say it.

"How about you first, Bree?"

"Fine." I pause for a minute to think about what I want to say. "Okay. Here's the thing about going to a real school. The only way to survive is by being popular, and you have to —"

"That's not true!" Melanie interrupts. "Don't tell them that!"

"When it's your turn you can say whatever you want. I'm telling them how I see it."

She grumbles but lets me continue.

"As I was saying," I say with a glare at Melanie, "you have to learn the rules of the school. You have to figure out who the popular kids are, and why they're popular. Each school will be different. In some schools the popular kids are the rich kids, or the best-looking, or the ones on a certain sports team. You'll need to find this out before school starts so you can be prepared."

"Wait a second," Ally says, her eyes still rimmed red. "How can I be prepared? I won't fit into any of those groups."

"You don't have to *really* fit in with them, you just

need to make them *think* you do. You can pretend you played a certain sport at your old school, but now your parents are making you focus on schoolwork so that's why you're not playing now. Or you can say you just moved from Beverly Hills and lived next door to movie stars. As the new kid, they'll try to put you in a category right away. Your job is to make sure it's the one you want."

Ally turns to Ryan. "Movie stars? This isn't helping."

Kenny says, "I don't know, it sort of makes sense. Like if I go in there on the first day and try out for the math team, then I'll be known as this math wiz, and no one in the entomology club will take me seriously."

"The *what* club?" I ask.

"Entomology," he repeats. "The study of bugs."

"Who told you there's going to be a *bug* club at your school?"

"You mean there won't be?"

Jack and Ryan shake their heads. I don't even trust myself to respond.

"Is it my turn yet?" Melanie asks.

"Yes, please!" Ryan says, shooting me a look.

"Sheesh," I say, pulling my sweatshirt tighter around me. "I was just trying to help."

"Okay, so let's say there are no bug clubs at your school," Melanie says with a lot more patience than I could have mustered. "Then you can start one. That's the great thing about living in a big town. You can do so many things. My sister might be a little obsessed with being popular, but she's right about kids wanting to put you in a box."

Kenny freezes.

"Not a *real* box," Melanie quickly assures him. Kenny breathes a sigh of relief.

"The trick is that as long as *you* know who you are, and what makes you happy, it doesn't matter how others see you."

I snort.

"It's true," Melanie argues.

"Yeah," Jack says, "if you want to get teased all the time."

Melanie shakes her head. "Kids respect you if you don't show fear. They think you know something they don't."

"Which is what?" Kenny asks.

I find myself leaning forward a bit to hear her answer. Jack does the same.

"Like if I'm at lunch, and I'm doing algebraic equations, I don't hide behind my book like I'm doing something wrong. I put it right there in the open. When people see I'm happy doing what I'm doing, it sort of takes the power away from them to tease you about it."

"So Kenny shouldn't be afraid to let people know about the things he likes," she continues, "and Ally, you'll still be able to do all sorts of astronomy things even though the sky won't be as dark. There are planetariums and astronomy clubs and lots of big bookstores and libraries and museums where you can learn about anything."

I glance at Ally's face, or what I can see of it by the glow of the single flashlight. Her skin is brighter already, less ashen. I'm surprised to find that I'm wishing it could have been me who made Ally feel better.

"Now, Ally," Ryan says, "It's your turn. Tell us what makes living here so great."

Ally takes a deep breath and sighs. "Where do I start? When you live out here, you feel like a part of the universe. The stars are so close and the sky is so wide, it's like the earth and the sky and everything in between are one. It's hard to remember that there are so many bad things going on in the world. It doesn't seem possible when everything around me is beautiful." She shivers. "Out here Kenny and I have grown up in this wonderful little bubble where you don't have to worry about how you look, how people judge you, or even what channel to watch on the nonexistent television. Our choices are so easy."

Kenny has been nodding during Ally's speech. "She's right," he says. "I couldn't have said it any better." He and Ally share a warm smile. I feel a stab of jealousy at their closeness. I don't like feeling jealous, but it's a familiar feeling. Every time I look in my Book at all the beautiful models I feel jealous. It's tiring.

Jack says, "Sometimes I feel like I live in my own little bubble. I'd rather live in this one. I don't have any friends in my bubble."

"You don't?" Ally says, her brows rising. "How is that possible?"

I know how it's possible, but I'm keeping my mouth shut.

Jack shrugs. "I don't like to do the same things as other people, I guess."

"What do you like to do?" she asks. "You know, when you're not organizing planet-hunting missions?"

They share a quick smile, then Jack goes back to pulling at the piece of loose string on his corner of the sleeping bag. Quietly, he says, "I like drawing, and reading science fiction novels and . . ." He says something else, but at the same time Kenny jumps up and yells, "It stopped raining!" and everyone springs to their feet and runs out. Except for me and Jack, who don't move.

"What did you say just now," I ask, "before Kenny cut you off?"

He seems surprised that I'm asking him and takes a little while to answer. "I said I can come awake in my dreams. I can fly."

"That's what I thought you said. Why do you want to come awake in your dreams?"

He shrugs.

I peer closely at him. The sliver of moonlight coming

from the open door casts strange shadows on his face. "Is it because you like the dream world better than the real one?"

With obvious effort, he meets my eyes. "It's not just that. When I fly, I feel free."

The shed door bangs open and Kenny comes back in before I can respond. I'm not sure what I would have said anyway.

"The rain has stopped for a while," Kenny says, "but the cloud cover is too great. All you can see is the moon."

"That's enough for me," Jack says, not wasting any time getting to his feet. "Let's take the scope out and at least take a look through it. We can leave the monitor and computer attachments here." He takes a quick glance back at me, then starts dragging the telescope toward the door.

I scoot out of the way. I've dreamt that I'm a famous model before. I've dreamt that I marry a prince and we have a huge wedding at a fab castle. But flying? I wouldn't tell Jack this, but it sounds like a waste of time. I think you should dream about things you really want to happen. That way, they're more likely to come true.

"C'mon out," Melanie says, interrupting my thoughts. "Come look at the moon."

"I've seen the moon before."

"Not like this you haven't."

I let her drag me outside where no doubt the mosqui-

☆

toes are buzzing in full force from the rain. The air is thick and soupy, and I can tell the lull in the storm is just that, a lull. Everyone has switched to their red flashlights even though only a handful of stars are visible.

I almost trip over the telescope cover, which is balled up on the wet ground. Ally has her eye pressed to the side of the telescope, and it takes me a minute to realize that's where the eyepiece is. "That's Dandelion Crater," she tells Jack. "It was named after a Ray Bradbury book."

Jack's face lights up. "Really?"

Ally nods and steps back. "Take a look."

Jack comes forward and puts his eye to it. I hear a sharp intake of breath. "It's so . . . so close!" he says. "Like I can touch it!"

Melanie pushes me toward the telescope, but I stand firm. For reasons I don't understand, I'm suddenly deathly afraid to touch it. Jack's not moving anytime soon anyway.

"You know, Ally," Jack says, not taking his eyes away. "You might not be able to see as many stars where you're going, but you'll always be able to see the moon."

"I've never spent much time looking at the moon. There were always so many other things to see."

Ryan says, "You can try to find all the craters on the moon instead of the Messier objects. I know it's not the same thing, but at least it's *something*."

Ally nods, but instead of answering, she turns to me and says, "Okay, it's your turn now."

Jack reluctantly steps aside and waves me forward.

I approach the telescope very slowly. "How about I use an empty toilet paper roll instead? I've heard that works great."

Everyone laughs, but Ally shakes her head and points to the telescope. I can't see a way of getting out of this. I take a deep breath and rest my hand on the side of the telescope for balance. Ally yells, "Don't jostle it!" But apparently I already did, so they have to locate the moon again, which requires looking through this small tube called the finder, and then adjusting knobs. You wouldn't think something as big as the moon would be so easily lost.

"I don't mind not looking," I tell them. "Maybe we should just go back in. It could rain again any second."

"It's all set now," Ally says, ignoring my suggestion and pointing at the eyepiece. "Just don't touch anything this time."

So having exhausted all other options, I close my left eye and let the rubber of the eyepiece cover my right eye, as instructed. And I look. The pockmarked face of the moon stares back at me, enormous and bright. It doesn't look anything like it does hanging above us in the sky. It's so beautiful and mysterious and powerful. This enormous rock controls so much of what happens on our planet. The tides, for one, and indirectly, the weather. I'm struck by the perfect way the universe fits together, like a big elaborate watch that keeps perfect time. Wait, why am I thinking about the tides and watches? What's wrong with me? I step back from it like I've been burned. My head suddenly feels heavy and I know why I was so scared to look into the telescope. The thing that I've smothered since third grade has resurfaced.

My inner geek has been released.

That's *so* not good.

JACK

6

Bree stumbles back from the telescope and Ryan, who is the closest, steadies her. The rest of us crowd around.

"Are you okay?" Ally asks, peering into Bree's face.

Bree nods slowly, but doesn't focus on any of us. She seems in a total daze or shock or something.

"Do you want to go back to your cabin?" Ryan asks. "We'll walk you down."

She shakes her head.

Melanie is standing next to me, so I whisper to her, "Is she going to be all right?"

Melanie's eyes are wide. She seems unsure what to do. Bree suddenly throws her head back and stares up at the moon, then back at the ground, then up again, almost like she's calculating something in her head.

"She'll be fine," Melanie says. "I think."

We continue to watch her for a minute, until she suddenly focuses on Ally and demands, "Where's that nail polish you found?"

"Guess she's back to normal," I joke.

But she shakes her head. "I don't want to paint my *nails* with it. I want to paint my *flashlight*."

Leaving the rest of us with our mouths hanging open, Melanie slips her arm through Bree's and they head to the shed, followed by Ryan.

A few minutes later, while Kenny is fiddling with the telescope, Ally says, "Jack, you told me you came here instead of going to school this summer. What did you mean by that?"

I don't really want to tell her, but I can't see how to avoid answering. "When you fail a class, you have to make it up over the summer."

"What did you fail?"

I can't even look her in the eye. "Science," I mumble.

"*Science? Mr. Silver* failed you?"

I nod, feeling like a total idiot. "And it's not like I don't think it's interesting. I just like sitting in the back and drawing better. It was dumb of me. I could have passed. He gave me plenty of chances." I can feel that familiar heaviness, that familiar disappointment in myself, start to settle in my chest.

Ally puts her hand on my arm. The feel of it makes the heaviness lessen. "If you hadn't failed that class," she says softly, "you wouldn't be on this hilltop right now. And neither would any of us. So I'm glad you sat in the back drawing."

I feel the ends of my lips curl into a smile. "Thanks, Ally. I guess I am too."

Kenny coughs, to remind us that he's here, too. It's

starting to drizzle again, so the three of us pull on the cover and push the scope back to the shed. Bree is done with her flashlight and shows it off when we get inside.

Kenny says, "We can make it down the hill before the rain picks up again. We won't have to sleep up here."

We all look at each other. Nobody makes a move to leave.

I'm the first to wake up the next morning. The sun is beaming through the small window. I have to get back to the campground to make sure no one from the tour needs anything, since somehow I doubt Mr. Daniels is going to do it. Kenny is starting to stir so I wait for him to open his eyes and then tell him where I'm going. He nods, and then closes his eyes again.

I tip-toe out of the shed, which isn't an easy thing to do when you're my size. The sunlight has a crisp quality to it that I've never really seen before. It must not be much past dawn. I dig my watch out of my pants pocket. Six fifteen. We hadn't gotten much sleep last night. It was pretty cramped with six people, and there was a lot of blanket stealing. Mostly we were talking though, telling stories, ghost and otherwise. Bree was still sort of out of it at first, but then she started talking about silly things she and her friends have done at the mall. Bree's someone who never would have spoken to me at school. And I never would have spoken to her either. But she's funny, and I don't think she's as confident as she wants people to believe. Up here everything's different. Up here *I'm* different. Back home I've tried to do what Melanie said and just be myself. But the kids didn't respect me like she said. They just ignore me. And that's not the same thing. I know I need to let it wash over me more and not worry what people think about me. It's so hard though.

I head to my cabin to make sure no one left a note for me. As I pull open the front door I realize that the shades are drawn. I'm sure I didn't leave them that way. I hear my mom's voice saying you never want to walk in on an intruder, but it's too late now. Enough light comes in behind me that I can see two people, one in each bed. On the floor at my feet is a crumpled t-shirt. I push it with my toe to get a better look: ECLIPSE CHASING: NOT FOR THE WEAK.

Right! I had promised those guys they could stay here if the storm came. I'm glad I left the door unlocked.

I quickly scan the cabin and don't see any notes or anything. I really want to change out of my pants, which are still damp, so I open the dresser drawer as quietly as I can and pull out the first pair of shorts my hand lands on. I'm about to make my exit when one of the guys wakes up and sees me.

"Hey, dude," he says, leaning up on his elbow. The cot creaks under his movement, but the other guy keeps snoring lightly.

"Hey," I reply.

"Thanks for letting us crash here."

"No problem." I turn to go again.

"Wait a sec. You just getting in? Where did you sleep?"

"Um, I was with some friends. We were trying to do this experiment thing and —"

"Dude," he says, holding up his hand, "you are a party animal," and he turns back over.

I hesitate. Should I tell him it was all in the name of science? Nah. It'll be good practice in not letting it bother me what other people think. I close the door quietly behind me. It's too early for breakfast, so I head to the Art House. Ever since I was in there with Ally I've wanted to go back. Once inside, I quickly pull off the stiff jeans and pull on the shorts. Walking slowly around the room, I carefully select a spot on the wall that seems the right size. Ally had said each person gets one square foot. You can fit a lot in that space. I didn't know until this morning what I would paint. I go to the table and pick out the right paints. Black and brown, white, blue and silver.

An hour later I drop my brush into the can of water. It's the best thing I've ever done. And not an alien head to be found.

Stomach growling, I hurry down to the pavilion for

breakfast. David and Pete are at the end of the line and I hesitate. I've been avoiding them the past few days, still embarrassed about not having the first-aid kit, I guess. But I get in line behind them and watch David pile eggs on a plate for both of them.

"Jack!" Pete says, grabbing hold of my wrist. "Where've you been? Did you hear that storm last night? Daddy said thunder is the gods bowling! Can you believe that? Bowling!"

"It must have been some game!" I say, smiling at Pete. I force myself to raise my head to David.

"You doing okay?" David asks. "We heard about Silver having to go home."

I nod. "He hopes to be back before the eclipse."

We stand there awkwardly until a familiar voice says, "Can't an old lady get some eggs or are you young men going to take all of 'em?"

I turn to find Stella, in a green sweat suit and a straw hat with a purple sash. If I ever draw her, I'd like to draw her in this outfit.

"By all means," David says, waving her toward the buffet. "Ladies first."

We all have breakfast together, and I fill them in on Mr. Silver's project. They listen intently, David often interrupting me with scientific questions I don't know the answers to. Ryan's grandfather puts his hand gently on Stella's shoulder. "Might I join you?"

"Of course," she says, reddening slightly.

The old man carefully brings his legs over the side

of the bench and sits down next to her. "My grand-son is bringing me breakfast today," he says. "I'm a lucky guy."

This is the first time I've seen Stella act shy. I'm try-ing to decide if I should tease her or not, when Ryan heads over and puts down two trays.

"Hey, Jack," Ryan says. "Don't eat too much. We're going jogging in an hour. Don't want you throwing up on my watch."

"I won't," I promise, watching Stella daintily cut her pancakes. I've eaten with Stella before. She usu-ally eats like a truck driver. I wonder if Ryan is okay with his grandfather getting friendly with another woman, even though it was his grandmother who did the leaving. I wonder what happened to Stella's own husband. I wonder why I never asked.

An hour later I'm panting my way across the Moon Shadow. I usually avoid running or jogging whenever possible. It's not a pretty sight. The only time I've run without being totally self-conscious is that time I had to get the first-aid kit. Ryan isn't even breathless as he leads me past the RV park. I wave at Sam and Max, the little red-haired twins. Their mom had been desperate for someone to watch them a few days ago, and I was the first person she saw who didn't run away when she approached. All the twins wanted to do was use the sidewalk chalk to draw dinosaurs. It was actually a lot of fun. I might take up babysitting when I get home. If Mike would ever let me live it down. I notice the dinosaurs were washed away by the rain and they'd been replaced by a big yellow SpongeBob.

"I really think . . . I think . . . I'm gonna pass out," I tell Ryan in between gasps for breath.

"Nah, you'll be fine. Drink plenty of water when you get back."

But all I can do when I get back to my cabin is collapse on the bed. Whichever t-shirt guy had slept in it was thoughtful enough to make the bed. Not that it would have mattered to me. The next thing I know there's a knock on the door. I groggily open my eyes and look at my watch. Three o'clock! I slept for five hours!

I scramble off the bed and hurry to the door. I open it to find Ally standing there, looking all clean and refreshed. I wince as I realize what I must look like. I wish I'd taken a shower after the run. I hope I don't stink. She holds up a big white paper bag and says, "I've got sandwiches."

I rub my eyes. "Sorry?"

"For dinner tonight. I figured we'd go up early. We need to make sure we can find the right star as soon as it's out."

I slept right through lunch! It's not like me to miss a meal. Those sandwiches smell good. "Don't you have to give one of your talks tonight?"

She shakes her head. "My mom's going to do it. She

243

feels so guilty about making us move that right now I could probably ask for a pony and she'd give it to me."

"You want a pony?"

"No. But don't all girls want ponies?"

"I have no idea."

"See, that's my problem."

"What is?" I know I just woke up, but I'm having a hard time following her.

"Being a girl."

"You seem to be doing a good job as far as I can see."

She shakes her head again. "No. I don't think I am."

We each sit down on a bed.

"I'm going to ask Bree if she'll help me."

"I'm a little scared of her," I admit.

"Me too," Ally says, then laughs. "Maybe it's because she's so beautiful. Don't you think she's the most beautiful girl you've ever seen?"

I shake my head. "I've seen prettier."

"You have not."

"I have." It takes all my courage to look up.

"Oh," she says, and blushes furiously.

And then because I can't believe I said that, I blurt out something even more embarrassing. "When I was ten months old I was in a Pampers commercial for plus-sized diapers."

"You were?"

I nod, mortified, yet unable to stop talking. "It was SD1's fault. That's Step Dad Number One," I quickly explain. "I don't remember him at all. But he knew someone who was looking for babies of a certain size. There was me and twenty other fat babies crawling around a park — on the jungle gyms, the seesaws, the sandbox, the swings, all in our non-leaking, moved-with-our-bodies, plus-sized Pampers. That commercial aired for six years. If I manage to get into college, it will be paid for."

"Wow," she says. "So you're kind of famous."

"I could have done without wearing a diaper on national television."

Before Ally can say anything we hear, "Dude! What are you *talking* about?" I look up to see one of the t-shirt guys sauntering through the door. He flops down on the bed that Ally's sitting on. "Mind if I chill here for a little? Kinda got used to the place."

Ally stands up. She's still holding her bag of sandwiches. "I've got to go anyway. Two hundred more people are checking in today."

"Two *hundred*?"

She nods. "It's crazy. I mean it's great, but just insane."

"And there's room for everyone?"

She smiles. "We've been planning this a long time, remember?"

"Right."

"Three more days!" t-shirt guy says, punching the air with his fists. I should probably ask his name. I'm not sure if I should kick him for interrupting my time with Ally, or thank him for keeping me from telling any more embarrassing stories.

I walk her to the door and we agree to meet at the shed at seven. She must have seen me eyeing the bag because she holds it out and says, "Would you like your sandwich now, by any chance?"

"Sure," I say as nonchalantly as possible. "Might as well save you the trouble of bringing it up later."

She opens the bag and pulls out a sandwich wrapped in tin foil. "I appreciate that. The bag was getting heavy."

"No problem." The sandwich is still warm. I wonder what it is.

"It's meatloaf," she says. "Left over from lunch."

I've got the sandwich open and am on my third bite before she walks down the last step.

"Dude," t-shirt guy says as I chew. "You gonna share that or what?"

I shake my head.

"Fine." He pulls a pixie-stick out of his pocket, rips the end open with his teeth, and pours it down his throat in one swig.

I leave him chanting "Three more days!" and go sit on the porch step. The campground is really hopping. People dragging suitcases, kids jumping and playing, couples holding hands. Last night's rain has made the ground pretty muddy, but I can tell it's already starting to dry up from the hot sun.

When I'm done with my sandwich I go back in, grab my towel, and head to the showers. And if I spend a little more time patting down my hair afterward than usual, I wouldn't admit it.

When I get to our site the first person I see is Ally. She's standing at the scope talking to Kenny and Melanie. Bree's in the doorway of the shed drinking a bottle of water. I quickly look the other way before Ally sees me because I'm suddenly mortified that I told her about the diaper commercial. What was I thinking? I'll have to remember not to carry on a conversation when I'm still half asleep. I'm putting so much effort into not looking at Ally, that I'm not looking where I'm walking. The next thing I know, I've tripped over something and am sprawled on the ground.

I hear a groan next to me and turn my head. "Ryan? Why are you on the ground?"

"Ungh," he moans. "Raw eggs. Trying to make protein shake. Barfed, like, ten times."

I get to my feet and brush myself off. "That's rough. Anything I can do?"

He shakes his head and grabs his stomach. "Go on," he says in a hoarse whisper. "Just leave me to die. If you find the planet, promise me you'll name it after me."

"You know I can't do that."

"Fine." He turns his head away from me. "Some

247

thanks I get for all I've done for you. When you start school next year twenty pounds lighter and fifty percent cooler, you'll remember you dissed me."

"I'll send you a thank-you note."

Bree heads over and kneels down next to Ryan.

"How's the patient?"

He groans in response.

"He's all yours," I tell her. It's time to face Ally.

I walk up to the scope as Kenny is explaining how to use the computer that he's re-attached to the scope. Ally smiles at me and I feel my cheeks get hot, but I manage to smile back.

"The first thing we have to do is synch up the telescope to our exact location," Kenny says. "I have to plug in the longitude and latitude of the nearest city, which we've already figured out. Then we'll need two bright stars to focus on. The GPS built into the computer will find those stars and then once it has those three points, it can find anything else we ask it to."

"It can go right to any star?" Ally asks. "Or planet?"

Kenny nods. "Or galaxy, or nebula, or even the International Space Station."

"So it can do the Messier objects?"

He nods. "If they're over the horizon at the time."

Her face falls and then she sighs. "It's all changing. What's the point of holding the Messier Marathon if you can just use a computer to find them?"

"Isn't the point to see them, not find them?" Melanie

asks. "It doesn't really matter how you get there, does it?"

"I guess you're right," she says. "It's just like those comet-hunting machines Ryan's grandfather told me about. I feel like I'm being left behind."

"They'll need someone to run the machines, right?" Melanie asks. "You could learn how to do that."

"You think so?"

Melanie nods. "Why not?"

I wish there was something I could add to make Ally feel better, but what little I know about astronomy I learned from her.

"Since we're just waiting around," Bree says, leaving Ryan twisting dramatically on the ground, "I thought of some more tips for Kenny and Ally. You know, on how to survive in civilization."

"Oh, great," Ally says, clearly suspicious.

Bree smiles and pats her on the arm. "Now these might seem really basic to your average four-year-old, but living out here you might have forgotten them."

"Should I take notes?" Kenny asks, poised to reach into his backpack.

I'm not sure, but I think he might be serious.

Bree rolls her eyes and Kenny pulls back his hand. "First, look both ways before you cross the street. You're not used to streets with lots of fast-moving cars and trucks and motorcycles. And most accidents happen within a block of the home."

"She's right," Kenny says when Ally groans.

"Second, always make sure your sneakers are tied so you don't trip in the hall and drop all your books. Nothing makes you look like a bigger dork than dropping your books."

Kenny looks down at his sneakers. "Mine are Velcro."

"Good move," Bree says, nodding approvingly. "Third. Wash your hands before you eat. Strange kids, strange school, strange germs. You aren't immune to the same things that most kids are. In fact," she backs up a few feet, "maybe we shouldn't get too close to you guys."

Ally narrows her eyes and then runs toward Bree with her arm outstretched. Bree screams playfully as Ally chases her across the hilltop, around the shed, past the scope, and over Ryan's moaning form. Even though it's rapidly getting darker, Bree's startling blue eyes are brighter than I've seen them. I finally glimpse what Ryan saw that first day. When she's happy, Bree's really pretty. But Ally's pretty all of the time.

"What's the last rule?" Kenny calls out when Bree's path brings her close by.

"Chew before you swallow," she yells.

"We do eat food out here in the boonies, you know!" Ally calls after her. "I'm pretty sure we know how to do it without choking."

Once they've exhausted themselves, we pass the time by pointing the telescope down at the camp. It's too powerful to focus in on such relatively nearby objects, but we can see people everywhere, in the Star and Sun Gardens, in the Labyrinth, finishing dinner in the pavilion. It's amazing how quickly these places have started to feel familiar. And in only four more days, it will all be over. I shake my head to rid myself of those kinds of thoughts. *Focus on the moment,* I tell myself. *It's all you have.*

Ally's walkie-talkie beeps and she pulls it off her belt loop. She presses the button in response and then holds it up to her ear. "It's my dad," she announces a few seconds later. "We got an e-mail from one of Mr. Silver's team members. From Scotland!"

I can hear noises coming through the walkie-talkie but not the words. Ally holds it up to her ear again and cups her other hand over it to hear better. Then she says, "over and out," and clips it back to her waist. By this point we're all gathered around her, closing in like a pack of hungry wolves.

Eyes gleaming, she says, "The guy in Scotland was able to rule out part of the transit window for sure! The other guy in Florida eliminated part of it, too. So tonight it comes down to us and a lady in Italy!"

This stuff is actually starting to make sense to me. Maybe I'm not as bad at science as I thought. "Mr. Silver said that if we catch a transit, then others will start tracking it to see how long the orbit is. And then a huge telescope somewhere will be able to tell if it's a real planet crossing in front of the star, or something else, like a smaller star."

"Not too much pressure," Kenny says. "But that's okay! We thrive on pressure, right, Team Exo?"

"Right!" we all yell. But one by one, we pick up the pages that Kenny typed out for each of us to make sure we know what we're supposed to do. No one wants to be the person who messes everything up. Least of all me.

And then it's all happening. The first stars come out, and Kenny immediately turns to the computer to align the "go-to" feature. He turns the scope to point at one star, waits to hear a dinging sound, then points it at another. "Coordinates found!" he calls out. Melanie records them, chewing so hard on her pen that I fear it's going to burst in her mouth. Then he asks Ally for the coordinates of the star we're assigned to monitor. She reads it from the logbook and he types it in.

"Right ascension of twenty hours. Declination of forty degrees, eighteen minutes, twenty-three seconds." She may as well have been speaking Klingon.

At first nothing happens and my heart sinks.

"Read me those again, Ally?" Kenny asks, his voice a little shaky. Ally rereads them, and Kenny retypes. He hits a few extra buttons, then steps back and crosses his fingers on both hands.

This time the telescope starts moving on its own with a low whirring sound. We all jump out of the way. When it stops, Kenny steps forward and checks the message on the monitor. "Object found!"

We all cheer, even though Mr. Silver warned me that that was going to be the easy part. "Okay, guys," I say, checking that the camera is ready. I glance at my watch. "Now we wait."

We take turns looking into the viewfinder at the star. It looks like any other star, twinkling and really far away. The gears in the telescope are humming faintly. It's starting to move again.

"Is it broken?" I ask, worried.

Kenny shakes his head. He's read the manual cover to cover, so he should know. "It has to keep the star in the frame. The Earth is spinning so it has to keep compensating."

"Oh." Just one more part of this whole thing that I don't really understand.

Ally points to the sky and says, "You know that Summer Triangle I showed everyone the other night?"

We all look up, and I'm shocked to discover that I can find it by looking for a triangle of three bright stars.

"Well," she says, "not to get too technical, but Earth, which is rotating on its axis at a thousand miles per hour, goes around the sun at 66,000 miles per hour. And then our entire solar system is hurtling toward the Summer Triangle at 45,000 miles per hour."

I turn away from the stars to stare at her. "How is that possible? How can we not feel like we're moving? How come we don't get left behind?"

Bree responds. "Ever hear of gravity?"

I turn to her. "Why don't you explain it, then."

Bree flips her hair at me and says nothing.

Melanie says, "I hate to interrupt this episode of *Who Knows Less About Science,* but it's almost time!"

We quickly assume our positions. I take a deep breath. *Here goes nothing.* Following Kenny and Melanie's careful instructions, I turn on the camera and pray it does what it's supposed to do. Every few seconds I call out the temperature readings and Melanie, sitting cross-legged on the grass, types them into Mr. Silver's computer. A cable from the camera to the computer sends more data at the same time. I keep calling out readings until my throat gets dry.

Bree is manning the viewfinder. I ask her if anything looks different. She says, "Nope."

"Nothing's supposed to look different," Ally calls to me.

"You mean we won't actually be able to see it?"

She shakes her head. "We can't see it because the planet is too small and the star too bright. But once the images are processed by the computer, we'll be able to see the light curve."

Melanie holds up the laptop, which shows a graph of the light curve. "Check this out! It looks like the star's getting fainter!"

We all crowd over her shoulder, even Ryan, who has finally gotten himself to a standing position. She points to a spot on the graph where a bunch of dots form a fairly straight line. Then she shows us how they're starting to go down, at a sloping angle. "Keep reading off the temperatures, Jack!" she says. "Let's see what happens to the pattern."

I return to my post. After another half hour of reading the numbers off the tiny screen, I'm getting delirious. I turn the position over to Ally, who later drags Bree up there to take her place. After more than two hours since we started, Melanie finally says, "Okay, you can stop." She jumps to her feet and turns the screen toward us. Then she clutches it to her chest and says, "Do you realize that what we just witnessed actually happened back when Napoleon was ruling France?"

We all stare at her. My brain is too stuffed right now to compute the whole thing about time and how long it takes light to travel. I'd find it interesting if there wasn't so much at stake here.

"Melanie," Bree warns. Melanie quickly turns the glowing screen around and holds it up triumphantly. The dots form a clear upside-down bell shape and then start to go across in that same straight line as before.

"That's amazing!" Kenny shouts. "We did it! We really found a planet!"

We jump up and down and high-five each other until Ryan says, "We found *something*. We won't know if it's a planet for sure until the data is verified."

This quiets us all for a minute. Then we start screaming again. Ally suggests we celebrate our success
Moon Shadow style. This turns out to be eating
s'mores in the hot spring behind her house.

An hour later, once we've moved all the equipment
safely into the shed and e-mailed the data to the ad-
dresses Mr. Silver left us, I find myself sitting with
five other kids, none of whom I knew ten days ago, in
what amounts to a really hot outdoor bathtub. This is
the first time I've seen Ally without the pouch around
her neck. It's such a part of her that it feels weird seeing her without it. Even though my clothes are getting looser these days, I'm still wearing my t-shirt
while everyone else is in their bathing suits.

I wipe off the thin line of chocolate dripping down
my chin and lean back. A zillion stars shine overhead.
They no longer feel threatening. I silently pick out the
Big Dipper, and then Polaris.

"Sometimes you can see the Space Station," Ally
says dreamily, "but it would have passed by here already. It looks like a shooting star but it moves a lot
slower."

"I don't think I've ever seen a shooting star," I admit. "I didn't even know a star could move."

She points east. "Wait." In less than a minute, we
collectively yell, "There's one!" Ally explains that a
shooting star isn't a star at all. It's a meteor, a speck
of dust from a comet or asteroid lighting up as it

hits our atmosphere. I see another before she's done talking.

I listen lazily as she tells Bree and Melanie that if they sit in the hot springs in the winter they can watch the colors of the Northern Lights flow like a river in the sky while the drops of water turn their hair into tiny icicles.

Bree frowns. Melanie says, "Cool!" Ally wipes a tear from her eye.

"Will we see it tonight?" I ask. "The Northern Lights?"

"Probably not. The summer's not a great time to look for them."

The conversation turns to the eclipse and I tune it out. The sooner the eclipse comes, the sooner I have to go back home. And when I go back home, I'll lose this feeling of belonging to something. Kenny says it's crazy how a single cloud can ruin an entire eclipse if it's right in front of the sun. I think about that for a minute, about how all these people came from all over the world to see it, and they might miss it through no fault of their own. A crazy thought flits across my mind. If I miss it, then it will be like it didn't happen, like this whole experience doesn't have an endpoint.

I tune back in to hear Melanie talking about a report she did in school about a Native American dance that you're supposed to do to guarantee clear skies. It's like the opposite of a rain dance. She says you have to do it every morning up till the day you need it to be sunny. She stands upright in the water and does a sort of whooping, bending, twisting dance. Everyone promises to do it first thing when they wake up.

No one notices that I haven't agreed.

ALLY

7

My bedroom is full of empty boxes and I am doing my best to ignore them. It's actually been pretty easy to do that since the last two days have been the busiest of my entire life. The Moon Shadow now has over a thousand guests. It is totally unreal. I've heard people are camping out on the main road, extending all the forty miles into town. Anyone that far away will only see a partial eclipse though. That's how narrow the path is. People camping on the other side of the lake will still see a total, but it will be much shorter. That's why our spot is so ideal. We're right in the centerline. My parents didn't want to turn anyone away, but we're already overbooked. People are crowded eight to a cabin. The RV park is full to capacity. Tents have popped up on nearly every plot of dry land. My parents' strictest rule is that the roads and paths are kept clear, and if anyone is seen throwing trash on the ground, they get one warning before they are kicked out. The pavilion has run out of food twice, and my dad had to call in a favor from a guy who works at a food distribution plant a few hours away. There is no hot water anymore, but so far we haven't had too many complaints. Eclipse chasers are used to being in remote locations.

I haven't seen much of the other Team Exo members after our middle-of-the-night dip in the hot springs. Kenny and I have been so busy running around the campground putting out fires (twice in the literal sense!) that I haven't had time to do anything even remotely social. I haven't been able to get near any of the telescopes in the Star Garden except to show the guests how to use them. I've had to say good night to Eta, Glenn, and Peggy with my binoculars, which isn't really the same thing.

Now, in five hours, barring the end of the world, the moon will obliterate the sun. On one hand I am so excited I can barely think straight. On the other, the eclipse means that everything will start happening really quickly. The guests will leave, including Jack and Ryan. Bree's family will move into our house. I can't see past that point. I read in a book once that if you can't picture something happening, that means it won't happen. But no matter what, the eclipse will be happening. Even if Alpha Girl had the power of X-ray vision, of flight, of turning lead into gold, the eclipse would still happen. I've done the clear-skies dance each morning, and that's all I can do.

Right now the clouds are of the fluffy white variety. But if they darken and get lower, it won't matter much if the eclipse happens or not, because we won't be able to see it. The sky will darken and it will get colder, but other than that, nothing. Good thing my parents have a no-money-back policy!

I hurry along the path, mentally wishing the clouds away and trying not to crash into anyone. It's so weird sharing the campground with all these strangers. And they're all so happy and excited. Sure, that's easy when they're not the ones whose lives will be turned upside down and inside out afterward. Kenny breaks through the crowd on the path and grabs onto my sleeve.

"C'mere, Ally! You've got to see this! Someone built a shrine in the field!"

I let him pull me over to the clearing behind the pavilion. This is where most people will view the eclipse. The huge projection screens are already set up and a crew is testing the sound system. This is what it must feel like before a concert.

"Look!" Kenny says, pointing to a crowd at the far side of the clearing. When we get closer, I see they are standing around a large cardboard box with a thin red blanket laid across it. On the top is a small oil painting resting against a wooden easel. I step closer. The painting shows two Asian men, in togas, standing next to an old-fashioned telescope. In front of the painting is a little printed sign that reads HO AND HSI, ROYAL CHINESE

☽

ASTRONOMERS, CIRCA 2000 B.C. IF ONLY YOU HAD WARNED THE KING ABOUT THE ECLIPSE. REST IN PEACE. All over the makeshift shrine people have left small gifts. A melting Twinkie still in the wrapper. A stick of Juicy Fruit gum. Two marbles. A yellow pencil. A book predicting eclipses for the next century. A green stuffed dragon.

I turn to Kenny. "Let me guess. The dragon was your contribution?"

"Yup! You know, 'cause the ancient Chinese thought an eclipse was a dragon eating the sun."

"And do you really think they ate Twinkies four thousand years ago?"

"If they were lucky," Kenny says, grinning.

I take a last glance at the painting. "Doesn't seem like luck was on their side."

"True. Can you imagine what it would have been like to live back then?"

I step away from the crowd and Kenny follows. We head toward my original destination, the labyrinth. "Well, even if they couldn't predict an eclipse accurately, they could see so much farther than we can now, even out here. Every night they would see the Milky Way streaming across the sky. Not blotted out like now. That I would have liked to see."

"Yeah," Kenny says. "But they didn't have indoor plumbing. I don't know if I'd trade that for being able to see the edge of the galaxy."

☽

I shrug. "I would. I prefer the hot springs to a shower any day."

"Hate to say it, but you're gonna have to get used to the shower."

He's right of course, but I hadn't thought of it before this minute. Wherever we wind up, one thing there won't be is a hot spring in the backyard. Yet another item to add to the endless list of things I'll be giving up.

Kenny goes off to finish photocopying the eclipse schedule brochures, a job that he actually volunteered for. He says he likes the sound the copy machine makes. I keep going till I reach the labyrinth. As I should have expected, I'm not the only visitor. In fact, there are at least ten people inside it and many more waiting their turn. I do a quick scan of the ground to make sure it's still smooth from last night. I've always thought of the labyrinth as a solitary thing. I can't imagine walking it with other people. You'd always be worrying about going too fast and bumping into the person in front of you, or going too slow and holding up the people behind you.

I should have come down at dawn, like I meant to. Maybe this is the Moon Shadow's way of telling me it doesn't belong to me anymore. My heart sinks, but rises a bit when I see Bree sitting a few feet away, on the slope that leads up to the Star Garden. As usual she's wearing her iPod. I don't think I've seen her without it for the past two days. She's watching the men lift the telescopes onto carts. They'll be set up in various places in the field, each one fitted with a special solar filter. The guests will be able to take turns looking at the eclipse through them. Dad put my favorite one aside for the family. I have specially fitted binoculars too.

I call Bree's name, but she doesn't hear me. Ever since the other night when she looked through Mr. Silver's scope at the moon, she's been stranger than usual. Not as angry as she used to be, but sort of in her own world. Jack's been a little strange too, but only about the eclipse. Every time I go to take care of one of the Unusuals, he's there. Or he's row-boating with that little boy Pete's family. Or he's babysitting the twins. But whenever I try to talk to him about the eclipse, he gets all weird and changes the subject. Maybe he's just anxious that Mr. Silver isn't back yet. He hasn't mentioned the whole "me being really pretty" thing again, and I'm beginning to think I heard him wrong. After all, who could possibly think I'm prettier than Bree? I've been paying more attention to my appearance though, or at least trying to make sure my clothes aren't covered in stains.

Static bursts through my walkie-talkie, and I grab it from my waist. Bree doesn't even look up, so I turn back onto the road and press the talk button. "Hey, Dad, what's up?"

It's not Dad though, it's Mom. "Come back to the

house, Ally," her voice cackles through the air. "I've got special news for you." There's so much interference from all the other walkie-talkies people brought with them that I have to ask her to repeat herself three times. When I finally understand her, my heart leaps! My fingers stumble over the right button to press. "We're not moving?" I ask, holding my breath.

"Of course we're moving! Just come —" She says more, but I turn it off and stick it back on my shorts.

When I get back to the house the first thing I see is Melanie doing cartwheels across the lawn. She runs up when she sees me. "Did you hear? Did you hear?"

"Hear what?"

Kenny comes running down the stairs to meet us, with Ryan a few steps behind. "What's going on?" I ask.

"Mr. Silver called!" Kenny says, shifting from one foot to the other like he can barely contain himself.

"He's still not here?" I ask, thinking of Jack.

Kenny shakes his head. "He's on the road, but it's pretty crowded. He might not make it in time. But listen —"

"We actually did it!" Ryan breaks in, laughing. "The huge telescope in Hawaii used our data and confirmed the planet!"

I gasp. "Seriously?" I had been convinced since we didn't hear anything right away that we had messed up somehow. And after getting my hopes up with the SETI project, I hadn't allowed myself to get too excited. But this is amazing!

"Not only that," Kenny says. "But we're famous! Mr. Silver said we're the youngest people ever to have found an exoplanet!"

"We didn't really *find* it, exactly," Ryan corrects. "We just monitored it. But he said this proves amateur astronomers can play a really important role in confirming exoplanets." His enthusiasm dampens a little. "At least for now. Until those planet-finding telescopes are launched into space in a few years."

"Let's not think about them," Melanie says. She looks so happy, with her cheeks so bright that it's impossible not to catch her enthusiasm.

"That's right!" I say. "And no matter how many planets they find, they didn't find this one!"

"We gotta tell Jack and Bree," Kenny says. "Does anyone know where they are?"

Still feeling like I could float a foot off the ground, I tell him I just saw Bree a few minutes ago by the Star Garden.

"I'll go find her," Melanie says. "I have to give her something anyway." She takes off running, does two cartwheels, and continues.

I ask Ryan if he's seen Jack.

He shakes his head. "Not since last night. I just went by his cabin but he wasn't there."

Kenny says, "He came by this morning to pick up the eclipse glasses for his group. I haven't seen him since though."

We all promise to keep an eye out for him. Ryan goes

off to find his grandfather while Kenny and I head in-side. I give the sky one last glance. Still a few too many clouds for my liking, but clouds move fast, and there's no way of telling what will happen this afternoon. I notice Kenny eyeing them nervously too, but he shakes it off as well and gives me a huge grin.

Mom and Dad each give us a big hug as we walk into the kitchen. "There they are," Dad says, beaming proudly. "The groundbreaking planet-finding astron-omers!"

"Isn't it amazing?" Kenny says, bouncing around the kitchen. "We're famous!"

"And you're finally talking to us again!" Mom says, clapping her hands.

"Oops!" Kenny throws his hand over his mouth, then brings it down in defeat. "Oh, all right! I give up."

"That's good," Dad says, turning to the huge dry-erase board they've set up on the table. "Because we have a lot to go over and the seconds are tick-ing away."

According to the board, Kenny's job is to finish printing the flyers and then to hand them out as peo-ple arrive at the site. He's also in charge of making sure no one is disturbing the peace or littering. For a ten-year-old with a sunny disposition, he can be very persuasive. People listen to him.

Dad's job is to oversee the technical aspects. Making sure the video cameras and projection screens are working, that the P.A. system is loud enough, that sort of thing, so that everyone can hear when it's safe to look at the sun without protection. Mom is on crisis duty — if anyone gets stung by a bee or faints, or if a kid gets lost, she's the one to take care of it. And my job is to go through the group and make sure everyone's eyes and equipment are properly protected during the partial phases. Besides listing the stages of the eclipse and telling the guests what to watch for at each stage, Kenny's flyers have a warning in big letters about not looking directly at the sun.

The security crew Dad hired will also be overseeing all these things, and even though every guest who registered signed something agreeing to take precautions, we want to make sure everyone has a positive experience. Dad tells us to meet in the roped-off area he reserved for us before totality hits. Otherwise it will be too dark to find each other. Ryan, his grandfather, and Bree's family are meeting us there too. I invited Jack, but he said he might have to be with his group. Then he changed the subject, as usual.

"This is it," Dad says, actually getting a little teary-eyed. "What we've been waiting for — planning for — all these years."

A lump forms in my throat. Kenny stops bouncing. We can hear shouts of excitement and anticipation drift in through the open windows as two different groups of campers run by.

"We should all be really proud of ourselves," Mom

says. "We're making a lot of people very happy. We're giving them a memory they'll never forget."

"That none of us will ever forget," Dad says firmly. He glances out the window. "No matter what happens."

"No matter what happens," we all repeat, placing our hands on top of each other's like a team before a game. Then we gobble down an early lunch and go our separate ways. I run up to my room to get my supplies, stepping over the empty boxes like they're bumps in the rug and nothing more. My backpack has been ready for days. Binoculars, logbook, red flashlight, camera, solar glasses, and a screen made of welder's glass. I've also packed many extra sheets of the solar filters in case people don't have them. I'm already wearing the t-shirt Mom had printed for us. It's bright yellow and has a picture of the sun during totality. On the front and back it says, in glow-in-the-dark lettering, MOON SHADOW STAFF. ASK US ANYTHING.

As I turn to run back out I take one last look at my room. The next time I'll see it, I'll have witnessed a total solar eclipse. How crazy is that?

By the time I get up to the field, it's half full. First contact isn't for another two hours, but clearly people want to stake out their claim to a prime spot. Not that any one spot is really different from another. The eclipse begins at 3:09 (and 42 seconds), when the sun will be high enough in the sky that none of the trees

☽

will block it. I drop off my backpack in the roped-off area that my parents set up for us. I watch one couple set up a huge pair of binoculars on a tripod, a telescope, and a video camera. They also have a collection of eclipse glasses, handheld screens, digital and regular cameras. If everyone has this much stuff, there will be no room left for the actual people. I do a quick survey to make sure they have the right lenses on the binoculars and the scope. They do.

But the next two families have forgotten to cover their viewfinders. You don't need the viewfinders to observe the eclipse, but someone could look through them by mistake. I give them a sheet of the specially-coated Mylar and watch to make sure they stick it on correctly. One of the families has a daughter who looks around eight years old and clearly doesn't want to be here. I can tell because when Kenny comes by and hands them a flyer, she makes a big show of spitting her gum into it. He hands her father another one without missing a beat.

Some people have gotten really creative. Instead of worrying about protecting their eyes, they've built these contraptions out of cardboard boxes that project an image of the sun inside of them. Some are six feet long! I see a lot of people with two pieces of cardboard, one brown, one white, with a pinhole through the brown one. I watch one kid as he holds them about a foot apart, with the pinhole facing the sun. A small yellow glow appears on the white one.

Along the west side of the field some enterprising eclipse chasers have set up booths selling solar glasses, bottles of water, disposable cameras, and other eclipse-related merchandise. All the venders had to get their wares pre-approved by Mom though. My parents decided a long time ago the only thing they would sell themselves are commemorative mugs and two t-shirts. One says I SAW THE MOON'S SHADOW AT THE MOON SHADOW. The other says I SAW THE MOON COVER THE SUN AND ALL I GOT WAS THIS LOUSY T-SHIRT.

Every few yards I see a familiar face. Most of the guests who have come to the campground over the years have returned for this event. I get a lot of comments like, "Oh, you're all grown up!" and "Wow, the place looks great!" It makes me feel good, and proud of what we've achieved, like Mom said.

The time passes in a blur of activity and noise and careful concentration on the faces of those setting up their equipment. Totality will only last for a little over three minutes, and while that's a pretty solid duration for an eclipse, it's not a lot of time in the grand scheme of things. One eclipse chaser wearing a t-shirt of all the eclipses he's been to is timing himself with a stopwatch. He shifts from checking his scope to his binoculars to his cameras and back again. It looks like a frantic little dance.

With half an hour to go before first contact, there is barely enough room to walk. I'm not the only one keeping an eye on the clouds. A light breeze keeps them wafting by. I wonder if it's too late for another anti-rain dance. I start to head back to my family's area when a tug on my shirt stops me. It's Bree. For once she doesn't have her earphones on. "What's that noise?" she asks, pointing to one of the big speakers. "Is it supposed to be music?"

I laugh. "It's a type of music, but not the kind you can dance to. It's the sound of the sun."

She squints. "Huh?"

"Astronomers can record the vibrations and echoes of all the activity inside the sun. The sun is like a huge musical instrument. My dad's playing a recording of it."

Bree covers her ears. "It just sounds like static to me."

"Don't worry, he's going to take it off soon. It's almost first contact."

She reaches into her shorts pocket where I see her earphones dangling. But she thinks better of it and follows me back through the crowd to our families. We get there to find Ryan, Melanie, and Kenny doing the anti-rain dance. Ryan's grandfather and Bree's parents are trying to follow along. I recognize the old woman with Ryan's grandfather as being on Jack's tour. "Have you seen Jack?" I shout over the increasing noise.

She shakes her head and holds up her glasses. "He handed these out about two hours ago. I haven't seen him since." She notices Bree and says, "Hello, future cover girl. Walked the labyrinth lately?"

Bree shakes her head. I look from one to the other, wondering how they know each other. For some reason I can't picture Bree walking the labyrinth. It hits me that once we're gone, it's going to be up to Bree's family to keep the Unusuals up and running. But will they? Bree's parents seem really nice and responsible, but still, they could get caught up in their own work and let things slide. Right now though, they're putting their all into the dance, arms and legs flying. It's pretty funny.

There's only one cloud now that can do any harm if it passes right over the sun.

Soon the solar music turns off and Dad's voice booms across the field. "Everybody ready?"

The crowd whoops and hollers. Kenny and I look at each other and giggle. It's weird hearing Dad's voice coming out of nowhere and filling the air.

"Glasses on!" he commands. In unison, a thousand people put on their glasses or goggles or hold up their solar screens. "Ten seconds to first contact!"

I look around for Jack, but still don't see him. I don't see Mr. Silver either.

Everyone starts counting down along with Dad. "Nine . . . eight . . . seven . . . six . . ."

My heart is pounding so fast I bet everyone can hear it, even over the din of voices. There's no sign of the approaching moon in the bright sky. An eclipse can only happen when the moon is in the new moon phase, when we can't see the sun reflecting off of it. So it's like looking for something invisible.

"Three . . . two . . . one!" everyone shouts, then collectively we hold our breath. All I hear is the loud chirping of the birds. Nothing happens for an endless second. My mind races. Were the astronomers mistaken? Is this the wrong day? What's going on?

And then I see it. A tiny nick out of the right side of the sun, like someone nibbled on it to see how it would taste.

"There it is!" people yell from all over the campground. The whoops and hollers start up again, but quiet down as everyone watches the tiny nick gradually increase into a thin crescent. It's going soooo slowly. Kenny's eye is pressed up to the telescope, so I peer through the binoculars. I can see tiny dark sunspots on the face of the sun. Through the welder's glass I had attached to the binoculars, the sun looks green. I put on the solar filtered sunglasses, and it's orange instead. I check my watch. There's still over an hour until totality, and I need to do a quick run through the crowd.

"Do you want to come check people's eyes with me?" I ask Bree, who is standing very still. "We'll be back in time."

She shakes her head, not tearing herself away from the sun.

"Okay. Be sure to give your eyes a rest though. The sun's still very bright."

She nods, half listening. Melanie and Kenny are excitedly going over the flyer and Bree's parents are holding hands and giggling like teenagers. I snake my way through the crowd, careful not to bump into anyone's scope. Under their glasses, one eclipse-chasing group is all wearing eye-patches over one eye. They look like a bunch of pirates! I've heard of people doing that, but didn't expect to see it. It's supposed to help your eyes adjust to the dark better when you take it off. "Ahoy, matey," one of them says as I pass.

"Ahoy!" I reply.

I pass by the girl who had spit her gum into Kenny's flyer in time to hear her say, "I don't get it. What's the big deal?"

It's true that besides the fact that the sun is slowly being eaten away, nothing looks any different on the ground. The light is just as bright. I'm forced to chastise two people shielding their eyes with their hands, but other than that everyone is being really safe. I pass the mother of the red-haired twins trying to calm down one of them, who is insisting that his brother is somehow responsible for what's happening above. I can't imagine living in a time before eclipses were predicted and suddenly the sun disappeared. How terrifying!

About half of the moon is covering the sun now, and the shadows of the people around me are starting to

☽

get shorter and sharper. The light still seems as bright, but the birds must sense something's going on. Their usual gentle tweeting and chirping is becoming more erratic, almost pleading.

I pass by the shrine to Ho and Hsi. It is now covered with little tokens, including a green Matchbox car, and about twenty of Kenny's flyers.

I climb up onto a bench near the side of the field and scan for Jack. My heart gives a leap when I see Mr. Silver racing across the field. A shout goes up from his tour group when they catch sight of him. Jack's not with the group though, nor with Mr. Silver. Where IS he? He must have found someplace else to view the eclipse.

I make my way back to my family. Mom is there now, looking in the scope. Bree is still standing where I left her. The sky is turning a darker, almost navy blue now, a color I've never seen before. I feel a slight chill in the air and shiver. It's definitely at least ten degrees cooler. The sun is about eighty percent covered and it's noticeably darker now. My heart starts pounding hard again, as Dad gets back on the loud-speaker.

"Ten more minutes till second contact," he announces. "And what does that mean?"

"Totality!" the crowd yells.

"Right! And when that happens, you can take off your glasses. You won't hear from me again until it's time to put them back on."

He steps off the podium and hurries over to us. A bundle of energy, he squeezes my shoulder before joining Mom at the scope. It's getting darker now by the second. The sun is slipping farther behind the moon. The clouds are still fluffy, which means they won't block our view. Our dances must have worked!

Kenny and Melanie are scrambling to check things off their list. The air is dark like dusk, but it has a greenish-yellowish cast that is totally unfamiliar. I know I'm supposed to be following Kenny's checklist, watching for changes all around me and scanning the sky for stars. But it's like I'm in a dream or something, and I can't think straight. I've imagined this moment my entire life, and now it doesn't seem real.

Suddenly it's dead quiet. The birds have completely stopped chirping. Tiny balls form a glowing circle around the black sun like a necklace of pearls.

"Baily's Beads!" people around us exclaim.

And as I watch, breathless, the beads fade into one thin circle of light. Gasps go up from around the field, and I hear people shouting about the moon's shadow passing over us, but I don't see it. I'm too busy watching the last bit of sunlight shine like a beacon through the deepest valley of the moon. It looks like a huge diamond engagement ring hanging in the sky where the sun used to be.

And then that last bit of light winks out. Totality! Everyone whips off their glasses. A flash of vivid red swirls around the outline of the moon, glorious in its contrast with the dark sky around it. This is the only time I'll ever see the sun's chromosphere, the thin atmosphere normally hidden to us. A second later it is fully engulfed by the moon. And then the main attraction arrives. The pearly white corona suddenly streams out from behind the dark moon in all directions, pulsing, looping, swirling, glowing, a halo of unearthly light. I feel like I could die from the beauty of it.

"Great Galileo's Ghost!" Kenny yells.

Then two things happen at once. The sounds of screaming and clapping and crying fill the air.

And someone slips their hand into mine.

BREE

7

The only other time in my life I've gotten up this early was the day the new shoe store opened in town and the first twenty people in line got a free pair of sandals. I had expected there to be roosters crowing at the crack of dawn, but apparently that's only on farms. I hurry to dress, grabbing whatever's nearby. I run my brush through my hair and then tie it back in a ribbon. Slipping on my sneakers I notice they're almost as dirty as the ones Ally loaned me when I first arrived. I bet Claire wouldn't even recognize me. I barely recognize myself. Melanie is just starting to stir as I slip out the door of the cabin. The eclipse is this afternoon, and I have a lot to do before then.

First stop — the labyrinth. I've tried every day since the day I met that old woman, Stella, but I haven't been able to step inside. Today I'm determined to change that. With the huge crowds of people here now, I figure this might be the only time I'd be alone.

But when I arrive, I see a woman in the center of the labyrinth, her head bowed. She's wearing a long black robe and a black shawl that even goes over her head. Doesn't she know white is the new black? She's saying something, but I can't hear. I move a little closer. It almost sounds like she's chanting, or praying. I turn to go because she's freaking me out a little, but manage to step on a twig. It cracks loudly under my foot. She lifts her head but doesn't stop chanting. I debate running off but force myself to sit on the bench and wait for her to finish. I might not get another chance for a while.

A few minutes later the woman threads her way back out of the labyrinth and heads toward me. I have no idea what I should say to her, so I just say an awkward "Hello."

"Are you here for the eclipse?" she asks with an accent that I don't recognize. She lowers the shawl from her head and drapes it around her shoulders. She's younger than I had suspected, not older than twenty-five or so. It's hard to tell under all those clothes. She must be hot, too.

"Yes." And then since she's still standing there, I add, "My family is actually moving here. We're going to be taking over the campground once the eclipse is over." This is the first time I've been able to say those words without feeling like throwing up.

"You are a lucky girl," she says. "This is a very beautiful place."

☆

Rather than commenting on my luck or lack of it, I ask her where she's from.

. "Egypt," she replies. "My family sent me here. My brother went to the last eclipse, and my sister will go to the next."

I blink. "You came all the way here from Egypt? Your family must really love eclipses."

She smiles. "We have never seen one."

"But I thought you said —"

"We come to pray during the eclipse. We pray for the sun's return."

"But you don't see it at all?"

She shakes her head. "I will keep my eyes to the ground."

Ally will NOT believe this. In defense of the eclipse I say, "But it's supposed to be really cool."

She laughs. "Yes, I have heard that. But this tradition goes back to the Prophet Muhammad. If he can miss it, I can miss it. It is for the greater good."

"Well," I tell her, "I'll tell you what it was like after, if that's okay."

"I would like that," she says. "Now I will leave you to your own task."

"I'm Bree, by the way," I call after her.

"Bellana," she says.

I watch her head back down the path and wonder what "my task" is supposed to be. Maybe the labyrinth will tell me. I step up to the opening and take a deep breath. This time my feet actually obey me and I

☆

take a few steps inside. But then they stop again. This is really starting to bug me. Why can't I walk the darn labyrinth? What am I afraid of?

I turn around and walk back out, staring at the circle of rocks before me. Ever since I saw the moon through that huge telescope, things have been so weird. Our parents had asked me and Mel about our night in the shed, and I'd wanted to tell them about seeing the moon, but what could I say? That in that one minute, I saw what *they* see? That the universe really is full of mysterious and amazing things? That we're on this piece of rock hurtling through space for this really tiny period of time and we better make the best of it? Which means whether or not my lip gloss matches my pocketbook really doesn't matter? How was I supposed to explain I got all that from looking at the moon through a telescope? They'd think I was crazy. And they might be right!

Well, no use sitting here anymore. I get up and go to the next stop on my list — the Art House. I have decided that I'm going to ask my parents if taking care of the Unusuals can be my job. It might help my case if I've actually spent some time in them. The Art House is empty when I get there, and I'm shocked to see that three walls are now completely covered! I guess with all the people here now, it shouldn't be that surprising, but it still is. I wouldn't have thought so many people could paint. No two are alike, even though a

☆

lot of people have painted different things in the campground.

I'm about to leave when one of the squares catches my eye. It's of a group of kids sitting inside a small, brown room. A big silver object in the middle takes up most of the space. I run up to the wall for a closer look. The kids are all laughing. I can see a rain-streaked window behind them, with a sliver of moon. One of the girls has shiny brown hair and blue eyes and she looks happy to be there. Is that *me*? Who painted this? Melanie's really good at art, maybe she did it. I have to force myself not to touch the scene with my fingers. Only one person has their back to the viewer. Jack. And he had said something about liking to draw when we were up there that night. The fact that the moonlight illuminates Ally's face so she looks like an angel confirms it. He did this, for sure.

I take one last look, then hurry off to the next Unusual — the stream where people pan for gold. People are starting to mill about now, and excitement is thick in the air. I've been noticing things like air lately, how it feels and how it looks at different times of the day. And the sounds of the campground, the birds constantly chirping, and the squirrels and chipmunks scampering through leaves and up trees.

When I get to the stream it's packed with kids dipping their pans in the water and bouncing the gold nuggets in the air. Kenny must have put a ton of nuggets in

☆

there, because no one is coming up empty. The Star Garden is next, but when I get there a few guys are loading the telescopes on carts. I haven't had my iPod on all morning, and I suddenly feel the need to take a break from all this nature. I put on my earphones and settle down on the slope to watch them. One of the guys slips on the still dewy grass and almost drops a telescope. I jump a little. I guess I must already be feeling a little territorial.

After listening to one more song, I head over to the Sun Garden. I haven't been there since I first got a tour of the place. As I wander through, I let my hand trail over the tops of the different sun dials. I wonder who made all these. The memory of making one in third grade out of a pencil and a paper plate comes floating back to me. I remember bringing it home from school and setting it up in the backyard. I'd keep running out to make sure it was still keeping the right time. Then a few days later it rained, turning the plate into mush. I threw it in the outside trash can and haven't thought of it since.

I want to stand in the big sun dial and see what it's like to tell time by my own shadow, but a guy and his son are in there, and I don't want to bother them. As I turn to leave, Melanie comes running toward me. "There you are!" she says. "I've been looking for you everywhere!"

"Looks like you found me."

"Mr. Silver called. Our experiment was a success!

☆

We're going to be written up in some scientific journal! Can you believe that? We're famous!"

No, I really can't believe it. *This* is what I'm famous for? I didn't even do anything, not really.

"Aren't you excited?" Melanie asks, her smile slacking a bit.

"I guess so. But I didn't really do anything. I just read off some numbers and tried to keep Ryan from throwing up on your data."

"That's important stuff!" she insists. "We were all in it together, and we all played an important part."

I think about that for a second. Written up in a journal. Me. Us. It's crazy. But not crazier than being here in the first place. I smile. "You're right. It's pretty cool."

"Hey," she says, "I almost forgot." She reaches into her back pocket and hands me a folded piece of paper. "This fax came for you while I was in the office today. It's from Claire."

I hurriedly unfold it. Life without text messaging has been soooo hard. Melanie heads over to the sun dials while I read the typed letter.

Hey there Breeziest Bree!

OMG, I miss u soooo much. come home! it's totally
not the same without u here. Lara is soooo not
u! she doesn't understand any of my jokes! and
she has this, like, weird toe on her left foot
that she never shows anyone—did u notice how she
never wears sandals? but i saw the toe when we

☆

were getting into my hot tub yesterday. it's like, all bent. she really should get that fixed.

ANYWAY, i wanted to let u know i started this class that's taught by that lady who led that modeling thing we went to? her name's Lulu, but i bet that isn't her real name. anyway, she called my house when i was in Florida and invited me to take it. i'm sure if i got invited to take it, that you would have, too. all of the B-cliquers are here and they're so obnoxious and I really, really need you! it's kind of expensive, but my mom said that she would pay for you to take it with me if your parents will let you. it's just for the summer and my mom said you could stay here for that long. so you have to say yes, say yes!! the class is reeeaaalllly good!! let me know as soooon as possible!

Love your bestest ever buddy,
Chocolate (egg)Claire

My throat tightens when I finish the letter. I can hear Claire's voice so clearly and picture her at her laptop, probably out by the pool when she wrote this. And then she took the time to print and fax it, and that was really thoughtful. I feel bad for thinking it, but part of me is glad that Lara has a freaky toe. I fold the letter back up and head over to Melanie. She's standing in the center of the large sun dial, twisting left and right, trying to cast the strongest shadow. It's late morning though, so her shadow won't be very long. I don't even know how I know that. As much as I try, I can't seem to squash down that inner-geek again. It's threatening to take over. I shiver at the thought.

"Did Mom or Dad see this?" I ask.

She shakes her head. "It came in while I was helping Kenny with the flyers for the eclipse. Why?"

"No reason."

"You're not thinking of going, are you?"

"You read my letter?"

She hops out of the sun dial. "How could I not have read it?"

"Easy. You just . . . oh never mind, it doesn't matter."

"You think they'll let you go?" she asks.

I shrug. "Maybe. If it's just for a few weeks."

She looks down at her sneakers and doesn't say anything.

I sigh. "This could be a really good opportunity. Mom was worried it was a scam, but Claire says it's really good."

"I know," Melanie says. "It's just that, well, what if something happens and you're not here?"

"Something like what?"

"You know, during the night. While I'm sleeping."

"You haven't had any night terrors since we've been here. And if you do, Mom and Dad aren't going anywhere."

"I guess," she says, still not meeting my eyes.

☆

"Don't worry, they'll probably say no. I'm not even sure I'll ask. C'mon, let's go have breakfast. Or lunch. Or whatever they're serving."

"I'll try to meet you there," she says, cheering up a bit. "I need to finish helping Kenny. You haven't seen Jack, have you?"

"Not since last night sometime. He was with that weird old lady in the Star Garden."

"What weird old lady?"

"The one who's always knitting that red scarf. You know, the really old one with the white hair?"

She shakes her head. "Nope. Well, if you see him, will you tell him the good news?" For a second I think she's talking about my modeling class, and then I remember about the planet.

We're about to part ways at the path when she stops and says, "So you were in the Star Garden last night?"

"Yeah, so?"

"So what'd you see?"

"What do you mean?" I ask, knowing very well what she means.

She rolls her eyes. "Stars, planets, the moon, space junk. You know, what did you see?"

"What's space junk?"

"Space junk is junk in space, like in orbit around the earth. Pieces that break off of satellites, or the Space Station, or rocket boosters. Nuts, bolts, astronauts' gloves."

Usually when Mel starts talking about anything science-related I tune her out, but this is actually interesting. "So these things are just floating around up there?"

"Not floating, more like zooming really really fast."

"Can any of it crash to Earth?"

"You mean like a meteorite? Like Ally has?"

"Huh? Ally has a meteorite?"

She tilts her head at me. "That thing she wears around her neck all the time? You never asked what it was?"

I shrug. I had figured that old pouch was some sad attempt at jewelry. When I don't answer, she sighs. "Why are you so interested in space junk?"

"I don't know," I say honestly. "I just think it's cool, and kind of creepy."

"You should learn about it then."

I gaze at her blankly.

She gazes back with the same "I can't believe we're related" look I so often give her. "When you're interested in something," she says very slowly, "it can be fun to learn as much as you can about the subject. Whether or not a teacher assigns it to you. You can learn about it on your own."

"That's okay," I assure her. "I'm not *that* interested."

She sighs again, then says, "You didn't look through the telescopes last night, right?"

I consider lying, but I'd probably mess up and name a planet that was destroyed by an asteroid or something. If that actually happens. "Right," I admit.

"Why?"

"I don't know," I tell her, starting to get annoyed. What business is it of hers?

She opens her mouth to say something but closes it again. "I'll see you later," she says instead. I watch her hurrying back toward the house that will soon be ours. I have a feeling she knew exactly why I didn't look.

Instead of heading to the pavilion to find something to eat, I go back to the cabins to find Mom and Dad. I knock and then go in, but they're not around. In only a week's time, they managed to turn their cabin into a duplicate of their office at home — books, papers, notes and computer equipment lay on every surface, including the floor. I pause before going back out, and consider actually picking up a notebook to see what they're working on.

But I can't do it. A lifetime of not caring is too powerful.

I hurry down the steps and almost walk right into Jack, who has his head down and is fishing something out of his backpack.

"Hey, did you hear the news?" I ask.

He shifts his backpack onto his shoulder, sticks a Twizzler in his mouth, and says, "What news?"

"Our data turned out to be right! They verified the

planet! We're going to be in some science journal, all of us."

His face lights up. "That's great! How'd you find out? Is Mr. Silver back?"

I shake my head. "I don't think so. But he called or something."

"That's really great," he says. "Thanks for telling me. Does Ally know?"

"I think so."

"Good," he says, mostly to himself.

I see my parents coming around the bend and say, "I've gotta go, but I'll see you at the eclipse later. Ally's family reserved a spot for all of us."

"I'm not sure I'm going," he says softly.

I turn back around. "You're not going where?"

"The eclipse. I'm not sure I'm going to watch it."

Sure that I must still be hearing him wrong, I say, "Huh? What are you talking about?"

"I'm just not that into it. Don't tell Ally, okay? I don't want her to worry about anything today."

"But it's okay if I worry?"

"I think you can handle it."

"But why would you miss it? Isn't that why you came here?"

He shakes his head. "I came here to get out of summer school."

"Oh. But still. The way Ally talks about it, well, are you sure you want to miss it?"

"I have my reasons, okay? Just don't tell anyone. I'll see you when it's over."

I narrow my eyes at him. "You know, Jack, the eclipse is going to happen whether or not you're there to watch it."

He shrugs. "It doesn't matter."

"I think it does matter. Believe me, I know how fast everything's going to go afterward. Everyone's going to leave, including Ally and her family, and it will just be me, Mel, and our parents. It's enough to freeze my blood."

He doesn't say anything, just kicks up some dust and pebbles with his toe.

I glance over at my parents, who are almost upon us. I really want to talk to them about Claire's letter. "Well, if you change your mind we'll be right next to the podium with the microphone on it."

"Thanks," he says, glancing toward the big field. It's already starting to fill with people.

My parents are next to us now. Jack says a quick hello and then takes off in the opposite direction of the field.

Dad takes my hand and swings my arm like he used to when I was little. "Are you excited, honey?"

"Um, sure, Dad." I'm very aware of the letter from Claire sticking out of my front pocket.

"We'd like to invite the Summers to stay here next August for the Star Party, what do you think of that idea?"

"What's a Star Party?" I get a crazy picture in my mind of flaming balls of gas dancing the night away. Two weeks ago I would have been sure he was talking about movie stars.

"It's a big event the campground holds each August during the Perseid meteor shower. People bring their telescopes and camp out."

"So sort of like this?" I wave my arm around at the rows of people heading toward the field, carrying telescopes or wheeling them in wagons.

Mom laughs. "Not quite this many people."

"Not nearly," Dad adds.

"I think it would be great if Ally's family came back next summer. In fact . . ." I'm about to suggest Ally stay *this* summer in my place, but instead I push the note farther down in my pocket. I don't want to argue with them. Not today.

I arrive at the field with about forty-five minutes to go. Apparently we have to wait through a whole partial eclipse before the total eclipse, which is what everyone came for. If I had been warned I'd have to stand there for an hour before the main event, I'd have found something else to do. But I'm here now so I might as well make the best of it. That seems to be the story of my life lately.

I head for the podium, snaking through a sea of people with telescopes and video cameras and lawn chairs.

☆

Some are totally manic, jumping around, testing and retesting their equipment. And some are totally mellow, lounging on their chairs and drinking from plastic cups. I hear snippets of foreign languages and I look around for Bellana, the woman from the labyrinth, but I don't see her. I hope she's drinking a lot of water to keep hydrated under that robe. At one point I stop and buy a key chain for Claire from a woman wearing a hat in the shape of a big stuffed sun.

A throbbing sort of noise suddenly fills the air. It sounds like it's coming from the speakers. I figure Mr. Summers must be testing the sound system. But it's not stopping. Just this rhythmic pulsing sort of thing. Almost, but not quite, like a really annoying heartbeat.

I see Ally's bright yellow shirt a few feet ahead of me and stop her. "What's that horrible noise?" I shout.

She laughs and claims that it's a recording of the sun. She doesn't seem to be kidding, either. I reach for my iPod to blot out the sound, but figure what the heck, how often does someone get to hear the sun?

I follow Ally back to our area. The rest of my family is there already. Melanie is leading them in that sunny sky dance of hers. That woman Stella is here with Ryan's grandfather. I overhear Ally ask Stella if she's seen Jack. My mind races for a response in case she asks me too, since I had promised Jack I wouldn't tell. But she doesn't ask. Stella asks me about the labyrinth

☆

again. There's no way I can tell her I've tried twice more but couldn't do it. I just shake my head. She smiles and squeezes my hand as she goes back to join the others. For some reason that makes me feel a little better.

Mom hands me the glasses right as Ally's dad starts talking. They're flimsy paper things with shiny silver lenses. These are supposed to protect me from going blind? Ally is in a state of frenzy next to me. She probably doesn't even realize it, but she's sort of buzzing. I put the glasses on as the countdown begins. The sky looks totally normal. Well, the sun is a little orangeish from the glasses, but isn't the moon supposed to be there, too? How else can it cover the sun? This is all very confusing. Then everyone shouts, "One!" And a few seconds later, out of nowhere, a black dot appears on the right side of the sun. This takes me utterly by surprise. Then the blackness grows slightly bigger and longer until it forms a crescent shape, like the sliver of moon I saw in the telescope. Except the rest of the moon is still invisible, and this crescent is black, instead of white. I can't tear my eyes away from the sun. It's disappearing right before my eyes. Ally asks me something, but I have no idea what she says.

I stand still and watch, turning away only briefly. As the moon creeps farther across the sun, the trees and grass turn a metallic color. It's like the life and color is being sucked right out of the world. Mom or

Dad or Melanie comes to talk to me and I almost can't bear to look at them. The shadows on their faces are really strange and almost scary. I shiver, and not only because it's noticeably colder. Everything is a little scary, actually, and my heart is beating faster than when I ran all the way to Claire's. I feel something warm and soft over my shoulders and look down to find Stella's red scarf draped over me. Her eyes meet mine and she mouths, "Keep it."

I smile gratefully and turn back to the sky. The sun is almost completely gone now, leaving a deep blue-black sky behind. All around the far horizon I can see a yellow-orange glow where the eclipse doesn't reach. It's like a huge circle of sunset. Ally's back now. I glance over at her. She's in a daze, just staring, frozen. I almost laugh, hoping I don't look like that, too. I take a quick look out at the crowd, just in time to see a huge wall of darkness push toward us from the direction of the sun. "The moon's shadow!" I hear Ryan shout. "Here it comes!" It zooms through us like a wall of ghosts, faster than I've ever seen anything move. It's exhilarating and terrifying at the same time.

And then a few seconds later the sun completely disappears, leaving a hole in the sky. I feel its loss in the pit of my stomach. I hear myself scream involuntarily, but it gets lost among a thousand other screams.

And as streams of light fan out behind the darkened

sun like the wings of a butterfly, I realize that I never saw real beauty until now. And one thought fills my head:

If this could be repeated every day for a year, I would never budge from where I stood.

JACK

7

I stuff my backpack with a flashlight, my sketchbook, two novels, a sweatshirt, and some bread and apples I took from breakfast. The conversation this morning was obviously all about the eclipse. People were comparing notes on how much totality they'd seen in their life, and how far they had to travel to see it. David invited me to a pre-eclipse party at their cabin, but I mumbled something incoherent and left as quickly as I could.

I had hoped Mr. Silver would be back by now. There are only a few hours to go before the eclipse. I had almost forgotten he had asked me to distribute the glasses.

I consider bringing a blanket with me, but those sleeping bags should still be in the shed so I'll have something to sit on besides the concrete floor. I guess I could just stay here in the cabin and close the shades, but if anyone came looking for me they'd try here first.

Better to stick with my original plan. I start to zip up the backpack and, as an afterthought, toss in my Game Boy and extra batteries.

I figure this is the best time to go, while everyone is racing about. Easier to get lost in the crowd. I have to admit, I've really enjoyed *not* being lost in the crowd. That's why I have to do this. I take a last scan of the cabin and head out. I haven't gotten five yards from my door when I run smack into Bree. Before I can stop myself, I've told her I'm not going to the eclipse. When she's done reading me the riot act, as much as I hate to admit it, I know she's right. And what would Mr. Silver say when he found out I didn't see it after all this buildup? I'd feel so stupid. With a sigh loud enough to make the family ahead of me turn around, I changed direction. I've got a party to get to.

When I arrive, I see the partygoers have spilled out of the cabin onto David and Hayley's porch. David sees me and clasps my shoulder. My backpack slips off my arm and crashes to the floor. "Hey, what ya got in there? You planning on camping out at the eclipse? You know it's in the middle of the day, right?"

"Hey, you can never be too prepared. Boy Scout motto." He laughs and heads off to refill the chips bowl. I slide the backpack against the wall so no one trips on it. I plop down on the top stair and before I know it, someone has stuck a soda in my hand. I turn around to see that it's Pete.

"Thanks," I say, taking a big sip.

He nods, but something's not quite right. His eyes are darting around a lot, almost like he's scared.

"Hey, are you okay?"

He nods, but too quickly. I pat the spot next to me. He sits down. "What's going on?" I ask.

In a low whisper, he says, "I'm scared. And there's all these people around."

"Do you want to go for a walk? We can talk where it's quiet."

He nods. I tell him to wait there while I go ask his parents if it's okay. When I find Hayley she seems relieved that I'm willing to watch Pete for a while. We agree that I'll bring him to the field before the eclipse, and we pick a place to meet. That gives me about a half hour to make Pete feel better. I grab my backpack and Pete and I head toward my original destination.

As I'd hoped, very few people are up on the hilltop, and those who are here are busy setting up all their equipment. The hilltop's been designated as a "flash friendly" zone, which means that up here people can take pictures with flashes, and set up lights with their video cameras, but down in the field they do so at their own peril. During totality, the people around them will be very angry since it will ruin precious seconds of their night vision. It's still early yet, but I don't think I'll be sharing my hilltop with many people.

Pete and I sit on the edge of the hill, watching all the activity below. We can hear the noise, but it's faint and muffled. Pete had been quiet on the way up, but now I ask, "Why are you scared?"

He shrugs. "I like the sun. I don't want it to go away."

"But it will be right back. You know that, right?"

He shrugs again. "How can you be sure?"

I think on that for a minute. I really CAN'T be sure, I guess. "I promise you, it will come back."

He smiles tentatively and says, "Okay, if you promise."

I unzip my bag and hand him my Game Boy. It always relaxes me. I take out my sketchbook and start drawing. Every now and then the shouts from below get louder, but I figure we have a few more minutes before it's time to meet Pete's parents.

"I think this is broken," Pete says after a while. "I can't see the screen anymore." He hands me the Game Boy. The screen is very dim. Then I realize with a sickening feeling that it's not the screen that's dim, it's everything else. I jump up. "How long have we been sitting here?"

Pete shakes his head.

"We've gotta go!" I shove everything back into my bag and then pull the pair of paper eclipse glasses out of my back pocket. "Here, put these on." I hand Pete the glasses. He has to hold onto them with one hand to keep them from slipping off. I grab his other hand. Together we stumble into the weird mustard-colored twilight. I risk a quick peek at the sun. The moon — black instead of white — is covering about three-quarters of it now. I force myself to focus on the ground as we slip and slide down the hill, not willing to go around to the path on the other side and use up more time.

We reach a grove of trees and stop for a second to stare at the tiny shadows on the grass beneath us. Streaming through the gaps in the leaves are hundreds, no *thousands,* of mini partially eclipsed suns. It's the coolest thing I've ever seen, and I've seen Saturn. Pete kneels down to touch them. I could watch the whole eclipse this way. But I don't want to. I want to watch it with Ally, in the field. With effort, we turn away and keep going. Pete is starting to breathe heavy, so I offer to carry him. He puts his arms up with no hesitation. I'm down the hill now, and running as fast as I've ever run, especially with a forty-pound kid in my arms and an overpacked backpack on my shoulder. Then a buzzing on my belt stops me short again. Out of habit I'd put my walkie-talkie on. The only person who had access to its mate is Mr. Silver. I put Pete down, grab it, fumble for the right button, and shout, "Hello? Hello?"

A very crackly voice comes through. "Where are ya, Jack?"

"Hang on! I'm coming!" The field is about a hundred yards away now. It's getting darker by the second. "Are you back?"

"I'm back!" he shouts. "You did it! You tracked that planet!"

It's easier to hear him suddenly because a hush has fallen over the field.

"I know!" I shout back.

"I'll be expecting a lot more from you in class next year."

I laugh and stick the walkie-talkie back on my belt. It's a good thing I've been running each day with Ryan because I'd be dead by now otherwise. The landscape around us has turned a strange metallic silver. Gone are the blues and greens — even the red of my t-shirt. I feel like we've stumbled onto some whole other planet. Pete's turning around in circles and pointing at the ground.

"Look! My shadow. It's gone!"

His eyes are wide with fright. I twist around to look at the ground beneath me. He's right. There's enough light that we should still be able to see our shadows. I'm sure there's some obvious scientific reason for this, but I feel a little deserted. If my walkie-talkie hadn't worked just now, I'd think I was dreaming.

"Don't worry, Pete," I tell him, scooping him back up. "It'll come back as soon as the sun does."

I run across the road to the edge of the field as Pete's thin voice says, "Promise?"

"Have I been wrong yet?"

He turns his head to look at me skeptically. Then he looks around at the crowd. "There they are!"

Sure enough, David and Hayley are running toward

us, relief flooding their faces. Pete scrambles to get down and runs over to grab his mom's leg.

"Our shadows went away, but they'll be back!" he announces. "And we saw tiny suns on the ground!"

I don't wait around to explain. Time's ticking away. With a quick goodbye, I race toward the podium. It quickly dawns on me as I watch everyone staring up that I gave Pete my only pair of glasses. Fortunately, a few feet away is a booth selling merchandise. I hastily grab the last pair of eclipse glasses from the tabletop and fish around in my pockets for money.

"No worries, man, just take it," the guy behind the booth says. I wave my thanks and put them on my face just in time to hear people around me yell, "There they are! The shadow bands!" I look up, but don't see anything other than the small chunk that's left of the sun. Then I see a crowd of people running over to look at something on the ground behind me. I turn to see a pattern of dark and light bands rippling across white poster boards. It's mesmerizing. Where are they coming from? I have to force myself to keep moving. I keep my eyes on the podium, trying hard not to knock into anyone.

I'm almost there when something big and black comes hurtling toward me and I duck, throwing my arms over my head. The laugh of a woman next to me makes me peek through my arms.

"That's just the moon's shadow, hon. It can't hurt you none."

I spring up, and if I had the time, I'd be totally humiliated. But as it is, I'm out of time so the humiliation will have to wait. I run the last few feet and finally see Ally, with Bree on the other side of her. They're facing away from me, staring up like everyone else. I almost trip again, over my own feet this time, but catch myself in time to see the last bit of light disappear. The campground erupts in screams and hollers as a whisper-thin circle of white flame appears above us. My heart skips a beat as I register the fact that the fiery circle is the only thing that proves the sun still exists. It's like a big eye beaming down on those of us lucky enough to stand beneath it.

I slip my hand in Ally's. She turns, and besides the tears running down her cheeks and the look of awe in her eyes, I can see surprise and relief when she realizes it's me.

"Hey," I say, squeezing her hand.

Thankfully, she squeezes back. "Where've you been?"

"Long story."

"You'll have to tell it to me sometime. Some *other* time."

We laugh.

So we stand there, part of a crowd a thousand people strong, beaming up at the sky with wonder. I know with a sudden certainty that wherever I am in the future — up in my treehouse, alone in the school cafeteria, or trying to figure out what my teachers are talking about, a part of me will always be right here, right now, with that giant eye in the sky shining down on me, telling me it's going to be all right.

ALLY

Epilogue

As we stand hand in hand, it takes me a second to realize Jack has tears streaming down his face, and a second more to realize I do too.

"Mr. Silver's back!" I shout over the screaming of the crowd.

"I know!" he shouts back.

"And our planet! We found —"

He laughs. "I know! Now look at the sky, not me!"

I laugh too. This is all so surreal. Kenny runs up and thrusts the binoculars at me. He's already taken the filters off. "Look at the prominences!"

With one more squeeze Jack lets my hand go. I point the binoculars at the sky. Small pink streamers loop out from the darkened sun, one after another, and disappear. It's so crazy to think the sun shoots those out all day long and we never see them. What beauty is hidden from us! I hand the binoculars to Jack and hear his sharp intake of breath as another one shoots out from behind the moon.

I finally remember to look for the stars and am surprised that I can recognize them. Normally I wouldn't be able to see these stars until winter, but now everything is reversed. It's Orion! I can't believe it!!! There's Sirius and Betelgeuse! Rigel and Capella! And there's Mercury and Mars and Venus, higher in the sky than they ever are at night.

I scream out the names of the stars and the planets and point wildly at them until everyone around me is laughing. I'm filled with warmth and gratitude for this new group of friends. All my visions of what this day would be like never included anyone other than my family and Ryan's. I always thought the only friends I'd be able to share it with would be Glenn, Eta, and Peggy. I never expected to have new friends on the same planet as me.

I don't notice Dad is gone until his voice comes over the speaker. "Everyone enjoying the eclipse?"

The hollers and hoots and screams are the loudest yet.

"As soon as I count to five, time to cover your eyes and equipment again."

The crowd boos.

"Remember, everything you saw is going to happen again, in reverse order. Hang on!"

I try to collect myself and focus. Kenny and Melanie gather around the white sheet they put down, trying to see the elusive shadow bands. But if I want to see the moon's shadow this time, I'll have to remain alert.

Dad counts down, and as soon as he gets to one, I throw on my glasses. The diamond ring returns, followed in quick succession by Baily's Beads. I feel an inexplicable loss as the light of that single beam shining through a crevice on the moon erases the corona from view. My brain freezes again as I try to burn the image of that billowing circle of light into my memory. That was both the shortest and longest three minutes of my life.

And I forgot to take a single picture.

Before I can berate myself too much, for the second time today someone puts their hand in mine. This time there's a sense of urgency. I tear my eyes away from the sky and turn to see Bree tugging on me.

"Now!" she cries. Suddenly a wall of darkness races toward us at a speed I never would have thought possible. It hits us straight on, rushes past, and leaves me breathless and blinking. Bree and Jack and I whirl around in time to see it speed over the crowd and out to the eastern horizon.

And as the shadow of the moon carries the darkness away, it takes something from me too. It leaves me lighter and freer and for the first time since I found out about our move, I truly feel like myself again. Everyone around me is bubbling over with joy. Bree's blue eyes are brighter than I've ever seen them. She looks lit from within. Oddly, she's now wearing a red scarf around her neck. It looks very nice on her.

Jack is wiping at his eyes and trying to hide it.

☽

We mull around our little corner of the field for a while, babbling and gushing to each other about the eclipse. Then Bree says, "We're going to see Mr. Silver. Come with us?"

I shake my head. "I'll meet up with you at dinner. I've gotta pack. Some girl is moving into my room."

Bree laughs. Jack says, "Are you sure?"

I nod. Jack squeezes my hand one last time and then he, Bree, Ryan, and Melanie run off into the crowd.

"Um, Astrodork," Kenny says. "You still have your glasses on!"

My hand instinctively reaches up and feels them on the bridge of my nose. "Yeah, well the eclipse is still going on, you know." It's true. The moon is still covering about a quarter of the sun.

"You're right," Kenny says. He pulls his out of his back pocket and slips them on. Mom and Dad do the same. Without a word, we sit down on the white sheet Kenny had spread out earlier. As the sea of people pack up their equipment and head back to the campground, we sit there and watch until the very last nick of the sun is gone.

"Well," Dad says, clearing his throat. "That sure was something."

"When's the next one?" I ask, half joking, half not.

Mom and Dad laugh, but Kenny rattles off the dates of the next six eclipses. I have no doubt this won't be the last one we see.

"We can come back here sometimes, right?" Kenny asks. "I mean, to visit?"

"Absolutely!" Dad says. "The Holdens have already asked us to run the Star Party next summer."

"Really?" Kenny and I say together, beaming at each other.

Mom and Dad nod. "We thought that would make you happy," Mom says. "We have to finish cleaning up here, but you guys are free to go."

I quickly throw my stuff into my backpack and say goodbye. I run all the way back to the house and up the stairs. Just as I suspected, my room does look different, post-eclipse. It looks smaller, like it can't contain me anymore.

After all, I've got a whole world to see.

BREE

Epilogue

Chocolate (egg)Claire,

i miss you too!!!!!!!! i wish you could have been
here for the eclipse two days ago. I really can't
describe it except to say it was really different from what I thought it would be. I tried to
describe it to this one lady named Bellana who
is very nice but "fashion-sense challenged," but
i don't think I did too good a job. My mom took a
lot of pictures and Mel just printed them out so
I'll stick one in this package and you can see,
and hopefully someday we'll see one together?
they have cruises where you can see it from the
ocean. how fab would THAT be? I'm sending you
this commemorative key chain even though you
only have one key. i'm soooo sorry I won't be
able to take the class with you, i'm sure you're
learning a ton and you'll be scouted at the mall
for sure and you'll have to tell me all about it.
i'm also sending your Book back because now that

you're in the class you might really need it and I have a lot of pictures of us in my own Book so I won't forget you, I promise.

I hope you can come visit me up here soon. it's different, too, from what i thought i guess. I'm still really scared, but not as much and there are things I sort of like, like you know that red nail polish on my toes from your party? it finally started to chip and I just let it, even though I had some red nail polish I could have used! but I bet it still looks better than lara's freak toe! :o)

xoxoxoxoxo,
Beach Baby Bree (who is currently very far from a beach, but there's a hot spring that looks sort of like a hot tub if you squint)

p.s. I finally did this thing today where you walk through these circles and there's like, a crystal thing in the middle on a tree stump with a dinosaur or a dragon or something, I can never tell the difference, and I'm not describing it very well, but I wanted to tell someone and I couldn't tell anyone here b/c they'd think it was weird that I couldn't do it before. Anyway, I'll show you when you come visit—you better come visit!

I print out the letter, and stick it along with the key chain and the Book into the thick mailing envelope Ally's mother gave me. I carefully climb over the piles

313
☆

of our boxes and suitcases that are now repacked and ready to be moved to our new house in a few days. Melanie is out on the porch. She's lying on her belly, propped up on her elbows, carefully examining a bunch of photographs spread out in front of her. I go out and sit cross-legged next to her. I hadn't even thought to bring my camera with me to the eclipse. I've only ever used it to take pictures for my Book. I hadn't even noticed Mom taking these.

"You'll like this one," Mel says, lifting one up and handing it to me. "You look really good in it."

She's right, I do. My eyes are bright, my hair has come lose from its ribbon, and Stella's scarf is waving around my neck. But that's not what I see when I look at the picture. I see three unlikely friends holding hands. And Ryan, Kenny, and Melanie are standing behind us, rapt.

And in the sky above us, I see a miracle.

"Can you make more copies for me? Maybe a little bigger?"

She reaches over to her bag and pulls out some larger sheets of photo paper. "I already did."

I want to hug her, and even though it's not the middle of the night, and she's not having a night terror, I do it anyway. Then I tuck Claire's package under my arm and carefully pick up two of the enlargements. My first stop is Jack's cabin, down the road. We haven't really had a chance to be alone since the eclipse, and I've been meaning to ask him something.

His screen door's open, and I can see him sitting cross-legged on his bed. I knock and he jumps a little, sending a little piece of charcoal flying through the air. He quickly closes what I take to be a drawing pad and tosses it on the floor.

"Sorry to scare you," I tell him, opening the door.

"That's okay," he says. "What's up?"

I see his sneakers and running shorts on the floor. "Hey, maybe tomorrow I can run with you guys?" My words surprise me.

"I'm not very good," he says. "Ryan's much faster."

"That's okay. I'm just starting out myself."

He glances self-consciously at his art book, and it reminds me of what I saw at the Art House.

"I saw your painting. The one of all of us in the shed?"

He reddens.

"It's really good. You're lucky you can do that. I don't have any kind of talent." I would have thought this would be hard for me to admit, but surprisingly it isn't.

"Sure you do."

"Yeah, if knowing which top matches which skirt is a talent."

He shakes his head. "You see things sometimes. Things other people don't. And you're not afraid to call it like you see it."

I size him up. "You know, you've really changed since you've been here."

"I know," he says offhandedly.

"I'm glad you decided to come to the eclipse."

"Me too. I can't believe I almost didn't."

"I have something for you," I say, holding out the picture.

He takes it and looks at it for a long time.

"I have one for Ally, too."

"Would you mind if I gave it to her?" he asks quietly.

"I'll make a deal with you," I say, sitting down on the empty bed across from him. "I'll give you the picture for Ally, if you do something for me."

"What do you want me to do?"

I take a deep breath. "I want you to teach me how to fly."

☆

JACK

Epilogue

The bus leaves in two hours. Stella said she'd save our seats in the back. The ride home sure will be different from the ride here. I look around the cabin that had been my home for the last two weeks, except for the night we all slept in the shed. I bet my treehouse is going to feel small now. The cabin looks strange without clothes and stuff everywhere. I toss my pile of books onto the bed when the piece of paper I was using as a bookmark falls out. I recognize it as one of the eclipse articles Mike had given me when I left. On the same page is a short sidebar I hadn't noticed before, called *The Death of Our Sun and the Beginning of Our Immortality*. I start to tuck it back in the book, but with a title like that I have no choice but to read it.

The article says how in a few billion years the sun will have used up all the hydrogen inside it and will swell up, absorbing the planet Mercury and making life on Earth uninhabitable. Then the sun will shrink until it's really small. And then a few billion years after that, it will eject gusts of matter from all around it, including what's left of the earth and the atoms of everyone who has ever lived there. The atoms will be sent out into the farthest reaches of space to become parts of other stars and planets and creatures.

I think of something Ally said one of my first few nights here. It was during her nightly lecture. She said that the atoms in our bodies came from stars that exploded. I guess what comes around, goes around. I tuck the article back into the book. For some reason, knowing that my atoms are going to one day arrive at the other end of the universe is kind of comforting.

The screen door bangs open. Team Exo has come to say goodbye.

"Gonna keep working out, right?" Ryan says. "I expect to see you here next year ready to beat me in a race."

I promise him I'll keep working out, but not to plan on me beating him in anything. Kenny and Melanie make me swear that if I'm falling behind in school to contact them for help. I'm not even embarrassed that they're just kids. I've stopped thinking of them that way. The three of them leave, and it's just me, Bree, and Ally. We stand around looking at each other and at the near-empty cabin. Finally Bree asks, "So what do you guys know about space junk?"

"Space junk?" Ally repeats.

"Yeah, you know, all that stuff zooming around in

318

space. It's a big threat, you know, to astronauts and satellites and lots of things."

"I know what it is," Ally says with a smile. "I just don't think I've ever heard you ask about anything, well, scientific."

I wait to see if that's going to tick Bree off, but she just says, "I'm going to have a lot of time on my hands soon. Might as well fill it up."

I put up my hands. "Don't look at me."

"My dad has some information on it," Ally says. "I'm sure he'll give it to you."

"Cool." And then, because she's Bree, she knows when to make an exit. "So Jack-in-the-box, keep it real. I hope we'll see you next summer for the Star Party. That is, if I make it a whole year around here without going stark raving mad."

"You'll make it," I assure her. "And I'm going to be here, even if I have to fail another class to do it."

She gives me a quick hug goodbye, just long enough to whisper in my ear, "Keep flying."

"You too," I whisper back. I'm glad Bree wanted to learn about the whole lucid dreaming thing. I think it will prove her inner life is bigger than she thought. My own goal is to do the opposite — to make my outer life as big as my inner one.

Bree turns at the door and calls to Ally, "Dinner at six?"

"You bet."

"Remember, tonight's music and television. Tomorrow is movies and fashion."

"I remember," Ally says.

The door closes behind Bree.

"She's teaching me the ways of the world," Ally explains. "She lent me her iPod and is testing me on it tonight. Testing me!"

"I have something for you too," I tell her, and reach over to my dresser. I hand her the picture on top. "No testing involved."

"Wow," Ally says, gazing down at the picture in her hand and then up at me. "You drew this? It must have taken forever."

"It didn't take that long." Actually it did, but I didn't mind. I don't tell her that I was so engrossed in making it that I almost missed the eclipse.

"That's me, right?"

I laugh. "Yes, that's you. Can't you tell?"

"I figured it was me, but how many times does a girl see herself standing on top of a comet in outer space?"

"What other girls do you know who could be riding on a comet?"

"None," she admits.

"And how many do you know who would be wearing a meteorite around her neck with the words *Alpha Girl* on their superhero outfits?"

"Again, none."

"Well there you have it, then. It must be you."

She runs her hand over it and I cringe a little, hoping the pencil doesn't smear. I'm going to have to get used to showing other people my stuff. After Bree told me she'd seen what I drew in the Art House, she made me promise to join the art club at school. She still scares me a little, and somehow she'll know if I don't do it.

"No one's ever done anything like this for me. I'm going to frame it and hang it up as soon as we get settled." She pauses for a few seconds and then says, "Jack, do you ever . . . do you ever worry you'll forget? About the eclipse?"

I shake my head.

She smiles. "Me neither."

"It seemed like it lasted a lifetime. But also like no time at all."

"I know exactly what you mean," she says.

"But if the memory does start to fade, you can always look at this." I whip out the photograph from Bree and hand it to her. Her eyes glisten as she looks up at me.

She holds it close to her chest and the gravity of her situation hits me fully for the first time. She's completely walking into the unknown and leaving behind everything she loves. But not every*one*. Seeing the way she and Kenny are together has made me wonder if there's hope for me and Mike.

Plus, she's Alpha Girl. She's going to do amazing things.

We don't talk as I throw the last few things into my duffel bag. Toothbrush. Souvenir mug. Sweaty running shorts. As I'm about to zip up the bag, she reaches in and grabs something. "What's this?" She holds up the stuffed bunny that I'd hidden in the duffel since my arrival.

The words I had practiced, *It's not mine, some kid left it on the bus,* spring to my head. But what comes out of my mouth is, "My dad put him in my crib for me when he left. It's the only thing he ever gave me. Well, you know, besides life."

I hold my breath as she gently rests the bunny back in the bag.

"He's a really special bunny," she says. "I can tell."

I don't say anything for a minute. "Ally?"

"Yeah?"

I take a deep breath and smile. "Wherever you wind up, I wish you clear skies."

"You too," she says. And when she hugs me goodbye, she smells like fresh air.

Author's Note & Further Reading

I'd like to thank my fearless editor, Alvina Ling, and her partner-in-crime, Connie Hsu, for encouraging me to pursue my interests and turn them into books. And a huge thank you goes to my writer-friends Pat Palmer and Betsy Reilly, who stayed up till all hours reading these pages and making them better.

For her help with all things eclipse-related, my deep appreciation goes to Nancy Tuthill. In only twelve years, she chased seven eclipses — from the Sahara Desert to the mountains of Bolivia. Her late husband, Roger (who chased twenty in his day), is a wonderful example of how fulfilling and exciting amateur astronomy can be. His invention of the Solar Skreen allows people around the world to safely view the partial phases of an eclipse.

Dr. Kathy Olkin was kind enough to take time off from working on the New Horizon mission to Pluto (and beyond!) to read an early draft and help with all things planetary. John C. Scala, planetarium director extraordinaire and all-around man-of-the-stars, taught me about the constellations and helped set up my own telescope. Without him, it would have remained an oversized coat hanger. I'd also like to thank the volunteers at the Sterling Hill Mine Observatory in Ogdensburg, New Jersey, for answering my endless questions and for showing me Saturn.

Thank you to the good folks at the Search for Extraterrestrial Intelligence (SETI), especially volunteers like Rohil Goutam, for teaching me how it works. You, too, can search for intelligent life on other planets by linking your computer to the seti@home program. Sign up at http://setiathome.berkeley.edu/ because hey, you never know.

Even though his planet-finding organization (transitsearch. org) had discovered a new *planet* that day, Dr. Greg Laughlin took the time to help me ensure the accuracy of the portions of this book that dealt with searching for exoplanets. He is a wonderful example of the scientific community's dedication to sharing their knowledge.

If you don't move from your chair, once every 300 years you'll be in the right place to see a total solar eclipse (although you'd have to go outside!). The next one in the mainland United States will occur on August 21, 2017. The path of the eclipse will extend from Oregon all the way across the country to South Carolina. So get up from that chair and go see it.

I also suggest visiting your nearest planetarium and joining a local astronomy group. All over the country astronomers are waiting, their telescopes at the ready, to show you not only the rings of Saturn, but galaxies and nebulae millions of light-years away.

If you are interested in learning more about lucid dreaming, a good place to start is with the books of Dr. Stephen LaBerge. I have him to thank for teaching me how to fly.

Every attempt was made to accurately describe the fictional eclipse at the Moon Shadow Campground. The following are some Internet sources that I found particularly helpful when doing research for this book:

www.skyandtelescope.com
www.space.com
www.eclipsechaser.com
http://eclipse.gsfc.nasa.gov/eclipse.html
www.astronomy.com
http://worldwidetelescope.org

I couldn't find anywhere in the book to put the following information, so I'm including it here. In 1977, President Jimmy Carter recorded a message that was sent along with the *Voyager* spacecraft on its way out of our solar system. It will take 40,000 years for *Voyager* to come close enough to another star system for anyone to find it, but hey, you never know. It's a wonderful message of hope and solidarity:

We cast this message into the cosmos. . . . Of the 200 billion stars in the Milky Way galaxy, some — perhaps many — may have inhabited planets and spacefaring civilizations. If one such civilization intercepts *Voyager* and can understand these recorded contents, here is our message: This is a present from a small, distant world, a token of our sounds, our science, our images, our music, our thoughts, and our feelings. We are trying to survive our time so we may live into yours. We hope someday, having solved the problems we face, to join a community of galactic civilizations. This record represents our hope and our determination and our goodwill in a vast and awesome universe.

I wish you all clear skies.

If you are interested in learning more about the universe, you can find hundreds of wonderful books on astronomy. Some that I recommend:

Astronomy for Dummies by Stephen P. Maran
Chasing the Shadow by Joel Harris and Richard Talcott
Cosmos by Carl Sagan
David Levy's Guide to Observing and Discovering Comets by David H. Levy
Deep Sky Companions: The Messier Objects by Stephen J. O'Meara
Eclipse!: The What, Where, When, Why and How Guide to Watching Solar and Lunar Eclipses by Philip S. Harrington
Find the Constellations by H. A. Rey
40 Nights to Knowing the Sky by Fred Schaaf
NightWatch: A Practical Guide to Viewing the Universe by Terence Dickinson
Out of This World Astronomy by John Rhatigan and Rain Newcomb
The Planet Hunters by Dennis Brindell Fradin
Seeing in the Dark by Timothy Ferris
See the Stars: Your First Guide to the Night Sky by Ken Croswell
Sky & Telescope and *Astronomy* magazines
Stikky Night Skies: Learn 6 Constellations, 4 Stars, a Planet, a Galaxy, and how to Navigate at Night — in One Hour, Guaranteed by Laurence Holt Staff
Strange Universe by Bob Berman
Turn Left at Orion: A Hundred Night Sky Objects to See in a Small Telescope — and How to Find Them by Guy Consolmagno
The Ultimate Guide to the Sky by John Mosley

Reader's Guide

1. At the beginning of the book, Ally, Bree, and Jack are introduced in separate, short chapters. The alternating chapters continue throughout the entire book. How does this format help compare and contrast the characters? What does each character want at the beginning of the story? Does this change as the story progresses?

2. What are the Unusuals and why are they important to the Moon Shadow Campground? Why does Bree resist walking the labyrinth for so long? What makes her finally walk it? If you were to visit Ally's labyrinth, what question would you ponder and what answer would you hope to receive?

3. Using three words, describe Bree's personality at the beginning of the book. Does Bree change during the story? What three words would you use to describe her personality at the end of the book?

4. What does Jack mean when he says he can fly? Why does he like "flying" so much? Where does he go when he "flies"?

5. Bree and Ally both have to move. What concerns do Ally and Bree have about moving? How does Ally's reaction to moving differ from Bree's? How are their reactions the same? Have you ever moved? If you were going to move, what do you think you would miss most about your hometown?

6. Bree and Ally come up with a plan to change their parents' minds about moving. Do you think it's a good plan? What would you do if you were in their position?

7. In regard to her friendship with Ryan, Ally thinks, "It's almost like nothing's changed. Except, of course, everything has." (213) What do you think she means? How has Ally's friendship with Ryan changed? Have you had a friendship that has changed as you and your friend got older? What happened to that friendship?

8. Several times Jack says he doesn't want to leave Moon Shadow Campground. Why do you think he feels that way?

9. Melanie and Bree have very different advice for Kenny and Ally about how to survive in a new school. Jack also offers his own take on fitting in at school. Which character's advice and experience at school do you identify with more — Melanie, Bree, or Jack — and why? Which character would you want as your friend in a new school?

10. How does the eclipse affect Ally, Bree, and Jack? How does it change their outlook and attitude for the future?

11. The author titled her book *Every Soul a Star*. The passage by Plato she included in the beginning of the book also contains a phrase similar to the title. Why do you think the author titled the book the way she did?

Also by Wendy Mass

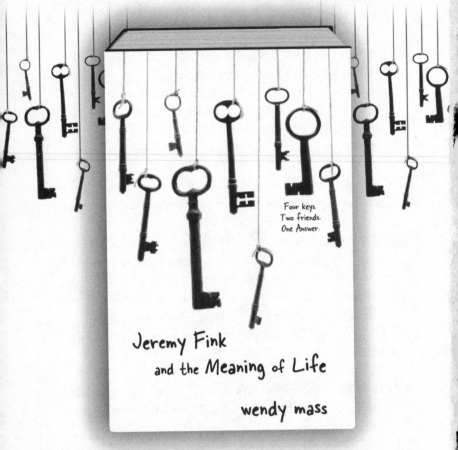

Four keys.
Two friends.
One Answer.

Jeremy Fink
and the Meaning of Life

wendy mass

Join Jeremy Fink and his friend Lizzy as they set out on incredible adventures in search of keys that unlock a box that just might contain the meaning of life.

Available wherever books are sold.

Little, Brown
Books for Young Readers

www.lb-kids.com